THE BRIGHTSIDERS

THE BRIGHT SIDERS

JEN WILDE

SQUARE FISH

Swoon READS

New York

SQUARE
FISH

An imprint of Macmillan Publishing Group, LLC
175 Fifth Avenue, New York, NY 10010
fiercereads.com

Our books may be purchased in bulk for promotional, educational, or business use. Please
contact your local bookseller or the Macmillan Corporate and Premium Sales Department
at (800) 221-7945 ext. 5442 or by email at MacmillanSpecialMarkets@macmillan.com.

Library of Congress Control Number: 2017957584
ISBN 978-1-250-30914-3 (paperback)   ISBN 978-1-250-18972-1 (ebook)

Originally published in the United States by Swoon Reads
First Square Fish edition, 2019
Book designed by Rebecca Syracuse
Square Fish logo designed by Filomena Tuosto

1   3   5   7   9   10   8   6   4   2

FOR EVERYONE JUST TRYING TO
DO THEIR BEST IN THIS WORLD

CHAPTER ONE

"Cheeseburgers!" I shout at the top of my lungs.

Jessie pulls me through the club, shoving people out of the way. "Move, people! We're getting cheeseburgers!"

"CHEESEBURGERS!" I shout again, but few hear me over the thumping of music and drumming of feet against the dance floor.

Everything goes dark, and I realize my eyes are closed. I take a sip of my drink and giggle as mystery shoulders rub against mine and Jessie's grip tightens on my hand.

"Em!" she calls. Her voice sounds miles away. "Wake up, babe!"

"I'm awake," I mumble, then open my eyes to find us walking past the bar toward the exit.

"Hey," a cute girl by the bar calls. "Are you Emmy King?"

I do a curtsy and smile. "Indeed I am. And what is thy name, fair maiden?"

Jessie snakes an arm around my waist. "Uh-oh," she says. "That's *Outlander* talk. You've officially reached peak drunkenness."

The girl at the bar holds her phone out. "Can I have a selfie with you?"

I stumble toward her and take her phone. "Aye, t'would be my most high pleasure."

"Um," the girl says. "What?"

Jessie laughs. "She means yes."

I start taking photos with her phone, sticking my tongue out and blowing kisses and crossing my eyes and giving the finger, but Jessie snatches the phone away and gives it back to the girl.

"C'mon, Em," Jessie says. "I'm starving." She takes my hand and pulls me away. We've been dating for almost six months, but she still gets a tad protective when fans pay me a lot of attention. It's kind of cute seeing her freckled nose scrunch up like that when she's jealous.

I bow to the girl, spilling some of my drink. "Fare thee well, my sweet, for I musteth findeth cheeseburgers, lest I waste away from hunger. My heart doth long for the day we may meet again!"

We walk through the dining area and I spot Alfie and Ryan in a booth in the corner. I give them my widest grin. Alfie Jones and Ryan Cho are my two bestest buds in the whole universe. And they're my bandmates. I get to rock out all around the world with my two fave people and get paid for it. Hashtag blessed.

Still grinning, I reach a hand out to Alfie as we pass. He takes it and stands.

"Where are you off to?" he says in my ear.

"CHEESEBURGERS!" I yell, and he laughs.

"I should have known," he says.

My best friend, Chloe, is dancing their butt off in the middle of the club. I wave to them and mouth that I'm leaving. They blow me a kiss, and I pretend to catch it.

Jessie pulls on my hand and I wobble off-balance, but Alfie steadies me.

"Whoa," he says. "You okay, Em?"

I nod. But then my stomach lurches, and I groan.

Alfie takes one look at me and furrows his brow. He taps Jessie's arm to get her attention.

"I think Em's gonna be sick," he says. I shake my head slowly even though they're not looking at me.

Jessie rolls her eyes. "She's fine."

"Nah," he says. "She's doing that face she always does before she voms."

They both look at me, and I smile, but it's delayed and lopsided.

Jessie sighs and pulls me closer to her. "Em," she says sternly. "Are you gonna hurl?"

I shake my head and pout. She gives Alfie a look that says *told you so* and turns to keep walking.

And then I barf all over the floor.

People around us jump away from me, shrieking in disgust, but I'm too drunk to care. I buckle over and heave again. Jessie stands over me, laughing and holding my hair, while Alfie takes my drink and rubs my back.

I stare at the puke-covered floor and laugh. "It's blue."

"It's from the cocktails," Jessie says.

Flashes of light hurt my eyes, and Alfie tries to cover the lenses of people's phones as they take pictures of me. Ryan joins him, spreading his arms wide to cover me.

"Let's get you some air," Alfie says.

With one arm around Jessie and one around Alfie, I stumble to the door of the club.

Jessie takes a moment to fix my hair, tucking some behind my left ear and letting the right side of my bleach-blond lob hang forward.

"Remember," she says. "Act neutral. And sober."

<hr />

Neutral. That's how we block the paparazzi. No weird facial expressions, no smiles, no frowns, nothing for them to use to spin fictional tales of our lives.

"Neutral," I say, nodding. I take her hand, and she opens the door to the busy West Hollywood street.

Immediately, paparazzi start yelling questions at me and sticking cameras in my face. I shield my eyes.

"Em! Emmy! Hey, Em!" they shout. I keep my gaze on my blurred feet, focusing as hard as I can so that I don't trip or stumble in front of them.

"What are you and your gal pal up to tonight?"

"Is Jessie your girlfriend?"

"Have you been drinking?"

"Aren't you underage, Em?"

"Are you going back to your place to continue partying?"

Alfie steps in between us and the cameras. They start pestering him instead. It's like I've disappeared. I keep my head down, letting my hair fall in front of my face.

"Hey, Alfie, did you get lucky in the club tonight?"

"What do you think about your ex being spotted with that basketball player?"

"Where's Ryan tonight?"

"Yeah, where's Ryan? Is there trouble in Brightsiders paradise?"

Meanwhile, it's taking all my brainpower just to put one foot in front of the other. I hold my breath like it's going to help me walk straighter. One stumble is all it could take for me to land on tomorrow's front pages.

Ryan emerges from the club, carrying a bottle of water. He catches up with us as we power-walk to the car and the questions start flying his way, too.

"Hey, Ryan!" a photographer says. "Where you headed, man?"

"You happy to see *Strange Welcome* still topping all the charts?"

The four of us ignore the interrogation and climb into Jessie's Range Rover, and I'm impressed with how well I did pretending to be sober.

"Alfie," Jessie says, turning to him from the driver's seat as he and Ryan climb into the back. "What are you doing?"

"Cheeseburgers," he says.

"Same," Ryan adds.

I laugh because *cheeseburgers* suddenly sounds like the funniest word in the history of all words.

"Cheeeeeeeeeeeeeeeeeezzze . . . ," I say. "Buuuuuurrrrgerrrrrrrr zzzzzzzuuuuuhhhhhhh!"

Alfie and Ryan cackle. Jessie glances at me, but I'm too far gone to understand what she's trying to communicate with me.

"Do you three have to do literally everything together?" she asks with big puppy-dog eyes. "Just because you're a band doesn't mean you have to follow each other around twenty-four-seven."

"Hey," Ryan says, handing me the bottle of water. "We're friends. Friends hang out."

I take a long gulp of the water, hoping I can keep it down.

"Can't me and Em have a night to ourselves?" Jessie asks.

Paparazzi surround us, sticking their lenses right up to the windows.

"Can we go, please?" I ask. "I don't feel so good. They can't see me throw up."

Jessie crosses her arms over her chest, pouting. "Why can't we just be alone? Just the two of us."

"You two spend tons of time together," Ryan argues. "We hardly saw Em all summer."

Alfie leans forward between the seats, a smile on his face so the cameras don't know we're fighting. "You're not seriously going to kick us out?" he asks.

Ryan groans. "You're going to leave us to the wolves out there?"

I stroke Jessie's shoulder. "Why are you mad? It's only Alfie and Ry. Let's just go. We can drop them home and have together time. It's cheeseburger time!" I drum my hands on the dashboard, but stop when a gross burp seeps out of me. "We need to go. Don't make me spew all over you."

"No," she says, then looks at them in the rearview mirror. "Get out."

"What the hell?" Alfie asks.

Ryan shakes his head. "You know kicking us out in front of everyone is going to start a billion rumors about the band breaking up, right?"

She shrugs. "I could care less."

I giggle. "Thy mean thy *couldn't* care less. Saying thy could care less means that thy *doth* care. Thou thinks thy doths care a lot."

Alfie laughs. "Wow, you really are wasted."

"Thus!" I say, springing upright in the passenger seat. "Hence! Why we should leaveth, lest the treacherous paparazzi uncover mine drunkenness."

Jessie leans back against her seat.

Alfie sighs. "Fine. Fuck you, too."

Before I can tell them to stay, Alfie and Ryan force their way out of the car and disappear into a sea of flashes and questioning.

"Whyyyyy?" I moan, resting my head on the seat. "Why did you do that?"

Jessie starts the engine and smiles at me like nothing happened. "I just wanna be alone with you, babe."

I pull out my phone and text Alfie and Ryan.

EM: sorry :(

ALFIE: not your fault

RYAN: All good, Em. Good luck not vomming!

ALFIE: drink lots of water :)

Jessie toots her horn at the photographers standing in front of her car before making a sharp turn onto the road.

"Huh," she says, glancing in her mirrors. "The paps are following us." I think I see a hint of a smile on her face, but maybe my vision is just blurry.

I turn in my seat to look out the rear window. Jessie slams on the brakes, the tires screeching across the asphalt. The Range Rover spins and skids to a halt, the force knocking me off my seat and into the dashboard.

"Shit!" Jessie cries, punching the steering wheel.

I rub my back where it hit the dash. "Ow."

Other cars in the intersection toot their horns at us, and then something hits us from behind. It slams into us so hard that our car moves forward into the middle of the intersection. We scream as another car skids to a stop just feet away from my side of the Range Rover.

I jump out of the car and immediately throw up. My arms and legs tremble from the shock, and when I wipe my mouth I see blood smeared across my hand.

Jessie runs around the car to reach me, taking me by the shoulders. "Em? Are you . . . Oh shit, your nose is bleeding." She lifts my chin to dip my head back and pinches the bridge of my nose. It takes a second for me to realize it hurts, and I swat her hand away from my face.

"Owwww." I lightly touch my nose. "I think it's broken."

More cars pull up, and the same group of photographers jump

out and run toward us, filming video and taking pictures. Jessie unleashes her wrath on them.

"Get the fuck out of here, you vultures!" she screams. "I'll call the police on you! I'll have you arrested! What kind of people see a car accident and take photos to sell instead of helping the victims?"

"Jess!" I call. "Stop!"

I can taste blood in my mouth.

"Victim?" one of the photographers says to Jessie, laughing. "Doll, you're the one who's about to be arrested if you've been drinking."

Jessie's hands fly up to her mouth, and then she throws a punch at him, missing completely. Sirens sound in the distance, and within minutes police cars arrive in a flash of blue-and-red lights.

The last thing I see before I pass out is Jessie swearing at the police while they handcuff her.

So much for neutral.

CHAPTER TWO

I wake up in a hospital bed with a bandage on my nose and a throbbing headache. The room spins, and it takes me a couple of seconds to see Alfie and Ryan sitting on either side of me, sleeping in their chairs.

I sit up and stretch my back, wincing when it hurts. "What happened?" I whisper.

Alfie wakes up with a start, almost falling off his chair.

"Em?" he croaks. "Do you feel okay? Do want me to get the nurse?" He stands up, but I pull him back down.

"No, I'm okay. Why am I here?"

His eyes widen. "You don't remember?"

I touch my nose gently; it feels sore and tender. "I remember being at the club."

Alfie scratches the back of his head, messing up the dark, wavy mane that runs past his shoulders. "Um . . . you were in an accident. You bruised your ribs and almost broke your nose."

I clutch my chest. "Like, a car accident? Was anyone else hurt?"

He shakes his head. "No. You're the only one in the hospital."

I try to remember something—anything—about the accident. But the last thing I remember is downing some blue slushie drink that tasted like pure vodka, then jumping onto the dance floor.

Tears fill my eyes. "I wasn't driving, was I?"

"Jessie was."

My heart is in my throat, and my stomach has curled itself into a ball, which is exactly what I wish I could do.

I look around the room. "Is she outside?"

He rests his elbows on the bed and frowns. "No, she was arrested, Em. They put her in the drunk tank for the night."

I feel sick, but something tells me I've already puked out everything in my stomach. "When is she getting out?"

"I don't know. This morning, I guess." He rubs a hand down his face. When he speaks again, his voice is louder, angrier. "Did you know she has a previous arrest for drunk driving?"

I lay back against the scrunchy paper pillow. "No. Is she okay?"

"Honestly, I don't give a shit if she's okay or not," Alfie says, leaning back in his chair and folding his arms. "You could have been killed."

Ryan wakes up and yawns. "Hey, Em. You okay?"

"I think so," I say quietly. "Just sore. And embarrassed."

They exchange a look.

"What?" I ask.

Alfie shakes his head. "Nothing."

"Try to relax," Ryan adds, but he's still giving Alfie a worried look. "The doctor said you need to take it easy for a few days." His phone buzzes, and he answers it in Korean. It must be his parents. He's first-generation Korean American, and his parents are some of our biggest fans—the kind who wear our band T-shirts to the supermarket so they can brag to the cashier that Ryan is their son. I adore them.

That's when I notice he and Alfie are still in the clothes they were wearing at the club. Alfie in a white tee, black skinny jeans and faux-leather jacket. The fluorescent lights make his creamy white skin look a sickly gray. I've always been paler than him, so I don't even want to know how they make me look right now.

Ry has the hood of his red-and-black flannel shirt draped over his head, flattening his jet black hair, which is usually perfectly styled into a high quiff. His light brown skin is washed out by the lights, too, and his faded Ninja Turtles tee is stained blue. Suddenly I remember all the drinks I had last night.

Ryan ends the call and sighs. "My mom just saw the news. Apparently they're saying you're in a coma. She was freaking out."

Oh, hell. "I'm so sorry, Ry. Is she okay?"

He nods. "Now that she knows you're okay, she's fine."

I hate how much this is already affecting the people around me. Ughhhh. What have I done?

A woman's voice echoes down the hall outside, and I sit up. "Oh no."

Alfie groans. "Sal's here."

Sal is our manager. Well, the head manager of our vast group of managers, agents, and everyone else who runs our lives. It's ridiculous how many people it takes to handle the hectic lives of three famous teens. All the times I dreamed of our band making it big, having an entourage organizing every minute of my day never entered my mind. Everything else, though—the fans, the money, the chance to share our songs with millions of people—that makes it all so worth it. Sitting on stage, slamming my drums while Ry rocks the guitar and Alfie belts out our lyrics, that's my happy place. And one day, I'll be singing lead on stage, too. At least, I hope I will. Maybe not, after this scandal.

"Emmy King's room, please?" Sal asks someone outside. I can already tell by the fast tempo of her voice that she's pissed. The door bursts open, and she glides in like a warrior in stilettos and sleek hair extensions.

She leans over Ryan and takes my hands in hers. "Emmy, are you all right?"

I nod and swallow nervously. She touches the back of her hand to my forehead.

"I'm fine," I say timidly.

She straightens and puts her hands on her hips. "Good, because I don't want to yell at a sick person." I hold my breath, preparing for her fury. "What the hell were you thinking, Emmy? Underage drinking? Driving under the influence?"

Ryan holds up a finger. "For the record, Em wasn't the one driving."

Sal throws her hands up in the air. "Do you think the press gives two fucks who was really driving? She's the celebrity, she's the seventeen-year-old role model with legions of teenagers looking up to her. Do you think their parents are going to shell out cash to buy your songs or go to your concerts if they think the Brightsiders are bratty party animals?"

Alfie drops his head into his hands. I sink lower into the bed and wish I could hide under the blanket and disappear. I feel like the worst person in the world right now.

"Just because you play punk rock music," Sal continues, "doesn't give you a pass to act like a little punk."

Ouch. That hurts, but she's right.

"I'm so sorry, everyone," I say.

Alfie reaches out and takes my hand, and Ryan gives me a tired smile.

Sal's phone buzzes. She looks at it and sighs dramatically. "Well, it's happening. All the videos from last night have officially gone viral."

My mouth goes dry. "Videos?"

Sal purses her full lips. "Don't act like you don't know."

"She doesn't remember anything," Alfie says, glaring at Sal.

She throws her head back and laughs. "Of course she doesn't. Well, allow me to refresh your memory." She holds her phone out to me.

"Don't," Alfie says.

"She doesn't need to see it right now," Ryan says.

They exchange that same worried look from before, and I realize this is what they weren't telling me. It must be really, really bad.

I take the phone and hit play. It starts off innocently enough: me dancing with Jessie in the club, flirting, laughing, the usual. Then there's me with some sort of blue concoction in my hand, gulping it down. Then another. And another. And soon I can hardly walk straight. Next, videos and photos of me puking my guts out all over Alfie's boots. Then me out on the street, my lips stained blue, my hair a mess, and my mascara smudged under my eyes.

Then it gets weirder. There's video of us in Jessie's Range Rover, and Jessie looks upset. I can see the vein that always appears in her forehead when she's mad at me. Alfie and Ryan get out of the car, and we speed off. The next shot is me falling out of the car in the middle of an intersection, blood running down my face, and puking again. The final nail in the coffin hits when I see Jessie swiping at photographers and getting arrested, while I fall unconscious on the road in the background, with my skirt hitched up and my lace underwear on show.

It's like a tacky montage from a bad frat party movie.

I give Sal her phone back with shaking hands, then promptly burst into tears. I've become the starlet of the tabloids, the celebrity train-wreck everyone talks about on the morning talk shows, chastising me over their mugs of coffee while an audience cheers. No one is ever going to take me seriously again. Every time my name is mentioned, this is going to be the moment they remember. Last night is going to be chained to me everywhere I go, for the rest of my career. For the rest of my life.

"My . . . life . . . is . . . overrrr," I wail.

Alfie and Ryan hug me, and even Sal seems to soften when faced with my tears of sheer humiliation.

"Come on now," she says. "Don't be so dramatic. You've got me, remember? We have a whole team of people who are already doing damage control. We're going to spin this into a positive."

I try to ask how, but her phone rings and she leaves the room to answer it. I turn to Alfie and Ry. "Tell me honestly, how bad is this?"

They don't answer me. They don't even look at me. But they don't have to. Seeing myself in that video, it's clear that I'm spiraling out of control. I can't keep doing this.

Ry presses the heels of his hands into his eyes. "When we heard you had been rushed to the ER . . ." He trails off. My stomach turns.

Alfie clears his throat, like he's trying to hold himself together. "But it's okay. You're okay." But I can tell by the tears in his eyes that he doesn't believe that. And neither do I.

I am not okay.

I need to get my shit together, ASAP. I wipe my tears away with the back of my hand. "I'm gonna fix this," I say. "I promise."

CHAPTER THREE

Later that afternoon, Sal sneaks us out the back exit of the hospital and drives us back to my place. I've been living in a hotel for the last six months, waiting out the days until I turn eighteen and can buy my own house. It's expensive, but anything beats living with my parents.

Paparazzi wait on the sidewalk outside the revolving doors and hold their cameras up to the windows of the car, tapping on the glass as we pull up to the curb. Hotel security forces the vultures back as Sal marches through them, creating a path for me. Alfie and Ryan walk on either side of me while I hide behind my oversize sunglasses and cover my bandaged nose with my hands.

The concierge frowns when he sees us walking through the lobby. I hang my head so my hair falls in front of my face, avoiding his judgmental gaze. Sal presses the button for the elevator, and I take in a deep breath, dreaming of my beautiful bathtub. I'm going to soak myself in hot water for at least three hours. The elevator takes us up to the top floor, where my neighbor, Dr. Bennis, waits with her little bulldog, Frenchie. I smile as we pass, but she turns her nose up at me and steps into the elevator. I'm not exactly the most popular resident here, but no one has ever snubbed me like that before. Oh God, she must have seen the videos.

"Okay, Em," Sal says once we're safely inside my apartment. "I know there's probably no point saying this, but try to stay offline for the next few days. No Twitter. No Tumblr. Not even Snapchat, okay? Maybe don't watch much TV, either, and definitely *do not* Google yourself."

"I won't," I say. She gives me a hug, and I breathe in the strong vanilla scent of her perfume.

"You'll be fine," she says. "I've got this under control. Just lay low this week." She turns to Alfie and Ryan. "You two keep her company if you can."

They both nod. Sal opens the front door but turns and points her finger at us before leaving. "And absolutely no alcohol or anything illegal! You hear me?"

"Yes, Sal," we all say. She closes the door, and a minute later we hear the ding of the elevator.

"Are you hungry, Em?" Alfie asks as he opens my fridge. "Jesus, you have, like, no food in here."

I can't look my bandmates in the eyes. "I usually just order room service."

Ryan opens my pantry, but that's bare, too. "We could order a pizza?"

"You two order," I say, yawning. "I'm not that hungry. I think I'm just gonna take a bath and go to bed."

I stand in front of my bathroom mirror and use my facial wipes to smear away last night's makeup and today's tears. Jessie's makeup is scattered all over my sink, concealers and lipsticks and eyeshadows, each a reminder that she's not here. God, I hope she's okay. The thought of her locked up all night, scared and alone, breaks my heart. She must be worried sick after seeing me pass out after the accident. I try calling her phone for the fifth time since I was discharged, but it's still switched off.

Before I've even started running the bath, there's a knock on my door.

"I've got it, Em," Alfie calls out to me. I press my ear to my closed bathroom door to hear who it is.

"Can I speak to Miss King, please?" I recognize the concierge's snooty voice. I walk out of my room to see him standing in the doorway with two members of hotel security behind him.

"Is everything okay?" I ask.

"I'm afraid not," he says as he steps past Alfie and into my apartment. The guards follow him. "I need to discuss something rather delicate with you." He glances disapprovingly at Alfie and Ryan, then adds, "*In private.*"

I narrow my eyes at him. "Whatever you need to say, you can say it in front of them."

He nods and holds his hands behind his back. "I've been told by management to ask you to leave the hotel."

"*What?*" I glance at the guards and realize they're here for me.

"As you are aware, we've had a number of complaints from the other residents and guests here," he explains. "Not merely about the noise from the many parties you've thrown, but also complaints about vulgar behavior directed at residents by you and your many guests." He side-eyes Alfie and Ryan, and I grit my teeth. "And given the, um"—he clears his throat—"recent events, management has decided to ask you to find alternative accommodation."

Recent events. Ugh. I want to fight, to argue my way out of this, but I'm just too tired. Alfie, on the other hand, jumps to my defense.

"You can't just kick her out," he says. "She has a lease."

"Yes, and in that lease it states very clearly that a resident who repeatedly breaks hotel rules and ignores warnings will be asked to vacate the premises without notice."

"What rules have been broken?" Ryan asks.

The concierge takes in a deep breath through his nose. "As I mentioned, rules regarding noise pollution and offensive behavior. There was also the incident with the *sand*."

Oh shit. I knew that would come back to bite me in the butt one day. For our three-month anniversary, Jessie threw me a beach party and turned the hotel rooftop swimming pool into an island, complete with tons of sand she had delivered. We first met at a beach; I was there shooting a music video and she was there for a bonfire party. So she was trying to re-create that day, which was super sweet. It was totally fun, and everyone was loving it—until the wind picked up and turned the roof into the eye of a sandstorm. We escaped the worst of it by running into the stairwell and back to my apartment, but the pool was clogged for days, and the rooftop was closed until professional cleaners collected every last grain. Some of the sand even fell to the lower balconies, resulting in lots of complaints. I ended up footing the bill, which cost more than having the sand delivered in the first place. So, yeah, that was my bad. I don't blame them for being pissed about that.

"Miss King," the concierge continues, "if you have further questions, I've been asked to refer you to our lawyers."

"Forget it," I say with a sigh. "Just give me a week or two to find a new place, and I'll be out of your hair."

He shakes his head. "I'm afraid I've been instructed to escort you out immediately. You have one hour to pack your things."

Alfie straightens his back, like he always does when he's mad and about to argue with someone, but I take his hand.

"Don't even bother," I say. "Just help me pack so we can get out of here."

The concierge gestures for security to follow him. "We'll wait for you in the lobby."

Once they're gone, Alfie turns to me, his brow furrowed. "You can come stay with me. I'll sleep on the couch."

I shake my head. "Thanks, but no. I'll just go back to my parents' place and tough it out until I turn eighteen."

"No way," he says. "They'll drive you crazy. Just come stay with me. I'd love to have you."

Ryan rubs the back of his neck. "I think Em's right. I mean, there's no way she can lay low at your place, it's in the middle of Hollywood."

"I'll just go back to Venice and hide out for a while. I'll be safer from the paparazzi there." I think of the house where I grew up and shudder. It's more like a museum than a home, a shrine to my mom and dad's short-lived music career. It's the last place I want to be right now, but it's the only place I can go where I won't have to worry about cameras peeking over walls or through windows. It's the only place I can go where I'll be left alone.

CHAPTER FOUR

"No one's home," I say as Alfie rings the doorbell for the third time. "I told you they'd be out on a Saturday. They're somewhere drinking mimosas with their friends."

"Don't you have a spare key?" Ry asks as he peeks through the window.

"Never needed one." I start walking through the bushes and around the side of the house to the backyard. It's littered with empty wine bottles and cigarette butts. A pair of red lace underwear floats in the middle of the pool. Looks like they had one of their Friday-night ragers and went straight to brunch. I slip off my heels and grab on to the vines that snake up the back of the house. Memories of all the times I snuck out to go to Alfie's house come flooding back.

Through the kitchen window I see framed portraits of my parents and roll my eyes. I'm not in any of the photos that adorn the walls and the mantel over the fireplace. If a total stranger walked through their house, they'd never even know my parents have a daughter. It's like I don't exist.

"Em?" Alfie calls from the front of the house. "You in yet?"

"One sec!" I yell back, then keep climbing. The vines are thicker than I remember; they've grown since I've been gone. But everything else here seems to have stayed the same.

I reach the roof and haul myself up, then rest for a second to catch my breath. Scaling a building after having my stomach pumped is probably not the smartest decision I've ever made, but desperate times call for desperate measures. When I'm sure I'm not going to collapse, I crawl over to my bedroom window. As usual, it opens easily, and I drop inside. Inside, everything is exactly as I left it. My walls and ceiling are plastered with posters of bands, a Pride flag hangs over the back of my bedroom door, and my desk is covered in notebooks filled with all the songs I used to write.

My bedroom was originally supposed to be their recording studio, but Mom got knocked up and, according to them, that's when everything started to turn to shit. Dad started cheating and drinking instead of writing music, so he was kicked out of his band. Mom started playing gigs in bars to pay the bills and began her own drinking habit after her shows. And I spent most of my time up in my room, way at the top of the house, separate from everything. Unfortunately, they never got around to soundproofing it, so I was constantly kept awake by their fighting or by Dad broodingly playing his guitars all through the night. The parties started when I was about thirteen, and the house was perpetually filled with loud nineties grunge and cigarette smoke. The night I got my first period, I had to sneak a tampon from the purse of some random woman who was passed out on our stairs because my mom was busy playing strip poker with a bunch of middle-aged dudes.

"Jesus," I whisper. "It's like I never left." I run down the stairs to let Alfie and Ry inside.

"Gross," Ry says as he walks into the living room. "It smells like all the furniture has been soaked in bong water."

I laugh, but I can't help but feel a little embarrassed. "Yeah. Sorry. The party never ends here."

Alfie gives me a sympathetic look. "Did you really expect it to?"

"I don't know," I say, shrugging. "Maybe."

If I'm honest, I did expect them to change. I thought seeing me walk out six months ago would have shocked them into cleaning up their lives. But from the state of the house, it seems all I did was give them free rein to go as wild as they wanted.

"You don't have to stay," I say, pretending not to notice the way Ryan is surveying the living room, his eyes landing on every lipstick-stained wine glass and empty beer bottle. Just add a tiger in the bathroom and it would be a recreation of the famous waking-up scene in *The Hangover*.

This is why I never invited friends over when I was growing up.

"Sorry," I say again. "Weekends always were the messiest here."

Ry rubs the back of his neck and chuckles. "To be honest, I was just thinking how it reminds me of your apartment after a big night."

I do a double take. "No way, man." His words feel like a punch to the stomach. "It doesn't look anything like this! That's totally . . ." But then I scan the room, seeing it as he does, and realize he's right. I've thrown a ton of parties lately, the kind that made my hotel apartment look like a tornado tore through it. Knowing that Ry sees similarities between me and my parents makes me feel so gross. I'm not like them. I'm a teenager; we're supposed to party, right? They're grown-ass humans. They're parents. They're supposed to be responsible and sensible and know their limits and all that adulting stuff. Mom and Dad are the ones looking bad here, not me.

———

Once we carry all my boxes and bags up to my room, I decide to soak my bruised body in a hot bath.

My back and ribs ache as I retreat into my bathroom and lock the door. I lean over my bathtub and turn the water on, then open the window to get some air. The afternoon sunshine casts a glare on the rooftops below and makes the glimpse of ocean sparkle on the horizon. I will never tire of the endless California summer, but the sky seems so obnoxiously blue at times like this, when it feels like my life is a rolling storm cloud.

The sliding doors to my living room open below, and Alfie walks out onto the pool deck, his phone held up in front of him.

"Hey, Kass," he says. I lean back so he doesn't see me. He's talking to Kassidy, my cousin who lives on the East Coast. She's probably calling to check in on me. I wish Kass were here instead of Boston. As comforting as Alfie and Ryan have been today, I really need her right now. She knows what my parents are like.

"Where's Emmy? I've been texting her all day, but she isn't responding," Kass says.

"I think her phone is off," Alfie says. "I don't think she wants to talk to anyone right now."

"Is she okay?"

"I don't think so. Can you blame her? The whole world is tearing her to shreds."

"I can't believe some of things people are saying," Kass says. "Some people are calling her an alcoholic and a slut. Can you believe that?"

A lump forms in my throat. I feel like such an embarrassment.

Alfie sighs. "You have no idea how much I want to just tell everyone to shut the fuck up. They don't know her; they don't know anything about what's going on behind the scenes. Em has had to go through so much horrible shit lately. She doesn't deserve this."

My chest tightens. I shouldn't be eavesdropping, but I want to hear what Kass has to say.

"Alfie, calm down," she says. "You can't say anything—it will just make things worse. You all need to lie low until this blows over. Focus on being there for Em."

"I know, I know," he says. "But I don't know how to do that. I can't tell her what to do with her life, you know? It's not my place. And it's not like her parents will do anything to help."

Alfie knows my parents; he's seen them at their worst, and been there when I needed to run away for a night or two. But, god, I hope he's wrong about this. I hope my parents see how much I need them right now. I hope coming back here will give us a chance to fix our relationship.

"She shouldn't be staying with them," Kass says. I can hear the bitterness in her voice. "That house is toxic, especially right now." There's a pause, and then my cousin speaks again, so softly I almost miss it.

"Alfie, can I tell you something?"

"What?"

She takes in a deep breath, and I lean forward. "I'm scared that if she keeps partying this hard, she's going to end up just like them."

I sink to the cold bathroom floor. Pain radiates down my bruised nose as I cry. Am I that out of control? I try to pinpoint the moment I started down this road. I don't remember seeing any signs, but it's clear now that the people around me did. Oh, god. Is this how my parents ended up the way they are? They just kept partying and partying until suddenly they're forty years old with wine-stained carpets and a house that reeks of cigarettes and regrets? This must be how the fighting started between my mom and her sister.

When I was twelve and Kassidy was fourteen, her dad got a job in Boston and they moved from three blocks away to three thousand miles away. I hated them for leaving me. Aunt Jo and Uncle Ben were the glue holding my parents together. They were their therapists, drinking buddies, and friends. But then Jo got a DUI while driving Kass and me home from school. She and Uncle Ben started going to Alcoholics Anonymous and told my parents they weren't drinking anymore. My mom thought it was ridiculous. She even laughed, saying they were being melodramatic. We started seeing them less and less, and then one day my mom's resentment reached peak level and she unleashed on Aunt Jo. It was the biggest argument I've ever seen. Kass and I spent most of it up in her room, pretending we couldn't hear it over the One Direction album we were listening to. But I heard everything my mom said: accusing her sister of being self-righteous, of thinking she was better than us, and of being a boring old woman now. Jo, Ben, and Kass moved to Boston two weeks later, and they haven't spoken to my parents since.

Within months, my parents went from backyard barbecues at Ben and Jo's to throwing three or four parties a week. It was like living in a frat house. Mom and Dad were trying to prove to Ben and Jo that they didn't need them, that they could have more fun without them.

I don't want to end up like that. Like *them*. I can't.

How did I go from being an unknown kid playing the drums in a garage to being the latest celebrity trainwreck?

Once the bathtub fills, I dab my tears on a towel and pull myself up to turn off the water.

I pull my T-shirt over my head and unclip my bra, gasping when I catch a glimpse of my back in the mirror. Bruises cover the middle of my back, sides, and left hip.

I don't know what's scarier: the fact that I'm covered in bruises, or the fact that I don't remember how I got them. With trembling hands, I slowly peel the bandage off my nose, and swallow back more tears when I see my face. The bridge of my nose is twice its normal size, and my eyes are black and blue.

I rest my hands on the dusty sink and try to breathe, then look myself square in the eyes.

"I am not like them," I say. "I am not like them, and I won't ever be like them. I won't, I won't, I won't."

I sink into the steaming hot bath, close my eyes, and try to think. All my dreams have come true. I have fame, money, friends . . . everything that's supposed to make me happy. So why am I crying alone in my tub? Why the hell am I making headlines for all the wrong reasons?

What is so fundamentally broken in me that I keep trying so hard to screw it all up?

CHAPTER FIVE

I wake up to someone knocking on my bathroom door. I sit up in the cold bathwater, and shiver.

"Emmy?" Alfie calls. "Are you okay?"

"Fine," I croak. "I'm fine. Fell asleep."

Teeth chattering, I lift myself out of the bath and wrap up in my old robe. When I walk out, Alfie is sitting on my bed and for the first time I notice how exhausted he looks. Dark circles hang under his eyes and his shoulders are hunched, like he's the one the world hates right now.

"Are you okay?" I ask as I sit next to him.

"Me?" he says with wide eyes. "Forget me, I'm fine. You're the one I'm worried about."

I try to give him a reassuring smile, but it hurts my nose and I end up grimacing. He reaches into his jacket pocket and pulls out a fresh bandage.

"The nurse gave this to me," he says, unwrapping it. "Here." He touches his fingers under my chin and turns me to face him. I close my eyes and hold my breath, waiting for the pain to come. But he's so careful, so gentle, that it hardly hurts at all. The pads of his thumbs slide over the edge of the bandage, smoothing it over my skin. When he's done, I open my eyes to find him staring at me.

Alfie tousles up his hair like he always does when he's nervous. The first time I saw him do it was when we were around fourteen, when he came out to me as genderqueer. After he told me, I did a lot of Googling and reading and watching of YouTube videos to educate myself and unlearn all the gender binary bull I'd been programmed to believe. I held his hand while he told his parents and asked them to use he/him pronouns for him. About a year later, he changed his name to Alfie. I still remember sitting on his top bunk in his bedroom while he told me how he'd been feeling.

"I just don't feel like I fit," he told me. "I've never felt 100 percent like a girl, but I'm not a guy, either. And I don't see why I have to fit. Why should I try to change myself to suit someone else's binary? It's like trying to fit a galaxy into a glass jar. I don't want to be poked and prodded into a glass jar. How am I supposed to breathe like that? Right now, I'm poking holes in the lid, letting the light and air in and freeing pieces of me star by star. And one day, I'm just going to shatter it."

He's definitely done that. Being thrust onto the world stage last year turned him into a powerful ambassador for nonbinary teens like him. And as a result of his coming out and all the hours we spent trading videos, articles, and books by people in the LGBTQIAP+ community, I realized I'm totally, fantastically queer.

I'm not officially out about that yet, though. I wanted to come out publicly the moment I heard our first song played on the radio, but I was worried about what the media would do. The media loves labels.

I knew they'd demand one of me or slap one on me themselves, so I took some time to figure out what label felt right to me. And I did: I'm totally bisexual. So far, I've only come out to the people closest to me. Then I started dating people of different genders and let the gossip blogs figure it out on their own. Getting comfortable with my bisexuality has been liberating; I've never felt more myself. One day soon, I'll be officially out to the world. I've just been waiting for the right moment. And okay, yeah, I'm scared. I've spent a lot time worrying that I'm not queer enough. I'm scared of being told I'm a poser or unwelcome or just trying to be on trend. I'm scared of screwing up and being called a "bad bisexual," even though logically I know there's no such thing. But fear isn't logical.

"I'm so sorry," I whisper. "I keep screwing up, and I don't know how to stop." The tears come again, and he pulls me into his arms.

"Hey, uh, Em?" Ry calls from downstairs. "I think your parents are home. And they brought company."

I let out a long groan. Alfie's shoulders tighten against me.

"Just stay at my place," he whispers. "You'll be so much happier there."

I shake my head and pull away from him. "If I crash at yours, the media will target you, too. You're in the center of town, so there's no way either of us will be able to hide. I need to stay away from everyone for a little while."

Just then, I hear voices downstairs singing an old Pearl Jam song. My dad is doing his best Eddie Vedder impersonation while his friends cheer him on. I can tell just by listening to them that they are wasted even though it's only five p.m.

A moment later, Ryan barrels up the stairs like he's running from a serial killer.

"Whoa," he says as he closes the door behind him. "There's, like, twenty people down there. And they're all singing."

I nod like it's no big deal, because this is my life. "Wait till they get to the Michael Jackson portion of the evening. Twenty drunk people trying to moonwalk. It gets dangerous." I smile, but I don't want them to see this. It's funny when my parents are characters in a story I tell to kill time on the tour bus, but seeing them up close . . . it's just sad.

"Stay here," I say. "Don't go down there without me." I grab a pair of sweatpants and a T-shirt from one of my suitcases and go into the bathroom to get dressed.

When I'm ready, we carefully sneak downstairs. I successfully help Alfie and Ry out the front door so they don't have to talk to my parents, but as I creep back up the stairs, I hear my mother laugh.

"Well, well, well," she says. "Look what the cat dragged in. David! Your daughter has decided to grace us with her presence!"

I freeze. Maybe if I stay incredibly still, she'll get bored and leave me alone. But then my dad appears, and I know I'm going to have to talk to them. "Uh, hey, guys."

My mom raises her mimosa in the air. "To what do we owe the pleasure?"

Dad nudges her on the arm. "I know why she's here. She needs a place to hide out after embarrassing herself last night." He turns to follow his friends into the backyard, then calls out to me, "I'd be embarrassed, too, if the whole world knew it only took three drinks for me to black out! What a lightweight."

He looks back over his shoulder and winks at Mom, and she laughs.

I wrap my arms around myself and lean against the wall. The only time I ever see my parents act like a married couple is when they're ganging up on me. Normally, Dad spends most of his time pretending Mom doesn't exist, while his mere existence seems to infuriate my mom. I sometimes think the only reason they constantly have friends and neighbors over to the house is so they don't actually have to spend time alone together.

Mom looks me up and down, then takes a sip of her drink. "I guess you can stay. But don't expect us to drop everything now that you're back. We have lives of our own, you know."

I just nod, then she wanders back to their guests. I drag myself to my room, close the door, and fall face-first onto my bed.

Welcome home.

The party finally dies down around sunset. I can tell because the sound of my dad's guitar fills the house, and he never plays in front of anyone anymore. Mom has probably gone to do her usual Saturday-night gig at one of the bars on the beachfront, so Dad is reliving his band days all alone.

A few hours later, I wake up to tapping on my window. "Hello?"

Tap, tap, tap.

"Alfie? Is that you?" I slide out of bed and tug the window open.

"Why would Alfie be sneaking into your room?" Jessie demands.

I sit back on the bed, and she climbs inside.

"Sorry," I say. "I didn't think anyone else knew I was here."

She stands over me, her silhouette tall and looming. "So? Why would *he* be at your window?"

"I dunno," I say. "I used to climb through his window, remember? I told you about that. I guess I just assumed."

She sits next to me on the bed, and even in the darkness I can tell she's tense. Sometimes I wonder if she's overprotective, or if she doesn't trust me. Either way, it makes it hard to breathe.

"I've been trying to reach you all day," I say.

"I couldn't exactly answer my phone from a drunk tank."

I find her hand in the dark and hold it. "Are you okay? You wanna talk about it?"

She softens, resting her head on my shoulder. "I don't remember much from last night. Thank god for booze. But I woke up freezing my ass off in a corner, surrounded by strangers. Three women were throwing punches about some guy. Another girl puked on me. And I had to shit in front of all of them. It took hours for them to finally let me go. But I lost my license for a while."

I cringe. "I'm so sorry, baby."

"Then," she continues, "the second I walked out of the precinct, paps attacked me like fucking zombies. I had to literally sprint away from them. Like, normally I don't mind being photographed, but I was not having it today." She throws her hand over her eyes. "I cannot believe you let me drive last night."

"Huh?" I must have misheard. "Me?"

"Yeah," she says, her voice steady, calm. "Why did you let me get behind the wheel? Didn't you see how wasted I was?"

Wait. Is she really saying this is my fault? I shift away from her in the bed. "I was too drunk to notice anything. I woke up in the hospital with no clue how I got there."

"I'd rather wake up in the hospital than a police station."

I don't say anything. I'm pissed. But she's so sure of what she's saying, like it's so clear that I should've stopped her and prevented all this. Maybe she's right.

My silence must tell her something's wrong, so she snuggles closer. "Are you hurt bad? Any broken bones?" she asks sweetly.

"My nose is busted. Hurts like hell."

She sucks a quick breath between her teeth. "Ouch."

I crawl farther under the covers, unsure of how I'm meant to be feeling. I don't think it's fair for her to act like the accident was my fault, but she's being so cute and caring now. Anyway, I'm too tired to argue, and it really does sound like her day was much worse than mine.

"I went to your apartment," she says, and I slap my hand to my forehead.

"Oh shit. I'm so sorry; I didn't get a chance to tell you about that."

She lets out an exasperated sigh. "Did you at least pack up my stuff?"

"Of course. It's all here."

"Good. I guess we're living here now."

I pause. I didn't realize we *were* living together. But now isn't the time to argue. "Guess so."

"With all the voicemails and texts you left me," she says, "you could've mentioned that."

"Please," I say, my last drop of energy drained. "Everyone in the world hates me right now. I can't bear to have you hate me, too. Can we just forget everything for a few hours? Please?"

Jessie wraps me in her arms. "Sorry. I've just had a day. Of course I don't hate you."

"Thanks," I say, wiping away my tears.

She's quiet for a few minutes, and I start to relax. But just as I'm drifting to sleep, I hear her whisper, "I still don't see why Alfie would be at your window."

CHAPTER SIX

The sound of Jessie's laughter wakes me up the next morning. I pull on new sweatpants and a T-shirt, then go downstairs to find her eating breakfast with my parents, the smell of eggs and burnt toast in the air. Dad stands at the counter, pouring coffee into a mug. Mom sits at the kitchen table, a mimosa in one hand and her iPad in the other. Jessie laughs as my dad tells her a story about his rock-and-roll days—probably one I've heard a thousand times. I take a seat between Jessie and my mom and start scraping the singed crumbs off a piece of toast.

"Emmy," Mom says, glancing up from her screen. "How long are you and Jessica planning on being guests in our home?"

"Um . . . not long, hopefully. Just until everything blows over."

She purses her lips. "And when do you think everything will"— she puts her iPad and mimosa down just so she can do air-quotes with her fingers—"*blow over*?"

She seems to think I actually want to be here.

Dad and Jessie keep talking and laughing. I wish I had sat on the other side of the table.

"Don't worry," I say dryly. "I'll be out of here as soon as possible."

Mom shakes her head. "I don't know why you think you can just run back here the moment trouble strikes. That's not how the real world works. I really shouldn't let you stay here, you know. I shouldn't spoil you like that. But I am your mother, after all."

This is where I'm supposed to thank her. We play this game a lot. She acts like she's Mother of the Century, and I'm supposed to grovel at her feet and beg forgiveness for being such a terrible daughter.

I don't say anything. I'm tired of this game.

"Oh, Emmy, Emmy, Emmy," Mom says, clicking her tongue. "When will you learn that you can't live in a bubble surrounded by yes-men forever?"

I furrow my brow. "What bubble? Which yes-men? You don't know anything about my life."

As though she prepared evidence for this argument in advance, my mom turns her iPad to me, showing the latest headline on TMZ.

IS EMMY KING HEADED FOR A BREAKDOWN?

"Are they right?" Mom asks. "Are you heading for a breakdown?"

Dad stifles more laughter. Jessie looks confused, like she's not sure if they're making a bad joke or just being assholes.

I stay calm and look Mom in the eyes. "If I was, would you even care?"

"Emmy." Mom puts the iPad down and pinches the bridge of her nose between her thumb and index finger. "Must you be *so* dramatic?"

Dad leans over the table and picks up the iPad. "What else is on here about you that we don't know about?"

"Lord knows you don't tell us anything," Mom adds.

"You never ask," I say.

Dad finds another article and squints to read it out loud. *"King Falls from Her Throne.* Ha! Now that's a smart headline."

Jessie shakes her head. I'm so embarrassed that she's seeing this.

I throw my head back and groan. I'll show my mother dramatic. "I cannot wait to get out of this fucking hellhole. Even one day is too much in this place."

Dad drops the iPad to the table with a thud. "Hey, missy. Show some gratitude."

"Yes," Mom says, even though she's smirking. This is exactly what she wanted. "You keep behaving this way and you'll end up on the street, just like you did six months ago."

"You didn't kick me out then," I say. "I left."

Mom chuckles. "And look how well that turned out for you. You need us. Remember that." She sips her drink, her pinky finger extended delicately. "And please, do tell us exactly how you plan to leave this 'fucking hellhole.'"

"I'm going to start looking for a place to live," I say quickly. "My plan is to buy a house."

She raises an eyebrow. "How nice for you."

My hips swivel ever so slowly toward Jessie in an attempt to extract myself from the conversation with my mother. I'm so done. But it doesn't work.

"Did you hear that, David?" Mom asks. "Emmy is going to buy herself a house."

"With what money?" he asks.

I clear my throat. "With *my* money."

He exchanges a look with Mom, like they're in on a joke I don't know about.

"Well," he says, "good for you. At least you'll have somewhere other than here to go when the green stops pouring in."

"Mm-hmm," Mom says. "Enjoy it while it lasts."

This whole time, Jessie sits next to me, eating her eggs. I nudge her, hoping she'll say something to change the topic. She looks at me, then shrugs.

"Your dad's right," she says. "Buy a house now, before Alfie leaves to forge a solo career and leaves you in the dust."

My jaw drops, and she starts laughing. So do my parents.

"Alfie wouldn't do that," I say.

"I'm just fooling around," she says. But when I don't smile, she puts a hand on my knee. "Sorry. It was just a joke, I swear."

Dad pulls up a chair at the table, shaking his head. "Don't apologize, kiddo. Someone needs to tell her the truth."

What the actual fuck is happening right now?

I guess I shouldn't be surprised at my parents. This fits nicely into their track record of behavior since my career took off. Instead of being proud of my success, they take offense at it, like we're in competition with one another. Then they do whatever they can to make sure I know I didn't earn any of it, and that I'll fade into a has-been before I can say "one-hit wonder."

"We're just saying," Mom says. "Enjoy it while it lasts."

That's what she said when our band won the Venice Battle of the Bands. Then she said it when we got a manager and a record deal. And again when our debut single climbed the charts. I'm sure she would've said it to me every day since if I hadn't walked out the door and not come back. Until now.

Dad gets up from the table, leaving his dirty plate behind. He shakes his head and laughs. "*King Falls from Her Throne.* That's gold."

I turn and stare at Jess, begging her with my eyes for help. She looks at me with sympathy, but I know there's nothing else she can do. Like Mom said, we're just guests in their house. We need to be on good behavior or we'll be out on the street, crashing on friends' couches until I turn eighteen and can finally buy my own place.

Dad reaches over and squeezes my shoulder. "Smile, girlie! Don't be so sensitive!"

"If you can't take the media's abuse," Mom adds, "you don't deserve the perks of fame, either."

I try to be good. To be quiet and go along with it. I force a smile for them, but I can't stop the tears from welling in my eyes. This isn't funny to me. It hurts. A lot. It's one thing for my parents to give me shit, but I never expected Jessie to join in on it. What she said about Alfie was not cool. She can't actually think that about him, can she? Ugh, this sucks. This is way too much suckiness for the breakfast table. I mean, at least let me eat my damn Froot Loops before you start trolling me about how much of a loser I am.

So I get up from the table and walk out the front door, leaving their laughter behind me.

I walk aimlessly for a few blocks, then find myself standing outside Alfie's old house. It's no surprise that I ended up here; from age twelve onward, this was where I would always go to escape my parents. Only now, there's nothing here except an empty house and a FOR SALE sign. Alfie bought his mom and dad their dream house in Malibu last year—a gesture that sent my own parents into a jealous rage.

"When do we get our Malibu beach house?" they asked.

I had already paid off their mortgage and given them expensive gifts, including a guitar once played by Kurt Cobain for my dad and a new convertible for my mom. I was doing everything I could to attain the title of Best Daughter, and still coming up short. Then they found out Ry flew all his extended relatives over to the US from South Korea to surprise his parents with a family reunion, and my dad suddenly remembered he had cousins in England he needed to visit. That was when I started to see that nothing I ever did would be good enough for them. And yet I still keep hoping that will change.

I walk into the backyard and climb the old jacaranda tree, using the same curves and branches I always used to haul myself up, up, up. In the spring, the tree would bloom purple and I'd pluck the flowers off and tuck them behind my ears. Alfie and I would sit on the roof, under the purple shade, and listen to music for hours. I felt like I could hide there forever and no one would ever find me. I was safe from the world.

Now, though, the flowers have fallen and wilted. There's no shade, nowhere to hide. Alfie's old bedroom window creaks open, and I slip inside, sitting cross-legged on the old carpet to reminisce. I could tell you exactly where every poster used to be on the walls. A huge Paramore poster made up the focal point of the wall by the window, surrounded by a collage of Fall Out Boy, Taking Back Sunday, and classic album covers from the Rolling Stones and David Bowie. More posters plastered the back of his closet door, mostly of Amy Winehouse, Lorde, and Ed Sheeran. They were originally on his wall with the others, but then Ryan accidentally kicked a hole in the door during one of our air guitar jam sessions, so we used the posters to cover it so Alfie's parents wouldn't find out. It's patched up now, but the memory of it still makes me giggle. Ryan hopping on one leg while he tried to free his foot from the door; the look on Alfie's face when it happened, his mouth hanging open, eyes wide. It was months before his parents finally noticed it.

I lean back and stretch out over the carpet, staring up at the ceiling fan. I always thought I'd have this place to go to when I needed it, and now it's empty. Soon a new family will be living here, and all I'll have will be the memories.

My heart hurts. Jessie's voice echoes in my mind, her words circling like vultures. I can't shake the thought that I've been here before, sitting alone before, feeling like shit because someone told me I was nothing. It's a kind of twisted déjà vu.

My stomach turns uneasily. I don't want to be here again. I moved out of my parents' place and into the hotel to escape this feeling, and yet here I am.

———————

"Emmy?" Alfie's voice echoes through the empty house.

I sit up, wondering if I'm hearing things. No one knows I'm here.

Footsteps bounce up the stairs. "Emmy? Are you here?"

Alfie stands in the doorway, a smile appearing when he sees me sitting in the middle of his old room.

"Hey," I say casually, like breaking into and entering empty houses is totally normal. "What are you doing here?"

He sits cross-legged across from me. "I went to your parents' house to see how you were. Jessie said you walked out, so I figured you'd be here." He flips his keys around his fingers. "Lucky I still have my key, or I would've had to Spider-Man it through the window like you."

When I don't say anything, his smile slips away. "You okay? Did something happen?"

I'm afraid that if I talk I'll cry, so I just shrug and lay back down on the carpet. I feel him stretch out next to me. My shoulders tense. I really don't want to talk about this, and I'm dreading the next words that come out of his mouth.

But they never come. Instead, he just lies beside me and lets me rest. I've never felt more grateful for him in my life. Out of everyone in the whole world, when you're feeling sad and don't want to say why but you also don't want to be alone, Alfie is the one you call.

When things got really bad at home, like strangers-passed-out-on-the-staircase bad, I'd sneak out and ride my bike to Alfie's house. I'd tap on his window, and he'd let me sleep in the top bunk. Just hearing him breathing, knowing I wasn't alone, not hearing the walls vibrating from music or loud, unfamiliar voices in the hallway, helped me sleep better than I ever did in my own bed.

"This reminds me of when we were kids," I whisper.

"Me, too."

"Do you ever feel torn between the past and the future?"

He rests his arms behind his head and looks up at the ceiling. "What do you mean?"

I chew on the inside of my cheek as I try to find the words to explain it.

"You're grateful for everything you have now," I say slowly, "and you wouldn't change anything, right? But you're also sad that everything has changed so much. And you can't ever go back to how things used to be."

"Do you want things to go back to how they used to be?" he asks, sounding skeptical.

"Not all of it, obviously. Just some things." I groan. "Never mind. I'm just in a weird place right now."

"I know," he says. "That's why I'm here."

CHAPTER SEVEN

Several days later, I pace back and forth in my room, not knowing what to do with myself. I don't remember the last time I stayed in on a Friday night, but Sal gave me strict instructions not to go out in public. I tried to convince Jessie to stay in with me, but she insisted on going to a birthday party at a club and will likely be out all night. I can't go outside, I can't go online, and all my friends are having fun without me. Even my parents are out doing a gig at a bar. This is a whole new realm of boredom.

But I refuse to sit around feeling sorry for myself, so I put on a swimsuit, a pair of denim shorts, and one of our Brightsiders baseball caps, then pad around the rim of my parents' pool and sit down. I dangle my legs in the water and stare up at the night sky, the stars glittering just like the rest of the city. I can almost feel the collective buzz of energy that spreads through the streets on a weekend like this. I must be the only person in Los Angeles who isn't getting ready to roam the city looking for the best party in town.

The doorbell rings, and I hear Chloe's voice. I haven't seen them since the night at the club, and I have to admit I'm a little nervous. I hope they're not mad at me for getting myself into trouble.

Chloe doesn't take anyone's bullshit—and they don't give it, either. If Chloe has a problem with you, they will let you know. That's what first drew me to them. We met when Alfie was a guest on their YouTube channel. Chloe is nonbinary femme and made a web series interviewing transgender and nonbinary people. After the interview, Alfie invited Chloe to one of our shows and we brought them onstage to sing our hit "All for You." We clicked right away and have been besties ever since.

"Em?" they call down the hallway. "You home?" My parents must have left the door unlocked when they left.

I look over my shoulder and see Chloe walking down the hallway, followed by Alfie and Ryan, carrying pizza boxes.

"Hey! What are you doing here?" I ask.

They walk onto the deck and put the pizzas on the outdoor dining table, pushing aside ashtrays and beer coasters stolen from bars around the city. They flick their sleek, dark mahogany hair over their shoulder and smile.

"We thought you might want some company," Chloe says. I relax, knowing that means they're not mad. They just want to hang out.

"You down for a pizza and Netflix night?" Alfie asks as he flips open one of the boxes. "I think we're way overdue for a Leo marathon."

This has been our thing since we were ten. Ry, Alfie, Kass, and I jacked ourselves up on junk food and soda, determined to sit through Leonardo DiCaprio's biggest hit movies. We made it all through the night but fell asleep at sunrise, right around *Catch Me If You Can*. Ever since, nothing cheers me up like binge-watching Leo with them and stuffing ourselves with KitKats and Flamin' Hot Cheetos.

"You don't have to babysit me," I say as I step up from the pool. "I know there are probably a thousand parties you could go to tonight."

Alfie scoffs. "Everybody knows the best party in LA is wherever Emmy King is."

I roll my eyes. "Not anymore."

Ryan pulls out a slice of pizza and takes a bite. "So," he says, sauce sticking to the corners of his mouth, "on a scale of one to ten, how bad is your FOMO right now?"

He's teasing, and I love it. Ryan always manages to break through my bad moods. "Actually, not too bad. Especially now that you're all here. I had planned to spend the night unpacking my bags."

"Boring!" Chloe sings, their Brooklyn accent coming out. "Those bags aren't going anywhere. This pizza, though, will be gone in a hot second if you don't get in before we do." They hand me a piece of pizza, knowing I'd never say no. There are three things Chlo and I share an unwavering love for: loud music, *Bob's Burgers* (Linda is their fave, Louise is mine), and triple-cheese pizza. Chlo looks amazing in tight denim short-shorts and a cropped white tee, paired with white wedges. As usual, their makeup is flawless and I found myself admiring their shimmery gold eyeshadow.

"I hope you're not letting the haters get you down, Em," Chlo says with a sigh. They get a lot of shit online for being nonbinary femme, black, and bi, so if anyone knows about standing up to hate, it's them. Not that what I'm going through is anything close to what they experience.

"I'll be fine," I say before taking another bite of pizza.

Chlo winks at me. "Yeah, you will."

"So," Alfie says, "Ry's written a new song he wants us to hear."

I swallow and give Ryan a punch on the arm. "That's awesome, Ry!"

He blushes and looks away. "Thanks," he mumbles. "It's not

perfect yet, but if we workshop it together I think it could be pretty rad."

"Oh, I almost forgot," Chloe says, taking their phone out of their pocket. "Jessie texted me yesterday. She wanted to know where you were. I was in the studio, so I didn't see it right away, and, uh, I guess she freaked out a little. She sent, like, twenty texts. Most of them were just question marks. I told her you were here. Was that an okay thing to do?"

"Yeah," I say. "She showed up at my window late last night. So sweet, right? She was so worried."

I pretend I don't notice how they all exchange worried glances. My friends have never explicitly told me they don't like Jessie, but they also aren't very good at hiding it. I get it—Jessie can seem pretty blunt and is prone to jealousy—but they just don't know her like I do. They don't see how sweet she is when we're alone.

"She's living here now, too," I blurt out, then immediately regret it.

Alfie puts his half-eaten pizza down. "Are you sure that's what you need right now?"

I shrug. "Why should I face my parents alone if I don't have to? Anyway, Jess lost her license after the accident, so it's just easier for her if she stays with me."

"I guess it's up to you," he says slowly. "You gotta do what feels right."

I nod, but I'm not sure. How does anyone really know what's right for them, anyway? All those parties I went to and drinks I had felt right to me at the time. Getting in that car with Jessie last week felt right.

Maybe my moral compass is defective. All I seem to do is make bad decisions.

Suddenly I don't have much of an appetite. I swallow the last bite of pizza and go upstairs to get into some sweatpants. My stomach turns at the thought of all the work I have ahead of me, of having to face the media circus my life has become, all because I was doing "what felt right."

I try to distract myself by putting on a new shade of lipstick I haven't had a chance to wear yet. It's metallic purple, and I was saving it for a big night out. That's obviously not going to happen any time soon, so I may as well use it to boost my mood. I drag the tip over my lips and pout in the mirror.

Some people call me shallow and superficial for being so obsessed with makeup and fashion, like it somehow cheapens my value to the world, but I call bullshit on all that crap. My hair is blond right now, but I've been known to change it when the mood strikes. And I don't dye my hair every color of the rainbow for anyone else's enjoyment but my own. It's not about covering my imperfections or attracting others; it's about expressing myself. It's a fun way to show the world how I'm feeling.

If I'm feeling creative, you'll see me painting my eyelids with multicolored eyeshadows and giving myself ombré lips. If I want to tell people to fuck off without saying a word, I'll wear black matte lipstick and a dark smoky eye. If I can't be bothered, I won't wear any makeup. See the pattern here? Whether I wear makeup or not depends solely on how I want to feel, never mind what anyone else says.

Besides, who's really the shallow one? The person who wears makeup because it makes them feel good or the person who judges them for wearing it? It's hypocritical, misogynistic bull like that that inspired me to write "Enough Already"—one of the songs on our first album.

Just thinking about our album brings a smile to my face. Two years ago, I was dancing around in my bedroom, singing into my hairbrush and dreaming of touring the world, playing our music to packed arenas. Now I'm living those dreams, our album is selling off the charts, and our shows sell out within minutes.

Putting lipstick on was a good idea; I feel better already.

"Hey, Em!" Alfie calls up the stairs. "You ready to hear Ry's song?"

"Be right down!" I call back. As I leave the bathroom, I have the urge to take a selfie and post it online. Then I remember I'm on a strict media break. It's been days since my fans have heard from me, and I can't wait until this mess quiets down so I can connect with them again. All this is really reminding me how much I love those beautiful people.

I skip down the stairs, feeling good and looking cute.

"All right," Alfie says, falling casually onto the couch. "Ry, let's hear the new song, man."

"Wait," I say. "Let me set the mood first."

I open the sliding doors to the backyard to let the warm breeze inside. The stars reflect in the swimming pool like glowing fireflies. I pick up one of my dad's guitars from its stand in the living room and hand it to Ryan.

Chloe and I sink onto the couch on either side of Alfie while Ryan sets up the guitar in front of the fireplace.

He clears his throat. "It's called 'And by the Way.'"

I've got an arrow in my heart and it's carved with your name . . .

> *. . . I didn't mean to, I didn't know I could . . .*

. . . at first I thought it was just a phase . . .

> *. . . the rhythm of my heart has stayed the same . . .*

. . . one day a switch flipped and then . . .

. . . all I could see was you . . .

. . . my heart just keeps comin' back . . .

. . . to you.

And by the way . . .

. . . I'm a fool for you.

Lyrics spill out, filled with angst and accidental love, unrequited. Our songs always lean more toward a punk or pop-rock sound, but this one has a classic-rock vibe to it. It would be rad with my drums and more guitars backing it up. By the time the last bars ring out, I've fallen head over heels in love with it.

"Well?" Ryan asks when he's done.

Alfie punches his fists into the air. "Yes! You killed it!"

Ryan smiles. "Thanks, man."

"Ryan," Chloe says. "Wow. Just wow. It's amazing on, like, another level."

Alfie turns to me. "Em? Thoughts?"

I cannot wipe the smile from my face. "I fucking love it. I think it's your best work yet!"

He laughs, but his gaze drops to the carpet. "Thanks, Em."

"Seriously," I say, standing up to give him a hug. "So many people will connect with those lyrics. They'll wish it was written about them."

"You think so?"

"Hell yeah! I wish it was written about me."

He laughs as he puts the guitar back on the stand.

"You know what," Alfie says, stroking his chin like he has a beard, "it would sound wild as a rock song, with Emmy as the lead."

I do a double take. "Wait, what? You want me to lead?"

Ryan nods. "Yeah, that's actually what I had in mind for it."

I twist my fingers in my lap. "But the studio will never go for it. I've already tried."

"Don't worry about them," Alfie says, waving it off. "I'll handle it."

"Oh my god, Em," Chloe squeals. "Do it!"

My heart races. This is the moment I've been waiting for. But I've already messed up so much. The band is hanging by a thread because of me. Stepping in as the lead on this song would just be one more thing to screw up. And Alfie would have to vouch for me to the studio, adding even more pressure. I can't let him down. I can't let any of them down. Not again.

I avoid their expectant gazes and shake my head. "I don't think that's a good idea. I need to fix my mess first."

CHAPTER EIGHT

Emmy,

　　Mr. Tucker and his colleagues have asked to meet with us to discuss recent events. I'm adding it to your calendar now. Nine a.m. tomorrow (Monday) at the record label.

Do not be late,

Sal

Ugh. Recent events. Obviously that's code for the Mess Emmy Has Made. Time to face the music.

It's my first time out in public since the Night That Shall Not Be Named, so I want to look better than I feel. I spend hours getting ready with my stylist, Zach, who chooses a smart white blouse, dark gray suit jacket, and matching pants. We tone down my makeup, keeping it simple with brown lipstick and matching eyeliner. Zach sweeps my hair over to one side and spritzes a dash of perfume on my wrists and neck.

Chloe offered to come with me to the meeting as moral support. They have been famous a lot longer than I have, amassing millions of subscribers on YouTube before striking it big as a solo artist. After all the years they've been hounded by the media, they're less shaken by the constant paparazzi presence than I am.

By the time Chloe arrives at seven a.m., I'm shivering with nerves.

"How are you feeling?" they ask as their driver turns onto the 405.

"Awesome," I say with a sarcastic laugh. "You?"

"Fine," they say, pushing their sunglasses up into their hair. "Freaking out about you, though."

Shame washes over me, and I have to look away. I open the camera on my phone and check my makeup. Even with all the concealer Zach piled on, the purple and black under my eyes is still slightly visible in the right light. Luckily, the swelling in my nose has gone down. As long as I don't sneeze, I shouldn't be in too much pain.

"Chloe," I say softly. I take in a breath, letting it fill my lungs slowly. Gotta hold it together.

"Yeah?"

"I'm low-key panicking right now."

"I know you are," they say. "But you've got this, Em. Just remember to own up to your mistakes and don't make excuses. They need to know that *you* know you fucked up."

I sigh. "Believe me, I know."

"Then you'll be fine." They reach over and pat me on the hand. "Just suck it up, apologize, and tell them it'll never happen again. And then the real work starts: proving to yourself and the world that you're better than your worst day."

Chloe's right. I've got a lot of work to do if I'm going to come back from this, but plenty of people have come back from much worse before me. I rotate my shoulders, trying to ease some of the tension.

Then a thought occurs to me, and it almost stops my heart.

"Do you think they're going to kick me out of the band?"

Chloe's jaw drops. "Emmy, no! Are you serious?"

I shrug.

"Em," they say, shaking their head, "they'd never kick you out. First of all, you are the heart of the Brightsiders. Alfie's the hot lead, Ryan's the prankster, and you are the badass bitch with a heart of pure gold. Secondly, Alfie and Ryan would never let that happen. It doesn't matter what you did—they would go on strike if you got kicked out. Thirdly, the fans would literally riot if you left. They adore you. There's no band without you."

I take in a deep breath. "Thanks, Chlo. Really."

Chloe takes my hand and squeezes it. "Anytime, babe."

When we pull up to the building, photographers and TV cameras are waiting. Chloe untwists the lid of their plum-brown lipstick and slides it over their bottom lip. I must have seen them wear it a hundred times, but it always looks amazing. It complements their brown skin perfectly. One of the many things we have in common is that we both wear makeup like knights wore suits of armor. I hope mine protects me from the arrows coming my way today.

The driver steps out of the car first, doubling as our bodyguard. Paparazzi rap their knuckles on the window. TMZ, *Entertainment Now*, and a host of other celeb gossip reporters are here, their lenses pointed right at me.

"Oh, God," I groan.

"Neutral," Chloe says. I nod.

I dab a fresh layer of powder over my nose, ease my sunglasses over my eyes, and step out of the car. I keep my head down as our bodyguard pushes through the crowd. I don't cry. I don't smile. Not even when the barrage of questions start.

"How are you today, Emmy?"

"Hey, Chloe! Are you on babysitting duty today?"

"Have you been drinking this morning, Em?"

"Where's Jessie this morning?"

"Are you an alcoholic, Emmy?"

"Emmy! How does it feel to hit rock bottom?"

Security ushers us into the foyer and we hurry to the elevators, desperate to get out of sight.

"You've got this," Chloe says when we reach the top floor.

───────

"You dodged a bullet the size of Air Force One, I hope you know that."

The executive at the head of the table glares at me from across the conference room. His name is Mr. Tucker, and he is a Dick with a capital D, emphasis on the *ick*. I've only met him twice, but both times he referred to me as "sweet cakes" and winked at me. It's like he binge-watched *Mad Men* until it melted his brain into a pile of sexist fuckboy goo. He's also the Big Boss at our studio, so what he says goes.

Alfie, Ryan, Sal, and I sit at the end of the long table. Our whole management and PR team is squished into this room to hear me state my case. I've never felt more intimidated in my life.

"I know," I say. I reach my hand up to remove my sunglasses, but then decide against it. I don't want them to see what I did to my face.

"I'm serious," Tucker says, leaning forward over the table. "In less than a week, you'll be eighteen. Time to grow up." He looks at Sal. "Did you tell her about the club?"

Sal sighs and turns to me. "The nightclub has been fined for serving alcohol to minors. They also banned you from going back there until you're twenty-one."

That's fair. They must have been fined for Jessie and Ry drinking, too. I know Alfie didn't drink because he never touches anything with alcohol in it.

I nod. "I won't be going clubbing again for a long time, anyway. Trust me."

Tucker smirks. "This isn't about trust, honey. It's about the reputation you've built for yourself. One that we don't feel fits with the Brightsiders brand. The majority of your fans are teenage girls, and they worship you." He points a finger at me. "More importantly, their parents shell out hard-earned cash to buy your music and merchandise and concert tickets. Do you think they'll keep doing that if they think their kid's hero is a drunk skank?"

I suck in a sharp breath. Don't cry, Em. Don't. You. Dare. Cry.

Alfie and Ryan speak up in my defense.

"There's no need for that," Alfie says, glaring at him.

"Yeah," Ryan adds, "give her a break."

Tucker shoots them an icy glare. "We've given her plenty of breaks, believe me." He starts counting on his fingers. "First there was that restaurant screaming match she had with her parents after the album dropped. Then there was the time she flashed her tits at everyone at LA Pride. And the time she pulled an all-nighter before the concert in London and almost missed the show."

I cross my arms over my chest and scowl down the table at him. For the record, the fight with my parents wasn't my fault. I hadn't seen them in months because the Brightsiders were touring the country and promoting our debut album, so when they asked me to have dinner with them at a beautiful, fancy restaurant in LA—something we had never done before—I was excited. I thought they wanted to celebrate the album release, and maybe apologize for all the times they told me I was a worthless piece of shit. But instead, all they wanted was to tell me my success wouldn't last, drink three bottles of expensive wine, and make me pay the bill. Then they asked for money. I started renting my apartment in the hotel the next day just to avoid having to go home.

As for flashing my breasts at Pride, that was a form of protest after a morning show host criticized me for not "acting like a lady." I stand by that.

But I can't argue with him about the thing in London. That's solely on me and my inability to say no to Jessie when she wants to party.

I don't say any of that to them, though. Arguing will only make this a thousand times worse, and they don't care about *why* I do anything, they just care about how it looks to the rest of the world. It's all about the "optics" to them. Besides, I'm not here to talk, I'm here to suck it up and listen. I take a deep breath. This is one of those moments where I have to choose between my dignity and my job. Do I tell Tucker he's a condescending, money-hungry jerk and risk my dream career, or keep my mouth shut and keep rocking out? I choose door number two, and make a mental note to fantasize about all the things I want to say later.

"Listen," Tucker says. "You've been begging us for months to let you sing lead in some songs. You want that to happen? You gotta be smart. You gotta show up and do the work."

"Okay," I say, holding my hands up. "Please stop. I know I've messed up. I've made one mistake after another, and I'm really, truly sorry. I'm going to fix it. All of it."

"Look," the exec closest to me says, "we just want to make sure you're okay. We need you to be at your best so the Brightsiders can be at their best. If you need anything—anything at all—tell us. You want to see a therapist? Go to rehab? Join a yoga retreat or start a juice cleanse? Whatever you need to do to feel better and be your best self, do it."

I resent the way he's patronizing me, but I nod anyway. "I'll straighten up. I'll show up to all the press junkets, the studio sessions, the events you want. I'll do the work. I promise."

Fucker—I mean *Tucker*—stares at his reflection in the window, checking his perfectly trimmed beard. "Awesome."

CHAPTER NINE

On Friday afternoon, I'm in our dressing room, sitting at the mirror with a colorful assortment of makeup products in front of me. Zach, our stylist, is juggling three different tools in his hands as he transforms my hair from flat and faded to luscious and sparkling. I open up an eyeshadow palette the size of an iPad and scan it for the colors I need—pink, purple, and blue. Tonight, we're holding a free show for attendees of a LGBTQIAP+ prom organized by a nonprofit, and I want to look like a walking Bisexual Pride flag.

Our team is buzzing around the halls backstage, making last-minute changes and double checking everything from lighting to costume to our set list. This is our first show since what Sal has taken to calling "the Incident," and I'm fucking terrified. Usually I love this part of performing: the hours and minutes leading up to a show, when the air is electric and the crew is frazzled, and I'm itching to get behind my drums. But tonight is different. I feel like

I'm suffocating. I keep thinking of all the eyes that will be on me, watching every move I make. Not just in the crowd, but online—the show is being livestreamed on Facebook, and I don't feel ready to be under that kind of scrutiny. I'm not strong enough yet, not prepared enough, not perfect enough. But we booked this show months ago, and I have to keep my promises. Plus, the hall will be filled wall-to-wall with queer teens. They are why I'm here. They are my people . . . even though they don't know I'm their people, too.

My phone vibrates among the makeup brushes on the counter.

> **JESSIE:** good luck tonight gorgeous!
>
> **EM:** aww thanks love xo

I'm ashamed to admit that I've sometimes wondered if Jessie just uses me for money and to get her name in print, but then she does something sweet like this and I realize she really does care. She just doesn't always know how to show it. She wanted to come tonight, but our PR team thought it best that we don't appear together in public for at least a couple more weeks. They're worried that seeing us would only remind people of the accident. Jessie wanted to tag along anyway, but I gently reminded her that I'm already on thin ice with Tucker and the studio. I can't do anything to piss them off. It would threaten my chances of ever singing lead.

Ryan waves a hand in front of my face, snapping me out of my funk. "Are you pumped, Em?"

His grin is contagious, and I smile at him in the mirror. "Pumped."

He claps his hands together and practically cartwheels out of the dressing room.

Everyone in the band handles the lead-up to performances differently. Ryan becomes even more restless than usual, jumping around, doing flips, riding his skateboard through the halls. Alfie gets intensely quiet and disappears. I can never seem to find him until ten minutes before we go out.

Me? I turn into a child who's downed ten Red Bulls. I talk a mile a minute. I giggle even when nothing particularly funny is happening. I'm a nervous pee-er, so I run back and forth to the bathroom every few minutes. I check the time a lot, because the clock seems to tick irritatingly slow when we're about to do a gig.

But tonight, time is moving much too fast. I don't want to go out there yet.

Zach sweeps the dye brush over my roots, filling in any patches. "So," he says, looking at me in the mirror, "we just wait for this to set, then rinse. Then do the glitter dip-dye thing up to here." He holds a hand next to my ear. "Yeah?"

"Awesome," I say, grinning. Tonight we're trying a style that makes it look like my hair has been dipped in cotton candy and glitter. I gave him my very technical instructions of "I want a rainbow-slash-glitter-slash-ombré look," and being the trouper that he is, he's pulling it off. I can't wait to show everyone.

While I wait for the colors to set, I start patting different shades of pink eyeshadow onto my wrist to decide which one to wear. Zach always offers to bring in a makeup artist for me, but I have too much fun doing it myself, so we only have one on hand to make Alfie and Ry look zit free and add some killer black liner to their eyes.

Alfie wanders into the room and starts rummaging through his backpack. He's wearing a pair of tight gold pants with rips at the knees, and a T-shirt that says:

~~BOY~~

~~GIRL~~

~~NONE OF THE ABOVE~~

UNICORN

I'm about to compliment it when he walks out of the room just as quickly as he came in, like he's running late. Something is up.

"Be right back," I tell Zach, then hurry into the hallway before I lose sight of Alfie. Unfortunately, Sal blocks my path.

"Nice hair," she says, chuckling. "How are you feeling?"

"Fine," I say, peering over her shoulder. Alfie is down the hall, tying his hair into a bun before disappearing out the back exit of the building. I don't know why, but I have a bad feeling. I need to get to him.

"Good," Sal says, patting me on the arm. "I don't want you to worry about anything. You're going to have an amazing show!"

Ry rides by on his skateboard, taking her attention away from me. She goes after him, begging him to slow down so he doesn't injure himself. Now's my chance to find Alfie.

I walk swiftly down the hall and out the exit, and find him leaning over a dumpster, puking his guts out. A strand of his long hair falls from the loose bun, and I move closer so I can hold it back from his face. Then I rub his back until it stops.

"I didn't want anyone to see me like this," he says as we sit on the steps under the door.

"Are you sick?" I ask. I place a hand on his forehead, but it seems normal.

"Nah." He presses his palms into his knees and stares up at the stars.

I move closer. "Then what's up?"

He clears his throat. "I puke before every show." He grips his knees and hangs his head a little. He says something else, but it's so mumbled I can't make it out.

I bend down to match his gaze, but his eyes are shut. "Alfie?"

He groans. "It's an anxiety thing. I have social anxiety disorder."

I furrow my brow. "Huh?"

He takes in a deep breath and looks me in the eyes. "I have social anxiety disorder. I've been taking medication for it."

I don't know what to say, but I can't just sit here staring at him in silence. "Oh."

"Yeah." He holds a hand over his stomach and takes in a few deep breaths.

A thousand questions run through my mind. How could someone like Alfie be socially anxious? He's literally a rock star. He's the light of every party we go to. He owns every stage he steps onto. And how could I be his best friend and not notice he was going through something? Am I that self-involved? Or have I just been too out of control?

I don't ask any of those, though. Instead, I ask the question I think he needs to hear most.

"Is there anything I can do to help?"

"Um, you could not tell anyone," he says with a quick smile. "It's hard to talk about."

I put my hand over my heart. "Promise."

"Thanks, Em." He picks up his water bottle from the ground and pulls an orange bottle of pills from his pocket. "Once I'm onstage I'll be chill. It's just the hours before that mess me up." He notices me staring at the bottle and turns it to show me the label. "Beta blockers. I'm supposed to take one a few hours before a show, but I forgot. Until I puked." He pops one in his mouth and washes it down with his water.

"Does it help?" I ask.

"Fuck yeah." He slips the bottle back into his pocket. "I mean, vomiting in a dumpster isn't my ideal pre-show ritual, but it's not as bad as it used to be."

"How did it used to be?"

He takes another sip of water. "Well, like, before I started taking meds and seeing a therapist, I'd be sick before every gig, every interview or photoshoot. I couldn't breathe, my hands would shake, I couldn't sleep. My stomach was constantly hurting, and I couldn't eat much. The more anxious I got, the more I'd worry that people would notice. I barely remember our first spot on *Jimmy Fallon* because I spent the whole day worrying I had vomit breath or clammy hands." He chuckles, but it's a shy chuckle, like he's embarrassed. I just want to hug him. "Now, when I actually remember to take the meds, I mean, I can do a show without feeling like I'm gonna die. The nervousness is still there, but I figure that's pretty normal. You get nervous, right?"

I nod. "It makes me pee a lot."

I happen to say that just as he's taking another swig of water, and he spits it out laughing.

"Well," he says, wiping his mouth with the back of his hand. "I'm glad it's not just me."

"Nope," I say, laughing with him.

He unties his long hair and musses it up with his fingers. "You don't have to stay out here. I'm okay."

"I want to stay."

I mentally go through every piece of advice I've ever heard about anxiety disorders and how to help. I want to ask him about it: if he likes going to therapy, if he knows what started it, how often he feels this way. I want to tell him that he doesn't need to feel embarrassed or ashamed, especially not with me. I chew on my bottom lip, holding back all my thoughts. I don't want to overwhelm him.

"I'm always here," I say softly. "If you want me. If you ever need to talk." I take his hand in mine and hold it tight.

With his free hand, he pulls his headphones from his pocket and hands me one. I pop it in my ear as he takes the other one and pops it in his, then hits shuffle on his phone. We sing along when we feel like it, but mostly we just sit, hold hands, and listen for a while. He seems to breathe easier after the third song, and that makes me breathe easier, too. I hate seeing him upset.

Eventually I hear Zach calling my name from inside the building.

"You're being summoned," Alfie says with a smile.

"I'll stay," I say. "He can wait."

Alfie shakes his head. "Nah, go. I'm fine now, really. Just having you with me helped a lot."

"I'm glad."

Zach calls my name again, and this time he sounds frantic. I give Alfie a quick hug and hurry back inside, wishing I could freeze time and sit with him all night.

CHAPTER TEN

The crowd chants our name. The lights fade out and thick clouds billow from the smoke machine. Alfie, Ry, and I scurry onto the stage to take our places just in time for the spotlight to illuminate us. The chanting turns into screams, the noise echoing off the walls of the concert hall. My heart rate speeds up in my chest. It's been a few months since we've performed a live show, and I forgot how intense it can get up here.

Alfie puts on his charm. "Well, hey there, gang. Thanks so much for the warm welcome." He says it smoothly, like he's chatting someone up at a bar. It drives the kids wild. "We're honored to be here to entertain y'all and help make this Pride Prom one to remember." More applause and cheers ring out. "We're starting with a song that's very close to my heart," he says. "I wrote it years ago, when I was trying to figure out my identity in a world of binaries. It's called 'Fluid.'"

He turns to look at me, gives me a wink, and then I start counting us in. I *tap, tap, tap* my drumsticks together, and then *BOOM*, I smash out the beat.

Ry starts strumming his guitar. People in the audience hold up rainbow flags, waving them proudly. Then Alfie starts to sing.

> *"The world says we gotta follow,*
> *All the rules we've been assigned . . ."*

My gaze is drawn to Alfie, his hair falling into his eyes as he sings his heart out. Something about the way his squeezes his eyes shut when he hits high notes makes me swoon a little.

Wait. Swoon? He's Alfie. Alfie doesn't make me swoon. I drag my eyes away from him and try to distract myself by looking at the crowd. A teen wearing a Brightsiders T-shirt under a suit blazer pumps their fist in the air. Someone with pink and blue hair screams Ryan's name. A cutie in a bright yellow dress holds up a sign that says MARRY ME EMMY! and I have to suppress my squees so I don't mess up my drumming.

> *"But who are they to tell me who I am?*
> *Who are they to decide?"*

We play straight into the next song, then another, and another. Tonight, our set isn't made solely of Brightsider songs. We've also added a few LGBTQIAP+ Pride faves and some epic dance tunes to really get the party going. Lady Gaga, George Michael, Prince, and Tegan and Sara are just some of the icons on our set list.

Now that I'm onstage, getting swept up in the beat, I feel alive again. It's hard to remember why I was so nervous about performing tonight—my fans never judge me the way adults in the media do. As long as I keep showing up, so will they. For the first time since the Incident, I'm truly happy.

Toward the end of the night, we get to my favorite part: the make-out song. During our world-tour concerts Alfie sang "Kiss Me" by Sixpence None the Richer, and the cameramen filmed cute people making out during the song and broadcast it on the big screens. It was our version of Kiss Cam, and it quickly went viral as a fan fave. Tonight, we don't have the big screens or the cameras, but we have a hall full of queer teens who are rocking out and making out and dancing and letting their rainbow flags fly, literally. And to me, that is so much better.

It occurs to me that if I ever want to come out, this is the place to do it. There's nowhere safer or more welcoming than right here, right now. A shiver runs down my spine at the thought, but it feels right. Now is the time.

After the last song ends, I stand up from my drum kit, walk over to the microphone and take it off the stand. My stomach flips like a gymnast on a high beam.

"Thank you so much!" I say. "What an amazing audience you all are! Seeing you with your rainbows and your gorgeous smiles . . . it feels like it's time for me to say something I've wanted to say publicly for a while." As though sensing what's about to happen, people in the crowd start screaming. I pause for a second, grinning at Alfie and Ry. "I mean, there are a ton of rumors out there about me. So why not just clear things up right now? Or should I say, *queer* things up." More screams ring out, and I laugh at my own bad pun. "I'm totally queer, my friends. Bi as hell. And I'm honored to be here with you all right now, and I thank you for giving me the courage to share that."

Ry comes over and puts an arm around me while Alfie stands by me and proudly applauds. People in the crowd cheer and make hearts with their hands for me. I sit on the edge of the stage, and a bunch of kids rush forward to take selfies.

"Your cheekbones look amazing!" one kid screams. "What do you use as highlighter?"

"Unicorn sweat and the tears of my exes!" I scream back, and they squeal with laughter.

There are dozens of phones in my face, and I can't keep up with everyone talking to me at once, but I'm having the time of my life. It's one thing to fend off paparazzi, and quite another to just have fun with people who love your music as much as you do.

I don't get home until three a.m., but I'm too amped to sleep. My parents are out and Jessie is nowhere to be found, so I hook my iPhone up to my speakers, put my iTunes on shuffle, and dance around my room. There may or may not be a lot of air guitar and singing into a hairbrush going on.

I fall onto my bed, sweaty and out of breath. But I'm still buzzing. I can't stop thinking about those amazing kids in the audience, waving their rainbow flags and having a blast. I get my laptop and go online to see the photos people have posted from the show. Sal finally ended my social media ban, thank god.

I open Tumblr and find that some clever person out there has already turned my answer to the highlighter question into a GIF. Someone else Photoshopped me riding a unicorn, my glittered hair sparkling like a disco ball. I grin and keep scrolling.

When I go on Facebook, the video of me coming out has already been shared thousands of times. I squeal when I see sites like the Mary Sue and Teen Vogue have already picked it up. And when I open my Twitter app to see my name trending, it's amazing to know it's not because of something I'm ashamed of.

I take a selfie to post all over social media, spreading the love far and wide. The only caption I add is rainbow hearts.

What a perfect night. I literally left a trail of glitter behind me everywhere I went, my Bisexual Pride eyeshadow and purple lipstick effing rocked, I didn't miss a beat on the drums, and I got to help the coolest kids celebrate themselves and one another. I could do this every night for the rest of my life and die a very happy girl.

High on fan love, I decide to commemorate the night with a new song. I call it "ILY" and start brainstorming lyrics.

Look at you with your hot pink hair,

Look at you with your sultry stare,

Look at you with my T-shirt on,

Look at you singin' my song.

You weren't born on the sidelines,

You entered this world with all eyes on you,

And that's the way you can live it, too.

Jessie creeps into my room and I jump into her arms, immediately telling her all about the concert.

"Did you see the video?" I ask excitedly. "I came out! I didn't plan it, but I was just so buzzed. The energy in that hall was something else. So I just went for it."

"Yeah," she says as she kicks her boots off. "I almost had a heart attack when I saw you trending. I thought you'd fucked up again."

My chest tightens a little, and I resist the urge to get defensive. She mustn't have meant that the way it sounded.

She grins and wraps me in her arms, holding me tight. "But yeah, so proud of you, babe. And now we can hold hands and go out in public without feeling like we have to hide anything. Everyone will know that you're mine."

We lay down to cuddle, and she points the remote at the television and turns it on to the news. "Let's see what the press are saying about it. I bet your PR team is relieved."

"Why?" I ask.

She raises an eyebrow. "Because this is a great pivot. You'll get great headlines, a butt load of praise, and everyone will assume that you've been such a screwup because you were in the closet and struggling with your sexuality. It was such a smart move, Em. I'm impressed."

Oh, god. I never even considered all that. I sit up in bed, suddenly feeling nauseous. "But that's not why I came out. And I wasn't struggling with my sexuality! I . . . this . . . It was *not* a pivot."

She laughs. "It's okay, Em. It's me. You don't have to pretend. Keep that act for them." She nods toward the television.

My jaw drops. "It's not an act. I didn't come out for the headlines. I did it for me."

"Okay, Emmy." She rolls her eyes. "Whatever you say."

First she accuses me of coming out to sway the media's perception of me, and now she's implying that I'm lying about it? Does she really think I would do that?

The gate to the backyard squeaks open, and laughter bubbles up through my bedroom window. *Great.* My parents are home, and they've brought company.

I reach for my noise-canceling headphones to help me sleep, but Jessie goes to the window to spy. "You know, from everything you told me about your parents, I expected them to be real assholes. But they're pretty cool. All they do is party."

I start to laugh because I think she's being sarcastic, but then I realize she means it.

"It might seem cool," I say. "But when you're a kid it's not so fun."

"What wasn't fun about it? They don't give a shit what you do. You could've gotten away with murder."

I don't even know where to begin. Jessie grew up in a loving home with parents who liked spending time with her. She has brothers and sisters she considers her best friends. I don't expect her to understand what it was like growing up in this house, but I definitely didn't expect her to think it was "fun."

"They don't give a shit," I say, my voice filled with more emotion than I expected. "That's the problem. They never gave a shit about me. They didn't even want me around."

I lost count of all the times they forgot to pick me up from school or couldn't help me with my homework because they were too drunk or busy entertaining their friends. And all the nights they stayed up fighting or crying or singing until the sun came up. It's scary when you don't know which version of your mom you're going to get when you leave your room. Or if you'll have to step over your dad in the morning because he's passed out on the kitchen floor again.

Jessie rolls her eyes. "Aren't you being a little dramatic? It's not like they beat you." I gasp and she laughs, as if it's a joke. I feel like I'm shrinking to the size of a pea.

"It's not funny," I say, my voice as small as I feel. "I think they really messed me up."

She shrugs like it's no big deal. "Everyone's parents messed them up. And let me ask you this: If you're so traumatized by them, what are you doing here? It can't be that bad if you chose to move back in with them."

So many answers run through my mind.

They're all I have.

I don't have anywhere else to go.

Even though it's messed up, this is the only home I've ever known.

I wanted this to be my one last shot at having a good relationship with my parents.

But Jessie has already moved on. She sits on the bed, scrolling through Tumblr and smirking at memes.

I put on my headphones and roll over so she doesn't see me cry.

CHAPTER ELEVEN

The television is still on when my alarm wakes me up. Jessie is asleep next to me, her arms and legs spread out like a starfish. I reach over her for the remote, but stop when I hear my name mentioned on the *Today Show*.

"Emmy King thrilled fans last night when she came out as bisexual during a concert in Los Angeles," the host says. They play a clip of me onstage, then introduce a panel to discuss it.

A middle-aged white guy with a graying beard claps his hands. "Well done to her PR team. This is clearly a stunt to distract from all her bad press lately."

I grit my teeth. Jerk.

"Wait a minute," a black woman in a blue dress says. "I think it's a touch cynical to assume this is all just a stunt. I say congratulations to her and welcome to the LGBTQ family."

"Thank you," I say to the television, feeling vindicated.

Another woman on the panel opens her mouth to speak, but Mr. Jerkface interrupts her.

"Give me a break," he says. "We keep seeing all these young celebrities coming out as 'bisexual.' Enough already. It's just another part of identity politics, a label they slap on themselves to seem hip and cool. Meanwhile, all these so-called bisexual girls always end up with a guy anyway. So what's the point?"

I turn the TV off, then throw the remote at the screen. What an ignorant, biphobic asshole. I flip my pillow over my face and groan into it, trying to let out all my bisexual rage.

My phone buzzes with an email, interrupting my fury.

> Emmy,
>
> Entertainment Now *wants to interview you for their live morning segment tomorrow. They want you to talk about your coming out and recovering from your accident. Let me know if you want to do it. I think it could be a great way to move forward.*
>
> Sal

My thumb hovers over the reply button. I don't know if I'm ready to face that kind of questioning. What if it's just like that panel?

But after thinking about it for a few minutes, I realize she's right. This could be my way to move on from all this.

> Sal,
>
> *If you think it's a good idea, then I'll do it.*
>
> Em

I hit send and immediately bury my head under the pillow, as though it will save me from having to go through with it. I've never been interviewed without Alfie and Ryan before, and *Entertainment Now* doesn't shy away from intrusive questions. And Sal said it will be live, so she won't be able to step in and pull me away if the reporter goes too far. This could make me or break me. I text Chloe in a panic.

EM: Going on EN tomorrow. I'm gonna die.

CHLOE: Woo! No dying allowed, missy.

EM: They wanna talk about my accident.

CHLOE: Of course they do. Do you want to talk about it?

EM: Maybe? What do you think?

CHLOE: Up to you. I would do it. Just to clear the air and shut people up. Then on to the next.

EM: Yeah. Get it over with.

CHLOE: Like a bandaid. Just rip through it.

EM: Ugh. Gonna die.

CHLOE: Well, let's do dinner tonight. It can be your last meal :P

EM: lol deal.

An email pops up from Sal.

> *Great! I'll set up a lunch with Andrew from PR to prep you.*
>
> *Sal*

I force myself out from under the covers and walk into the bathroom. I've met with Andrew dozens of times before interviews, but never alone. He's a nice guy, but very blunt and just a little condescending, yet Sal says he's a PR star, so I do what he says. I slide my bathroom window open to let the early morning sun in, but am greeted instead by voices calling my name from the street below. A group of photographers and reporters are staked out at the gate. They've found me.

"Creeps," I mutter, and close the window again. I guess this was inevitable. It was only a matter of time before a neighbor spotted me and sold me out, or a pap followed me home. I'm public property now.

———

I wait at a table at the back of the restaurant, avoiding the curious eyes of people at the other tables. Jessie slides her chair closer to mine and takes my hand, lifting it onto the table. I blush a little, but I can't help but feel uncomfortable. Like we are being gawked at. I didn't even want Jess to come to this lunch—after all, it is business. But for some reason that I just can't explain, I have trouble saying no to her. So here I am, bringing my girlfriend to my PR meeting.

Andrew walks through the door and his eyes go straight to the back, narrowing when he sees me with Jessie.

"Emmy," he says when he reaches us, stretching out his hand for me to shake. "Great to see you again! Who's this?"

"Nice to see you, too," I say. "This is Jessie, my girlfriend."

She nods at him and shakes his hand.

"Just to clarify," he says as he sits across from us. "Jessie isn't doing the interview with you, right?"

"Oh no," I say. "She just wanted to tag along for lunch."

He makes a face, and I can't tell if he's annoyed or just thinks it's odd. I immediately resent Jessie for coming, and wish I'd objected a little harder. I don't want to, but every time she does something like this I grow more and more irritated. I try to push those feelings aside and focus on the meeting.

Andrew briefs me on the kinds of questions I'll be asked tomorrow, and I listen carefully, trying to take it all in. The more he talks, the more nervous I am. It's starting to feel like the rest of my career depends on five minutes of airtime. No pressure, though. Ugh.

"All right," he says, clasping his hands together on the table. "Let's do a practice run. I'll throw some questions at you and you answer like you would on the show."

I lean forward, ready to go.

"So, Emmy, recently you made headlines after a night of underage drinking that landed you in a car accident and then the emergency room. How are you recovering from that?"

I swallow hard, hoping he's just throwing me the worst-case-scenario question and that he doesn't actually think they'll ask me this. "I'm doing okay. Thank you for asking. I made a terrible mistake, and I've learned a lot from it. I'm very lucky that I wasn't seriously hurt, so I'm grateful for that, and I'm looking forward to moving on from it."

He nods slowly, thoughtfully, like he's analyzing every word of my answer.

"Good," he finally says. "Are you sober?"

"Yes."

"This and other scandals have littered your short career so far, resulting in a Bad Girl reputation. Are you saying you're trying to turn things around and clean up your image?"

I open my mouth to answer, but Jessie speaks before I do. "I thought this interview was about her coming out?"

Andrew looks at her, then at me. "It will be, but this is also Emmy's first interview since that night, so they will ask about it. I guarantee it."

"Huh," Jessie says as she leans back in her chair. "Well, can't you just tell them not to ask about that?"

I turn to her. "It's okay. I want to clear it up."

"But the whole point of you coming out was so that people would stop talking about that night."

My cheeks warm and my chest burns. "No, it wasn't. I told you that's not why I did it."

She runs her hands through her hair. "Whatever. But I don't think you should answer those questions. Talking about it more isn't going to make it go away."

Doubts start to swirl around my mind. Is she right? I glance at Andrew, whose thumb is tapping on the table impatiently. Seeing the discomfort on his face makes me realize how unprofessional this is. I should never have let Jessie come to this meeting. My embarrassment quickly turns to anger.

"Jess, Sal and Andrew are the professionals," I say to her quietly but firmly. "They know what they're doing, and I trust them."

Her eyes widen. "Oh, and you don't trust me? Is that what you're saying?"

"No." My shoulders slump. "That's not what I meant."

She points to Andrew. "So you'll listen to this guy over me?"

Andrew sighs. "Listen, I've got another meeting. If you want to go over some more questions later, give me a call." He gets up to leave before I can say anything. I want to run after him and apologize, but I'm too embarrassed.

"Jess," I snap. "This has nothing to do with you." I try to match her gaze, hoping my pleading eyes will make her calm down. But she's too busy looking around the restaurant. At first I think she's looking for the exit, but then I see her turn slightly to face someone at a nearby table. Someone with their phone pointed straight at us. Is she doing this on purpose? Is she provoking a fight with me to get attention?

My fists clench, and I lean in close to her ear. "Get. Out."

She doesn't leave, so I do. I hurry by all the people whispering and glancing my way, and before I've even made it out the door, I've made a decision: I have to break up with Jessie.

CHAPTER TWELVE

I don't see her again until three a.m. when she stumbles into my room and shakes me by the shoulders to wake me up.

"Babe," she mumbles, her breath thick with the smell of fruity cocktails, "you awake?"

I press the heels of my hands into my eyes. "I am now."

"Your dad is on the couch downstairs," she says.

"I know." My parents were up until midnight, arguing about money. I only heard bits and pieces of it before I put my headphones on, but it sounded like they're in a lot of debt. He was yelling at her to stop buying drinks for all her friends when they go out, and she was screaming at him to stop buying old guitars. I'm expecting them to ask me for money in the morning. But I'll save that problem for tomorrow; right now Jessie is all I can handle. I'd tried to wait up for her, my breakup speech all planned out and rehearsed, and if I don't do it now I might chicken out.

Jessie starts pulling the covers back to slide into bed, but I stop her.

"I don't think you should stay here tonight," I start.

She ignores me and jumps on the bed. "I'm already here, though, so."

"Okay." I sit up. "I don't *want* you to stay here tonight."

She groans. "Is this about what happened at lunch today?" I feel her hand snake around my waist. "It's okay, baby. I forgive you."

"You forgive me?" I screech. "You embarrassed me in a work meeting!"

Footsteps creak on the stairs, and I hope I didn't wake my mom. The last thing I need right now is for her to come in here in a mood.

Jessie's arms pull away from me fast. "Hey. I was trying to help. If you didn't want me there you should've said so."

"You're right," I snap. "I should have said so then. But I'm saying it now. I didn't want you there then, and I don't want you here now. I want to break up." My voice trembles, and my heart beats like a drum in my chest as I wait for her reaction.

She starts to moan. She must be crying. I resist the urge to hug her, to try to comfort her. I can't let myself give in. Then she gags and suddenly she jerks forward, puking everywhere. I leap out of bed and turn the light on to see my bed covered in blue sludge. It looks like a Smurf exploded all over my comforter.

Once Jessie has emptied her guts, she leans back and rests her head on my pillows. "Sorry."

"You okay?" I ask. She nods, and I'm glad because I'm still not ready to give up on this breakup. "Jess, I'm sorry, but you need to leave."

She waves a hand over the bed. "But I'm sick!"

"I can see that." I pinch my fingers over my nose. "And smell it.

But the only thing that's gonna change is my sheets. I need some space from you. Please go. I'll order you a Lyft." I pick up my phone and open the app, feeling very proud of myself for being so real with her.

Jessie finally gets out of the bed. But instead of leaving my room, she comes over to me and tries to pull me in for a hug. I back away, my eyes still on my phone.

"Come on, Emmy," she says with a laugh. "You know we'll just get back together again in a week. Stop being so dramatic." She leans in like she's going to kiss me, her lips stained blue. I duck and swerve like a boxer, dodging her puke breath just in time.

"Jessie, I'm being dead serious," I say. "Your ride will be here in three minutes. Please. Just go home."

Her jaw clenches. She kicks my dresser so hard that a glass of water I left there topples onto the floor and shatters.

"Jessie!" I yell, and point to my door. "Get the fuck out!"

"How could you do this to me?" she screams back. "Is there someone else? Is it fucking Alfie?"

I run into the bathroom to get a towel and start cleaning up the broken glass. She keeps yelling.

"It's Alfie, isn't it? Don't lie to me! It's so fucking obvious that he's into you. How long have you been screwing him?"

I want to scream, so I do. "Shut the hell up. There's no one else. I'm just sick of the way you make me feel all the time."

"What are you talking about?"

My bottom lip quivers. "Whenever I'm around you, I just feel like shit. You make me feel like . . . like . . ." I search for the right words, but I don't know how to explain it.

"What?" she yells.

"Like I'm wrong!" I finally spit out. "You make me feel like I'm wrong all the time. I feel small and inferior and like nothing I do or say matters."

She crosses her arms over her chest. "I don't make you feel like that. That's not true."

I throw the towel back onto the floor. "You're doing it right now! I'm always wrong or acting crazy or being dramatic. You never just listen or trust that I feel the way I feel for a reason. You always doubt me, and I hate it."

"This is bullshit," she says, totally proving my point. "I don't buy it. There's someone else. And I know it's Alfie."

I clutch my head. "What is your obsession with Alfie? He and I have never ever been anything more than friends. He has literally nothing to do with this."

She marches toward me and shoves her index finger in my face. "He has everything to do with this. I know it."

I slap her finger away, then open my bedroom door. "Out. Now. I'm done."

Finally, she leaves. I slam the door shut, lock it, and listen as she stomps down the stairs, still screaming.

"I knew it! You're fucking Alfie! You fucking slut!"

Her ranting spills out onto the street but disappears after another minute or two. And then I breathe for what feels like the first time in days. More tears run down my face as I strip my bed of the blue-stained covers and dump them in the hamper. My mind races with all the ways Jessie could try to get back at me. No doubt there will soon be headlines out about our breakup, citing an "unnamed source." But I'll know it's her. Ugh, what a shitstorm I've just unleashed.

But as hard as it was, and as messy as it's probably going to get, I know it was the right thing for me to do. I didn't realize it until I blurted it out just now, but being with her really did make me feel worthless. And I was growing to hate the person I was when I was around her. I don't want to be someone who only cares about being the life of the party. I've seen what that leads to. I don't want to feel like I'm wrong all the time. I don't want to feel inferior, especially not to the person I'm supposed to be equals with. And most importantly, I don't want to feel worthless.

I deserve better than that.

With fresh sheets and covers on the bed, I wrap my arms around myself and wait until the tears slow. I have to get up in two hours, and my eyes will be puffy for my interview, but at least I'm free.

CHAPTER THIRTEEN

"Emmy," the makeup artist whispers. I open my eyes and smile, acting like I didn't just fall asleep in the makeup chair.

"You're done," she says, smiling back at me like she knows I fell asleep.

I look in the mirror, grateful to whoever invented concealer. The dark circles under my eyes are gone, the puffiness of my eyelids virtually invisible under all the glittery eyeshadow and feathery false lashes. No one will be able to tell I spent last night cleaning up the vomit of my newly ex-girlfriend.

A producer pops her head into the dressing room. "Five minutes!"

Sal looks up from her phone and locks eyes with me. "How are you feeling?"

"Great," I lie through my teeth. I don't feel anything close to great. I feel like I'm about to walk into a courtroom to hear the final verdict: innocent or guilty. Hero or heathen. When I leave this studio, I'll either have a stamp of approval or a scarlet letter branded over my heart.

"Okay," Sal says. "You know what to do. Make it clear that you know you made a mistake, you're ready to move on, and then pivot to other topics. They want to talk about your sexuality, but don't do anything that makes you feel uncomfortable. And try to talk about the band and working on the next album. Bring it back to the music."

I nod with every instruction she gives, repeating it all over and over in my mind. Made a mistake. Moving on. Music. Those are my main talking points.

I stand up and walk with Sal down the hall toward the set.

"Smile," she adds. "Back straight, legs closed. Hair out of your eyes. Make sure you appear open and calm even if you don't feel that way."

It doesn't matter how many times I get prepped for media appearances, hearing stuff like that always makes me cringe. It feels so forced, so fake, so unnatural. But I remind myself that if I just grin and bear it for now, one day—when my career is more stable and my music more recognized—I'll be able to make my own rules. I'm still a newcomer. The Brightsiders might be a hit with teenagers my age and younger, but adults are more cynical. They're snobs. They won't take us seriously until we release a few more albums, win awards, prove we have staying power. They don't trust that people my age know what's good and what sucks. They don't trust people my age, period. I can't wait to prove them wrong.

My phone buzzes with a call from Jessie, and I ignore it. I'm standing just off-camera, waiting to go on, when it buzzes again. I ignore it once more, then switch it off. Not today, honey.

The show goes to commercial break, and a producer hurries me onto the set. I take a seat on the high chair that looks more like a bar stool while my mic is checked.

"Nice to see you again," the cohost, Chelsea, says as she shakes my hand. "Welcome to the show."

"Thanks for having me," I say.

Someone from the control room must be speaking into her earpiece, because she presses her fingers to her ear and starts to nod.

"Seriously?" she says quietly. "We have that ready? Okay. Okay. Okay. Yes. Okay." She glances at me, and I swear I can see a hint of excitement in her eyes. "Mm-hmm. Right now? Okay. Great."

She shuffles her papers around, then reaches over and puts a hand on mine. "Whatever happens, just go with it."

I nod, but I feel a strong sense that something isn't right. Why would she say that? *Whatever happens?* Like what? Images of everything that could go wrong flash through my mind. Visions of Jessie walking out to hoots and hollers, like an episode of *Jerry Springer.* Or Dr. Drew being called in for a surprise live intervention. I look around the set, as though it's going to give me answers. Sal smiles at me hopefully and gives me a thumbs-up.

The countdown begins, and my mouth goes dry. Oh no. I can't swallow. I've stopped producing saliva. I can't speak. I have literally lost my ability to form words. I lift my glass of water from the table with two hands so no one sees me trembling, and sip it slowly. And then we're live.

Chelsea beams at the little red light. "Welcome back to our morning edition of *Entertainment Now.* Right now I'm joined by Emmy King, known to teens everywhere as the drummer from the hit band the Brightsiders. Emmy, good morning and welcome to the show."

Smile. Smile, dammit. "Good morning, and thank you so much for having me."

"Now, I wanted to start by asking you about your recent underage drinking-and-driving scandal," she says. My heart stops. "But we just got some breaking news. TMZ just released a tape recording that I want you to listen to and then get your thoughts on. Let's hear it now."

I freeze like a deer in headlights as the tape starts to play.

"You know we'll just get back together again in a week."

Oh. Fuck. No. I recognize the voices instantly. It's Jessie. And me. Breaking up. I stare wide-eyed at Sal, who looks just as panicked as I feel. The tape keeps playing. Our strained voices fill the studio. Then the glass shatters, making one of the cameramen flinch. My words are bleeped when I scream at her to get out. And then Alfie's name is dropped, and I realize how bad this is all going to look. The internet is going to break over this.

Time slows down. When they finally stop the tape, the whole room is silent except for my heartbeat. I hope the mic doesn't pick it up. Chelsea watches me carefully, like she's waiting for me to shatter to the floor in a thousand pieces.

"Wow," she says. "Obviously, that was a very emotionally charged conversation."

My panic turns to anger as I piece everything together in my mind. They ambushed me for ratings. And Jessie must have been recording our argument. I'm going to kill her.

"What are your thoughts on what we just heard?" she asks.

I have to lie. There's no way I can say what I'm really thinking, which is: Fuck all of you for doing this to me.

"It's hard to explain," I spit out. "It's not what I expected to be talking about when I sat in this chair, that's for sure."

"Mm-hmm." She nods, like she really cares. "I can imagine. How are you feeling?"

I laugh because if I don't I'll scream. "Stunned."

"Can you tell us a little about what we just heard?"

I think for a moment, wondering what the hell I'm supposed to do. "I don't know what to say, honestly. I'm lost for words."

I squirm in my chair, wishing I could shrink to the size of a quarter and dive into the empty water glass in front of me. Chelsea glances behind the cameras toward the booth, then nods.

"Okay," Chelsea says. "We need to go to a break, but we'll be right back to get more of Emmy's side of the story."

The second we're off air, I'm out. I hurry off the set, push past Sal, and run back to the green room. My chest feels like it's being crushed. I sit on the couch and bend over, keeping my head between my legs to help me breathe. I'm going to hyperventilate or throw up or die, I can feel it. I thought things were bad before, but this is the worst of the worst. How did this happen? How could Jessie do this? Does she hate me that much?

Sal walks in and closes the door behind her. "You have to go back out there."

I laugh because I've never heard a more ridiculous sentence in my life. "Fuck that."

"Emmy," she says, crouching down in front of me. "I know it's bad, and I'm so sorry they just did that to you. I promise you I'm going to fight them on this later. But right now, people are watching, waiting for you to respond to that tape."

I swallow back my sobs. "You can't ask me to do this. She's going to eat me alive."

Sal sighs. "She's going to try, but you can stop her. If you leave, she's definitely going to eat you alive."

"I've been trying so hard to do the right things," I say, fighting the lump in my throat.

Sal rubs my knee gently. "I know, honey. And you've been doing so well. This isn't your fault."

I throw a hand toward the door. "They don't care about that! They just want ratings. And headlines."

"Yes, they do. This is going to give them great clickbait. But the headlines will be even more scathing if you run away from this."

Shit. She's right. If I run from this, it'll just make the story bigger news. People will call me a diva. Reports will say I stormed out of the interview like a spoiled brat.

I have to go back out there.

CHAPTER FOURTEEN

"Now that you've had a moment to gather your thoughts," Chelsea says, "can you tell us about the tape we just heard?"

I'm about to answer when one of the producers decides to roll the tape again. I sit still as a statue, every muscle in my body tensed as the audio echoes through the studio once more. When it ends, Chelsea looks at me expectantly.

"It was a private conversation," I say slowly. The bright lights of the set make me feel like I'm in an interrogation room. "Obviously, I didn't know I was being recorded."

Chelsea nods sympathetically. "To be clear, the voices on the tape are you and Jessie Wilson, who has been romantically linked to you in the past."

"Yes." Chelsea looks at me like she's waiting for me to say more, but I don't plan to give her any more information than is absolutely required. If that means a whole interview of one-word answers, fine.

"When did this conversation take place?"

"Last night."

"Oh, wow," she says. "So it must still feel incredibly raw to you."

It hurts like hell, so thanks for playing it for the whole fucking world to hear. "It does."

"And that shattering sound," she says, looking at the camera then back at me. "Did she throw something at you? Was this relationship violent?"

"No, and no. A glass fell." This is too much. I glance at Sal, whose brows are pinched together like she's trying to set Chelsea on fire with her mind. I can't take any more of this.

"And what was said about Alfie," she says, looking down at the papers in front of her. I can see Alfie's name scrawled in big letters, circled and with a question mark. "Is there any truth to that?"

"None. But if you don't mind," I say before Chelsea can continue, "I don't want him brought into this. Even though someone felt the need to record and share this with the public, it's still very much a private issue. I'm not going to say anything more on the matter."

I hold my breath, almost in awe of how mature and calm I just sounded. I'm handling this better than I thought I would. I actually feel a little proud of myself.

"Absolutely," Chelsea says. "Just one more question."

Ugh. Surprise, surprise.

"What is your relationship status?"

I take in a deep breath through my nose. "I'm single."

"And did you make this recording?"

So much for one more question. She's not going to give up easily. "No."

"Who did?"

"I'm not going to say anything more on the matter."

Chelsea laughs like I made a joke, then flicks her hair back. "Okay, let's move on to something else everyone has been talking about. You recently came out as gay—congratulations!"

"Bi," I say.

"I'm sorry?"

"I'm bisexual. And thank you, I feel really happy to finally be open about who I am."

For the first time during the interview, I smile an authentic smile.

She leans forward over the table. "So what inspired you to finally come out?"

"It was something I'd wanted to do for a while," I say. "But I was afraid. It was seeing the fans that gave me the courage to do it. They make me feel safe, and they love me for who I am. And I love them back."

"Aww, how sweet." She turns to the camera. "That's all we have time for, I'm afraid. Emmy King, thanks so much for talking with me. We'll be right back after the break."

The red light goes dark and she holds a hand out to me. "Thanks a lot. No hard feelings, okay?"

I shake her hand but don't reply. Any answer I give is not going to be one she'll like, so I stay quiet.

Sal is by my side in a second, whisking me off set and out the back door. Security keeps the photographers at bay while I'm ushered into the waiting SUV.

The first thing I do is turn my phone back on and call Jessie.

"Hey," she answers.

"Why did you do it?" I demand.

"Huh?"

"Why?" I ask again. "Are you that petty? Or was it for money? How much did you get for it?"

I hear her breathing. And then she says, "Emmy. I didn't release that tape."

"Bullshit," I spit. "Don't lie to me."

"I swear to God," she says, her voice growing louder. "It wasn't fucking me."

I roll my eyes. "So who did, then, huh?"

Sal slides closer to me in the backseat and hands me her phone. On the screen is an email from PR:

> *Sal,*
>
> *Checked with my sources at EN—they say they paid Mr. King $20,000 for the tape early this morning.*

"What?" I gasp. "My *dad* sold it?" I turn to Sal. "Are you sure? Like, one hundred percent sure?"

She frowns. "I'm so sorry, Em."

"What?" Jessie says through the phone. "What's happening?"

Tears fill my eyes. "It was my dad." He must have heard us fighting and come upstairs to record us. And now he'll use the money to pay off my parents' debts. "Sorry," I say. "I gotta go."

The moment I end the call, I burst into tears.

———————

By the time we've made it through LA traffic and pull onto my parents' street, the recording has been turned into a dozen different memes online. I shield my face from the cameras as the car enters the driveway, not wanting them to see me crying.

"Are you sure you don't want to go to a hotel?" Sal offers for the third time.

I shake my head. "Later. Right now, I need to talk to my parents."

Alfie is waiting on my porch when I get out of the car. "Em" is all he says. I walk straight into his arms.

"You saw the interview?" I ask.

He nods against my shoulder. "I came straight over. And Sal just texted me. Is it true about your dad?"

"Yeah," I say with a sigh.

His grip tightens around me. "I knew they were assholes, but I never thought they'd sink this low."

I start to cry again, then pull away from him.

"You can't stay here," he says, but it sounds more like a plea.

I nod. "One thing at a time." I walk by him and through the front door. My stomach churns from nerves as I walk through the house, searching for my parents. When I find them, Dad is smoking a cigarette by the pool and Mom is sitting at the outdoor table, talking on the phone.

"Yes," she says, her phone voice all pleasant and proper. "I'd like half of that to go toward our credit card, please."

"Glad to see you're already finding that money useful," I say, scowling at them.

Mom holds a hand over the phone. "Emmy, I'm on the phone. Don't be so rude."

I storm over to her and yell, "How's this for rude? Dad recorded a private conversation and sold it!"

She swats me away, apologizing profusely to the person on the other end, and quickly ends the phone call.

"Sorry, Em," Dad says with a shrug. "We really needed the money. You know how it is."

"You could've just asked me for it," I say. My voice cracks a little at the end, but I stand tall, trying my hardest to appear stronger than I feel.

Mom scoffs. "Ask you for it? After the way you behaved last time? I don't think so."

"So you thought it would be better to humiliate me instead?" I yell.

"Relax," Dad says. "It'll all blow over. Tomorrow some other pop star will get a DUI or get someone pregnant, and this will all be old news."

Mom takes a sip of her coffee. "Yes. I really think you're over-reacting, Emmy. No one really cares what you do."

"No," I say. "*You* don't care what I do. *You don't care.*"

Dad gives me a blank stare, like he's surprised it took me so long to figure that out. Mom just scowls at me.

"We are the only people who do care," she says. "Come on, you're a smart girl. Do you really think Sal cares about you? Jessie obviously doesn't. And Alfie and Ryan will both move on the second they see an exit. We are all you have."

They're doing it again. They're trying to make me doubt myself. To make me feel wrong and stupid and worthless, just like they used to. Why did I think things would be different if I came back here? I bury my face in my hands.

"No," Alfie says as he walks through the door. "Emmy, none of that is true. Don't listen to her."

"Oh," Dad says, laughing dryly. "Here comes the hero."

"Leave Alfie alone," I say through gritted teeth.

Dad raises an eyebrow. "Better be careful not to be seen around him, Em. You don't want everyone to think Jessie was right about him. People already think you're a hot mess. You don't want them think-ing you're a whore, too."

Something snaps inside me, and I launch myself at my dad, fists swinging. Alfie holds me back, his arms wrapped tight around my waist. Dad jumps back, his mouth hanging open in surprise. I keep struggling forward, punching the air, but Alfie's grip is too strong, and I give up. Once I've calmed down, Alfie releases me and steps in between me and my dad.

"How could you do that to her?" he asks, his own fists clenched by his side. "You heard her screaming and instead of coming to see if she was okay, you decided to record her instead? What kind of father are you?"

Dad flicks his cigarette to the ground, then storms through the yard and out through the side gate, slamming it behind him. Mom sighs.

"Now look what you've done," she says. "You hurt his feelings. I think it's time for you to leave."

Alfie takes my hand, and we do as she says. I don't say good-bye. I don't look over my shoulder. I just collect my things, walk out the front door, and let Alfie take me away.

And I don't ever want to go back.

CHAPTER FIFTEEN

"That's it," Chloe says. I'm watching them pace back and forth in their living room. I asked Alfie to drop me here after we left my parents' place. He wanted to stay, but Sal set up an emergency PR briefing with him and Andrew, so he knows the right things to say when reporters ask him about the tape.

"You're staying here," Chloe says. "And I'm not taking no for an answer."

I don't even try to argue. Not only is Chloe stubborn, but in this case they're right—besides, with Alfie's place under constant watch by paparazzi and Ry's apartment only a one bedroom, I don't have any other choice. But once I turn eighteen, I'm legally free from my parents, and I can make a new home for myself.

"Thanks, Chlo," I say. "I promise I won't stay long. I'm sorry for just showing up like this." Guilt sits in my stomach like a brick. I hate that my own shit is spilling into the lives of my friends. First Jessie got arrested when I was the one who wanted her to drive me to get cheeseburgers, then Alfie's name got dragged into my breakup-tape scandal, and now I'm dumping myself on Chloe. I feel like such a burden. On top of that, the burst of relief I felt after breaking up with Jess seems to be turning into guilt, too. I feel bad for kicking her out of my house in the middle of the night when she was drunk and upset. And that tape doesn't make her look great, either—some Brightsiders fans have been trolling her hard on social media.

Chloe stops pacing long enough to put their hands on their hips. "Don't give me that. Enough. You can stay as long as you like. I love you. You're my best friend, and I won't let you go back to that house. Ever."

They finally sit down, and I hug them close. "Thank you so much. I'm so sorry. This is all my fault."

They pull away, holding me at arm's length. "What the hell are you talking about?"

"If I hadn't broken up with Jessie, this never would have happened." I slap a hand to my forehead. "Maybe I made a mistake. I overreacted. She loves me. And if I had just shut up, that tape wouldn't even exist."

Chloe looks at me with pity in their eyes. "Jesus, Emmy. Please tell me that's not what you really think."

I shrug, too embarrassed now to admit it's true. They take my hands in theirs.

"Nope," they say sternly. "Nope. We're not having that. You know I'm the first one to tell you when you've fucked up, but this isn't one of those times. I won't watch Jessie or your parents gaslight you anymore."

I cock my head to the side. "What do you mean?"

"It's an abusive tactic," they explain. "People treat you like shit, and when you call them out on it, they act like you're crazy." They sigh and look down at their hands. "I know I don't talk about my mom much, but there's a reason for that. Our relationship is . . . complicated. You know she's white, right?"

"Yeah." It's rare for Chlo to talk about their folks. I got a vibe from Chlo that family was a sensitive subject for them, so I never asked much about their mom and dad. I remember seeing photos of them on Chlo's Instagram. Their mom is tall, thin, white, and blond. Their dad is black and even taller than Chlo's mom, and Chloe has his wide, beaming smile. Other than that, all I know about their parents is that they got divorced before Chloe was even five years old, and their dad moved across the country for work so they've never been that close.

"Okay, so," Chloe continues. "My mom never wanted to acknowledge my blackness. Except for when she uses me as a shield to prove to other white people that she's not racist." They roll their eyes. "Whenever I try to talk to her about my experience as a black person in this country, especially lately, she dismisses me. It makes her uncomfortable. *I* make her uncomfortable. She'll say I'm being too sensitive or I'm just imagining the racism or transphobia or whatever other thing some bigoted asshole threw at me that day. Last time I saw her I was wearing my Black Lives Matter T-shirt and she acted like I did it just to make her mad. She said I was being disrespectful to her. We got into a huge fight, and I haven't spoken to her since."

I rub Chloe's back. "I'm so sorry. That's awful." I feel my blood boiling with anger, and all I want to do is call up Chlo's mom and scream at her.

"And then," they add with a quick breath. "There's her subtle homophobia and not-so-subtle transphobia. She refuses to respect my pronouns. But when I call her out over it she calls me melodramatic and tries to guilt me, acting like I'm trying to hurt her. That would have worked five years ago, but not now." They run a hand down their face, rightly frustrated. "Don't even get me started. Anyway, my point is that sometimes, parents can be toxic, and sometimes, we're better off without them."

I pull them into me, wanting to shield them from pain forever. "You know what? Our parents suck. But we have each other. And we have Alfie and Ry and Kass. They're our family, okay? Our chosen family."

Chloe pretends to move hair out of their eyes but is really wiping away tears. I pretend not to notice.

"Chosen family," they say, smiling again. "I like it."

They clear their throat. "Now you know why it's so hard for me to see you blame yourself for what's happening. The doubts you're feeling aren't the truth. It breaks my heart to see you like this."

Then we can't fight it anymore and we both start crying. They reach for the Kleenex on their coffee table. I take one and twist it around and around in my fingers while everything they said hits me. Hard. I've heard of gaslighting before, but it never even occurred to me that I would experience it.

All the shitty things my parents have said and done run through my mind. Then I think about all the times Jessie was just as mean and manipulative.

"How did I not see it before?" I whisper, almost to myself.

Chloe strokes my hair and cries with me. "It's hard to see a storm when you're in the eye of it."

I cry so hard my throat hurts.

"Listen," they say once our tears soften. "Don't beat yourself up over this. This isn't on you."

I nod and wipe my cheeks on the back of my hand.

Chloe smiles through their tears and pokes me in the side. "It'll be hard to move on from this, but please don't let me find you texting Jessie in a fit of regret, okay?"

I laugh. "I'll delete her number right now." I pick up my phone and do as I said, and then Chloe gives me a celebratory high five.

"I know it hurts," they say. "But honestly, I think this is good for you. I mean, yeah, feel shitty all you want right now. It's your right as someone who just got her heart crushed by people you trusted to feel shitty and mope around and whatever, but I think you'll soon see that this is a fresh start for you."

They pat me on the leg. "Hey, remember last year when Paris broke up with me and I was all set to try to win her back? And you sat me down and told me to wait it out, see how it feels to be apart from her and then decide if a relationship was what I wanted?" I nod. "And what happened?"

I sigh. "You realized you were happier without being in a relationship."

"Exactly. So take your own advice."

I close my eyes and let out a dramatic groan. "Fiiiine."

"You and I have the same problem, you know that?" they ask.

I chuckle. "Yeah, we're surrounded by assholes."

They laugh, nodding. "Okay, so maybe we have *two* problems." They count on their fingers. "Surrounded by assholes, and people pleasing. You know what happens when you combine the two? You get taken advantage of. You try to save people. You become a helpaholic."

I don't try to deny it. It's not the first time someone has called me out for being a people pleaser. Kass would always try to get me out of the people-pleasing habit in school. I was that kid who was so desperate to be liked that I lent people money, gave them the answers to all the tests, let them copy my homework. Once, in ninth grade, a girl stole one of my photo prints for photography class and handed it in to the teacher as her own, and I did nothing because I wanted to be her friend.

Kass wanted to kill me when she found out I gave my parents money last year. She always said I let them walk all over me.

And now that I'm famous, people are falling over themselves to be friends with me, and yet all I do is exhaust myself trying to please them. I don't know why, maybe I'm just super insecure, but I have this intense need to be liked. If someone doesn't like me—or even expresses a different opinion than me—it makes me judge myself. I know it's unhealthy and screwed up and destined to be a massive failure, but my self-esteem is entirely dependent on what other people think of me.

"We need to stop," I say. "Like, right now."

"The dating assholes or the people pleasing?"

"Both."

Chloe fake cries. "But assholes are always so hot!"

I laugh. "Hey, hotness fades. Assholery is forever."

They laugh and slide closer to me, resting their head on my shoulder. I stare at the framed print of Marilyn Monroe on their wall, deep in thought about how I'm going to get through this.

"No more trying to save people," I say.

"No more being helpaholics," Chloe says.

"I wish there was a rule book," I say. "Like, *Rules for Recovering People Pleasers and Asshole Magnets*."

We laugh some more, but I'm dead serious.

"*Rules for Recovering Helpaholics*," they say, writing in the air with their index finger.

"Or," I say. "*Rules for Recovering Trainwrecks*."

"Mm-hmm." Chloe nods. "I would read that book cover to cover."

"Same." I push my hair off my face. "We could always make our own rules, you know?"

They grin and clap their hands. "Yes! Rule number one: Self Care Comes First."

I nod enthusiastically. "Yes, yes! Love it. Number two: umm . . ." I tap my fingers on my chin. "Oh! Follow Your Heart."

Chloe giggles, and I blush a little.

"Too corny?" I ask.

They laugh louder. "Maybe just a little. How about: Go with Your Gut. We won't do anything just because someone else wants us to."

"Perfection," I say. I'm starting to get excited about this. "Okay. Three: No Doubts. We gotta stop doubting how we feel."

"So important," Chloe says, nodding. "And that includes not questioning our own ideas and talents, yeah?"

"Yep." But even as I say it, doubts start to creep in. Are we being silly right now? Could I ever live up to these so-called rules? What if I fail? "Ugh, this is going to be hard."

"Hey," Chloe says. "What's the worst that can happen?"

I stick out my bottom lip in an exaggerated pout. "I'll get called a diva. Or a bitch."

"Pfft," they say, waving it off. "So what? You'll be a happy bitch."

I groan and lean back against the fluffy couch cushions. "I need a change. Like a tattoo or a vacation or something. I need to get out of LA for a while."

"Ugh, saaaame," Chloe says. "Too much time in this town destroys my soul. We should do it. Just get the fuck outta here."

I shake my head. "Everywhere I go right now, cameras will follow. I'd rather just lay low. Crawl under a rock and wait it out."

They purse their lips. "Well, *that* sounds super healthy."

"Super," I say with a roll of my eyes. "But I'll take that over sitting on a beach, worrying about people hiding in the bushes to get a photo of me just so trolls can body shame me online."

Chloe cringes. "I hear you. But you can't hide forever."

CHAPTER SIXTEEN

I hum to myself as I walk down the stairs the next morning. It's my birthday, and I'm buzzing with excitement. What's that saying? Today is the first day of the rest of your life. Well, I'm eighteen today, and that's exactly how I feel. As of today, my parents don't have a legal hold on me. I leap over the last step and almost trip over suitcases stacked in Chloe's hall.

"Huh?" I mutter as I take a closer look. "Chlo? You going somewhere?"

"HAPPY BIRTHDAY!" Chloe, Ryan, and Alfie yell as I turn into the living room. I scream and jump a mile, right into Alfie as he jumps out from behind me.

"Ow! Motherf—" he curses, cupping his hands over his face. Blood drips down his chin.

"Alfie!" I gasp. "You're bleeding!"

"Yeah," he says as he hurries over to the kitchen sink. "Happy birthday."

I follow him and tear some paper towel off a roll on the counter. Chloe runs to their freezer for some ice. Ryan's too busy wetting his pants from laughter to help.

"Shit," I say as I hand Alfie the towel. "I'm so sorry."

"It's all good." He tries to give me a smile that says it's okay, but his teeth are stained with blood. "Wait, Chloe, don't let this ruin the surprise."

I glance from Alfie to Chloe and back again. "Huh? What's happening?"

Chloe smiles and hands me their phone. On the screen is an email from Hawaiian Air, confirming a flight to Hawaii that leaves tonight.

"You're going to Hawaii?" I ask, grinning.

They shake their head. "Nope."

My eyes narrow. "It's way too early for my brain to figure out what's happening right now. I'm going to need more information."

"*We* are going to Hawaii!" They wave Ryan and Alfie in closer.

My jaw drops. "Wait. What? We? What we?" I can't even manage a full sentence, and Chloe laughs.

"Hey," they say. "We want you to have a birthday you'll never forget. Anyway, you said you wanted to get out of LA, right?"

"Uh-huh," I say, still in disbelief.

Chloe raises their arms in the air. "Well, we made it happen. We leave tonight, so get your butt upstairs and pack a bag, or four."

All three of them stare at me, eyes as wide as their smiles. I stand in front of them, dumbfounded. I look at Alfie, knowing that if this is one of his pranks, I'll be able to see it in his face.

"For real," he says, like he knows what I'm thinking.

Ryan bounces on his heels excitedly. "It's a done deal. Charlie, Alyssa, and Will are coming, too."

I open my mouth to say something, but I'm speechless.

"Em?" Chloe says, trying to meet my gaze. "You okay?"

Alfie chuckles. "I think she's in shock."

I nod. "But what about paparazzi? And everything that's happened . . . Is this really what I should be doing? Does Sal know?" The questions roll off my tongue so fast they can't answer them.

"Whoa, relax," Chlo says, flattening a stray hair on my head. "Everything's taken care of."

"Yeah," Alfie says. "Sal's cool with it. We all think getting out of LA is exactly what we need. And we've arranged it all in secret, so the media won't know until we're gone."

"Chill," Ry says. "It's all organized."

"Come on," Chloe says as they start running up the stairs. "I'll help you pack."

My shock turns into excitement as I follow them. I don't know whether to jump with joy or ugly cry. All I know is that I have the best friends in the entire freaking world.

―――――――――

"Hey, y'all!" Alfie calls from downstairs an hour later. "Our Lyft is on the way!"

"Coming!" Chloe and I call back. I zip up my suitcase and run into the bathroom to put on some lipstick. "Which color should I wear?" I turn to Chloe, holding out five different shades.

They think for a moment, then say, "Go with Your Gut." They wink at me, reminding me of our rules. I tap my foot on the bathroom tiles as I look from one color to the next. I really love the purple, but I've never been brave enough to wear it outside of a concert setting.

"Fuck it," I say as I drop the others back in my bag and untwist the purple one.

"Ooh," Chloe says. "Nice choice."

They watch my reflection as I slide it on thick. "Thanks!" It dries into a matte look, bright and bold.

"How do you feel?"

I straighten my back and admire myself. "Tough. No one messes with the girl wearing purple lipstick." Oh, that would make a killer line in a song. I look at Chloe. "Do you mind if I write something on the glass?"

They raise an eyebrow, looking intrigued, then nod. "Go for it."

I pop open my purple lipstick and scrawl it on the bathroom mirror.

DON'T MESS WITH THE GIRL WEARING PURPLE LIPSTICK.

The words stare back at me, and I smile.

Chloe claps their hands. "Bad. Ass. I need to snap this."

We take a collection of mirror selfies, making sure to get my purple writing in the shot. Then I grab my suitcase and backpack and we run downstairs, meeting Alfie and Ry in the car.

———

A few hours later, I'm staring out the window of the plane as we lift off the tarmac. Chloe is beside me watching *Veep,* and Alfie and Ryan are seated in front of us, playing a video game. Our friends Will, Charlie, and Alyssa are meeting us in Hawaii in the morning.

Alfie shifts in his seat in front of me, resting his head on the window as he hits the button on the video game controller. Seeing his disheveled hair gives me an idea. I open Snapchat and slowly reach a hand out to him, preparing to take advantage of his fear of spiders. I hit the record button and tickle the back of his head, moving my fingers over his hair like spider's legs. He sits up with a start, whipping his hair around and messing it up with his hands. He stands up and flicks his hair forward, shaking it out.

Ryan leans away from Alfie's haphazard hair flicking. "What the hell are you doing?" he asks.

"I felt something in my hair," he whines. He shoves his head in Ryan's face. "Do you see anything?"

By this time, I've recorded three Snapchat videos and posted them. But I can't hold my laughter in anymore, and I erupt into a fit of giggles.

Alfie turns to me, spots the phone in my hand and the tears of laughter streaming down my cheeks, and slumps. He tries to glare at me, but his lips twitch into a smile.

"That's how you wanna play it, huh?" he teases. He kneels on the seat and leans over it, trying to snatch my phone from my hands. I slap his hand away and hold my phone above my head, laughter pouring out of me.

Chloe groans next to me. "Children," they say, "if you don't calm down, I swear, I'm going to turn this plane around."

Other passengers in first class side-eye us, but I ignore them.

Alfie grabs my phone and starts filming himself. "Emmy doesn't know it yet," he says, "but that was an act of war." He narrows his eyes dramatically. "All the *Fright*sider pranks I've pulled before will be nothing compared to what's coming. This time, it's personal."

He hands me my phone back, giving me an evil grin.

I roll my eyes. "Oh, I'm *so* scared, Alfie."

"You should be," he says. "I've got six hours to sit here and come up with a way to get you back." He slowly sinks down until all I can see are his eyes. He widens them, waggles his eyebrows, then sinks lower until he's disappeared from my sight. I shake my head, chuckling to myself.

But soon I find myself staring at the black screen in front of me, unable to relax. I thought I'd be more excited by now, but I feel strangely ashamed, like I don't deserve this. And to top it off, I can't stop thinking about Jessie, leaving her behind to deal with the tape scandal without me. Just because we broke up doesn't mean I don't want her to be happy.

But then I remember all the cruel things she said, how she treated me like I was nothing to her. I force myself to admit that she has always treated me like that, from our very first date. I couldn't—or wouldn't—see it at the time. I put her up on a pedestal the size of the Empire State Building, convinced she could do no wrong. Every time she belittled me or made fun of me, I laughed it off. Every time she made me pay for dinner or drinks or her plane ticket to London so she could be with me. I did it all willingly, just because I wanted her to love me. Even the sweet things she did for me benefited her more than anyone else. Maybe Chloe was right—maybe Jess and my parents have been gaslighting me this whole time. Maybe I just didn't notice it because it was all I've ever known. Feeling worthless has been normal my whole life.

I deserve better than that.

Don't I?

Ugh. I'm just so tired of feeling like I'm not good enough, of trying to gain everyone's approval all the time. I'm sick of feeling like the world is more interested in the fictional version of me that the press creates than in who I really am.

And most of all, I need to stop treating other people better than I treat myself. It's killing me.

Once we're in the air, I unlock my phone and go through the selfies I took back at Chloe's, letting the badassery of it burn into my mind. There I am, smirking, wearing bright purple lipstick, with my new motto written on the mirror behind me.

DON'T MESS WITH THE GIRL WEARING PURPLE LIPSTICK.

Excitement buzzes in my stomach. This is it. This is the beginning of something huge for me, I can feel it. Clean slate, fresh start, second chance—whatever you want to call it, this is the moment it all kicks into gear. From now on, I'm firing on all cylinders, living by my own rules.

I add the caption *True story* to one of the selfies, and then post it online. Instantly, notifications begin pouring in from my millions of followers.

"Em," Chloe says, staring at their phone, "that pic you just posted is fire."

Alfie and Ry pause their game to peek at my pic on their phones.

"Jesus," I hear Aflie mutter. "Looking good, King."

"Hot," Ry says. "You're definitely going to win this breakup."

I go through my notifications and smile. "I'm not trying to win the breakup. I'm trying to win my life back."

CHAPTER SEVENTEEN

"No peeking!" Chloe says. Their hands are cupped over my eyes, making sure I don't see the big surprise. Apparently, there's more to my friends' plan than a spontaneous birthday trip to Hawaii, and I'm bursting with curiosity and excitement. Someone takes my hands and leads me forward.

"Who's this?" I ask, squeezing the mystery fingers.

"Moi," Ry says.

My senses give me clues to our location. There's the unmistakable sound of waves, and the salty ocean air fills my lungs. I take a few more steps forward, and the ground beneath me becomes unstable, rocking gently, like we're on a pier.

"Whoa," I say, steadying myself with Chloe and Ry's help.

"Better get your sea legs ready," Ryan says.

"Shut up!" Chloe hisses. "You'll ruin it!"

Footsteps run past us, and I hear Alfie muttering to someone.

"Can I look yet?" I ask. "The suspense is killing me here."

"No!" Alfie calls, his voice sounding far away.

The ground angles up suddenly, and I almost trip.

"Oops!" Ry says. "My bad."

They lead me up the ramp slowly, and I hear the sound of water lapping up against something. It becomes clear that we're climbing aboard some sort of boat, but I don't want to let them know I've figured it out.

"All right," Chloe says, a smile in their voice.

Ryan helps me sit down on a cushioned seat. Chloe keeps their hands over my eyes.

"I'm going to let go," Chloe says. "But you still can't look. If I even see one eye open—"

"I won't look," I say, grinning. "Promise."

Chloe takes their hands away, and I keep my eyes shut. All I hear for the next few minutes are my friends running around frantically, moving things and whispering and giggling like children who are up to no good.

I feel a hand on my shoulder unexpectedly, and I jump.

"Chill," Chloe says. "It's just me. Come here; stand up." I do as they ask, and they put an arm around my shoulder. "Okay, Em. Open your eyes."

It takes a moment for my sight to adjust to the bright sunshine glaring down on us. And then I squeal.

"Whaaaaaat?" I scream. My hands fly up to cover my mouth.

We're on a yacht. A gigantic, sprawling, fancy-ass yacht that's fit for the likes of Beyoncé or Kim Kardashian. I'm standing in the center of the outdoor lounge area, with couches lining the edge, a round daybed behind me, and a dining table in front of me, covered in food. My friends stand around it, wearing costumes.

"Happy birthday!" Chloe squeals.

"No way!" I say through my giddy laughter.

Alfie spreads his arms out wide. "It's a Leonardo DiCaprio–themed birthday party!" The moment he says it, I recognize his costume; he's dressed as Leo's character Romeo, from *Romeo + Juliet*. He's wearing the shining armor from the party scene.

Chloe, in a blue shirt, suspenders, and brown pants, is Jack Dawson from *Titanic*.

Alyssa Huntington and her girlfriend, Charlie Liang, stand hand in hand on the other side of the table. I met them through Chloe a few months ago, and we got along instantly. They all started out as YouTubers around the same time, then one by one grew their careers and eventually ended up living in LA. Alyssa is black, has long lashes, a shaved head, and a collection of awesome tats down her arms. Charlie is Chinese Australian and, like me, dyes her hair based on her mood. Today it's a light blue that matches the ocean around us. They met last year at SupaCon and they are legit the most adorable couple I've ever seen.

Their costumes are easy to guess: Alyssa is dressed as Amsterdam Vallon from *Gangs of New York*; and Charlie is Jay Gatsby from *The Great Gatsby* in a white three-piece suit. The other two are harder to figure out. Ryan and Will are both wearing suits.

I first met Will Horowitz at last year's Teen Choice Awards when the Brightsiders presented him the award for Best New Talent. He's an actor on a hit CW show *Silver Falls* about werewolves and the people who love them.

"I don't get who you two are . . . ," I say, tapping my chin as I think. "Leo wears suits a lot."

Ryan reaches into his jacket pocket and pulls out a spinning top toy, twirling it on the table.

"*Inception*!" I say. Then I point to Will. "So, if Ry is Cobb . . . Will, are you—?"

"They call me the Wolf of Wall Street," he says in a thick Queens accent while he fixes his tie. I can already tell he's loving playing the role of Leo as Jordan Belfort right now.

"Is this . . . ," I start, looking around the amazing yacht. "Is this really all for me?"

Alfie runs up to me, pulling me into his arms. "Em, you only turn eighteen once." He walks me over to the table.

"And we know how hard the last couple of weeks have been for you," Ryan says with a sympathetic frown.

Alfie nods. "We wanted to do something that would blow your mind."

"Mission accomplished," I say.

Chloe smirks, then Alfie walks around the table to the tinted sliding doors. "Kid, we're just getting started," he says, then pulls the door open.

The indoor living area is even more glamorous than the outdoor one. Glossy mahogany walls, white couches, wide windows that provide an amazing view of the ocean. And every surface is made of marble. I've never seen anything so glamorous. It leads into a kitchen fit for a world-class chef, with a twelve-seater dining table under a chandelier to the left of it.

Alfie leans against the nearby bar, a smug smile on his face. "Did we crush it, or did we crush it?"

I nod excitedly. "Crushed it to smithereens."

He holds his hand in a fist over his chest. "Yes!" He reaches behind the bar. "Oh, and we have a costume for you, too." He pulls out the other iconic outfit Leo wore in *Romeo + Juliet*: the blue Hawaiian shirt.

"Yeesssss!" I say as I snatch it from his hands. I slip it on then and there, finishing with a twirl. "How do I look?"

"Very Leo," he says.

But my heart sinks when I notice that the shelves behind the bar have been stripped bare. My friends don't trust me enough to be here without eliminating every last trace of alcohol. Do they think I'm going to go on some kind of drunken rampage? I had one bad night; it doesn't mean I can't control myself.

Alfie notices me staring behind him at the bar. "Um," he says, running a hand through his hair. "We have another surprise for you." He pulls his phone out and starts filming me. "Consider this payback for that spider prank you pulled on the plane." He cups a hand over his mouth and yells, "You can come out now!"

A bear appears from the hallway. It's not a real bear, obviously, but someone wearing a not-at-all-lifelike bear costume. Everyone starts chuckling as the bear runs toward me, the head bouncing unnaturally.

"Whoa, whoa!" I say as it lunges at me. It lifts me up and spins me around while I scream and choke on fake fur.

"Bear hug!" a voice yells from inside the mask.

"I know that voice!" I squeal, hugging the bear tighter. "Kassidy?!"

"Nah! It's not Kassidy. I'm the bear from that movie!" she says. "Rawr!"

"*The Revenant*," Chloe says, laughing. "I knew you'd forget what it's called."

She puts me down and lifts her mask off so I can see her freckled face grinning at me.

"Surprise!" she says.

I haven't seen Kass since our tour went to Boston last year. Alfie and Ryan had their families show up for them at so many of our concerts, even cousins and extended relatives, to cheer them on. My parents were passed out in front of the television, surrounded by half-eaten McDonald's and stained wine glasses whenever we did shows in LA. But Kass, she showed up for me. That concert was the highlight of the whole tour. Even though we've been on opposite sides of the country for years, she always shows up when I need her. And, God, have I needed her lately. I've lost count of all the nights I fell asleep while FaceTiming with her, crying over the latest horrible thing my parents had said to me.

I throw my arms around her again, tears spilling down my face. "But . . . When did you . . . How?"

She nods to Alfie. "This one offered to fly me out to surprise you."

I glance over my shoulder to Alfie, who looks away shyly. I'm too emotional to talk, so I pull him into the hug, too.

"Happy Birthday, Emmy," he says as he hugs me back.

"Yo!" Ryan calls from the outdoor dining table. "No more of this gushy stuff. We've got Leo-themed food here that isn't gonna eat itself."

We all sit around the dining table and dig in to cupcakes with Leo's face on them, and then two waiters emerge from the level below with my all-time favorite food: nacho pizza.

My tongue hangs out of my mouth and I pretend to drool. "Oh my god, yes!"

The yacht leaves the dock while we eat, and by the time we've cleaned our plates of every last bite, the islands float on the horizon.

CHAPTER EIGHTEEN

"I'm so sorry I wasn't here," Kass says when we get some time alone after dinner. We're sharing watermelon by the swimming pool of the yacht, mostly talking about her life in Boston and college and boyfriends she's had. But I knew we could only go so long before the conversation turned to me. "I should've left Boston the second I found out you were in an accident."

I shake my head. "I was fine."

"Did your mom and dad pick you up and take you home?"

"No, Alfie and Ry drove me there."

She looks confused. "Wait, so you *voluntarily* moved back with them?"

I shrug. "I didn't think I had anywhere else to go."

Kass rubs her fingers over her eyebrows. "That place is toxic. Especially if you're trying to get your life together."

"I know," I say, staring down at the water lapping up against the boat. "I just wanted to try to have some kind of relationship with them."

She digs a seed out of her piece of watermelon and flicks it into the ocean. "I'm sorry they screwed you over like that. They're evil assholes."

"How embarrassing is it that I actually thought they'd changed?" I ask, more to myself than Kass.

She puts a hand on my shoulder. "Hey, there's nothing wrong with hoping your parents aren't dicks. You're allowed to get angry about this. Or feel sad or hurt or bitter as hell. Feel however you wanna feel. You have every right."

Hearing those words lifts a weight off my shoulders that I didn't even know I was carrying. "Thanks."

We're quiet for a few minutes. I let everything she's said sink in, and the more I think about a life without my parents dragging me down, the freer I feel.

She stifles a yawn, and I giggle. "You must be exhausted. I'll let you get some sleep."

We go inside and I walk with her to the other end of the yacht, where our cabins are.

"Night, Emmy-Wemmy," Kass says as she squeezes me against her.

"Night, Kassy-Wassy," I say. "Thanks for being here."

"Wouldn't have missed it for all the Tom Hollands in the world." She blows me a kiss. And with that, she disappears into her room.

I'm about to go back upstairs when Alfie turns into the hall, meeting me in the middle.

"So, how does it feel to be eighteen?" he asks.

I sigh. "Like freedom. Also, I'm a proper adult now. That's weird."

He laughs. "Hey, I'm almost nineteen, and I still don't feel like an adult."

I elbow him in the ribs. "You don't act like one, either."

"Good!" he says. "Being an adult is overrated. That's why we became rock stars: We don't ever have to grow up."

I think of my parents and frown. "I'm glad to be growing up. Mom and Dad don't have a claim on me anymore. I can start my life."

He gives me a sad smile. "I'm sorry they didn't wish you a happy birthday."

"It's okay," I say, avoiding his gaze. "Any contact with them would have ended in an argument anyway."

But really, it's not okay. Even though I knew the chances of them calling me were slim—they didn't even reply when I texted to say I was moving to Chloe's. Still, I have to admit that it hurts.

Alfie shakes his head. "It's their loss. They don't deserve to have you in their lives. You're like a magical unicorn, and they were trolls trying to keep you under their bridge."

I can't help but smile. "I am totally a magical unicorn."

We stand by the door to his room for a moment, just smiling at each other. It's not anywhere near as awkward as it sounds. Nothing is ever awkward with Alfie.

"I'm glad you liked your surprise," he says, smirking.

"Well," I say, flicking my hair back. "Come on, Leo cupcakes? What's not to like?"

He laughs. "True story."

"Seriously," I say. "Thanks for flying Kass all the way out here. You have no idea how much I need her right now. This was, by far, the best birthday ever. I'll remember it forever."

Alfie beams, and I can tell he's proud of himself. He opens his arms wide, and I step into him, sliding my arms around his waist.

One thing everyone knows about Alfie is that he smells incredible. It's become almost like an urban legend now—entire articles have been written about it. I guess that's what happens when you become the official face of Burberry cologne. I close my eyes and breathe in the woodsy scent.

He rests his chin on my shoulder and sighs. "It's so good to see you so happy," he says softly.

"Back at you," I say.

He releases me and I lean back, but we're still holding on to each other.

"Beautiful birthday girl," he says, giving me a half smile.

I rest my forehead on his shoulder, smiling into him. I find myself not wanting to let go. I look up at him, and suddenly the energy between us is different. He's looking at me like he knows what I'm thinking, but how can that be when I'm not even sure what I'm thinking?

I know that look. I've seen it hundreds of times before. It's the look he gives the camera at photo shoots or people at clubs that he wants to hook up with. It's pure heat and sex and intensity, complete with pouty lips and eyes that don't waver from you for a second. I never thought in a million years that I'd be on the receiving end of that stare—or that I'd enjoy it.

His hands rest on my hips, and I move mine over his shoulders. It's like my body has a mind of its own, and I'm watching from the sidelines as I lift my chin. Alfie leans in, and then it happens.

He's kissing me. I'm kissing him. We're kissing each other, and it's not weird or uncomfortable or awkward. It's soft, and warm, and feels like the most natural thing in the world. Alfie links his hands on the small of my back and holds me closer. I dip my head back and tighten my grip around his neck until he's leaning over me and my back is arched. The yacht rocks against a wave, knocking us off-balance. I fall back against the wall and rest against it to stabilize us. We don't break our kiss for even a second. Goosebumps wash over me, making me shiver. I never want this moment to end.

Until I hear laughter rolling down the stairs and into the hallway. Alfie and I jump away from each other. I fix my hair while he shoves his hands in his jeans pockets, acting all casual.

Will and Ryan turn into the hall, laughing hysterically.

"Oh, hey!" Ry calls. "What's with the disappearing act? It's not a party without the birthday girl!"

Alfie and I glance at each other. I can feel my cheeks warming.

"We were just showing Kass to her room," I say, a little too defensively.

"Are you coming back up?" Will asks, still method acting as Leo.

Panic rises in my stomach. "Um, actually . . . ," I start, trying to think of an escape route. "I'm pretty wiped. Maybe I should call it a night."

Ry shoots me a perplexed look. "But we're just getting started!"

"Yeah," I say, stepping backward down the hall. "It just hit me." I fake a yawn. "Must be all the excitement. But we can . . . uh, keep the party going all week, right?"

Will grins. "Absolutely."

I give him a thumbs-up. "Cool, cool." I pretend to yawn again and turn toward my bedroom. "Night, everyone!"

"Night, Em!" Ry calls.

"Happy birthday!" Will adds.

"Yeah," Alfie says, looking amused at my freak-out. "Sweet dreams."

Before I close my bedroom door, I see him watching me. He's still got that look in his eyes, paired with a devilish smirk that makes me want to invite him into my bed right now. I close the door and lock it to stop myself from going back out there. My phone buzzes a minute later, and I see a text from him.

ALFIE: well, that was an interesting development.

I cannot for the life of me wipe the stupid smile from my stupid face. Now that I'm away from his intoxicating scent and taste, I'm starting to think clearly. And I'm realizing just how very bad this could be.

> **EM:** That's one word to describe it.
>
> **ALFIE:** here are some other words I would use . . .
>
> amazing.
>
> mind-blowing.
>
> hot.
>
> **EM:** Dangerous.
>
> Mistake.
>
> Trouble.
>
> **ALFIE:** inevitable.
>
> **EM:** Not inevitable.
>
> **ALFIE:** not over.

I chew on my bottom lip, staring at those last two words. He's making a promise, and I'm surprised at myself, but I desperately want him to keep it. I drop my phone onto my bed and go into my bathroom, smiling the whole way. I lean over the sink and stare wide-eyed at my reflection.

"Emmy," I whisper-yell. "What the actual fuck? What did you just do? Fuck, fuck, fuck!"

I should be horrified. I should be worrying about what this all means for us, for our friendship, for the band. I should be beating myself up—after all, Jessie totally called this. But I'm not doing any of that. It doesn't feel real. It doesn't feel serious; it feels fun. We were just two kids blowing off steam.

It must be a side effect of being newly single. It's a rebound thing. I just want to distract myself from the trash fire of my life lately, and there's nothing wrong with that, right?

I take in a calming breath, trying to shake off the wild electricity bouncing off of me. My skin feels like an exposed wire—one touch and I'll burst into flames.

I look at the ceiling through the mirror, knowing Alfie is up there somewhere. I wonder if he's jacked up like I am, if he's walking around in bewilderment, too. Knowing him, though, he's probably already forgotten about it. Electric kisses are probably a regular occurrence for him, being the heartthrob that he is.

I hum to myself and pull one of my makeup-remover wipes from the pack, swinging my hips back and forth. I suddenly feel like dancing, like sneaking off this boat, finding a club on the island, and rocking out on the dance floor until the sun comes up.

But that is not what recovering trainwrecks do. I should make the smart decision and go to bed to get a good night's sleep. Besides, even if paparazzi aren't waiting for me back on land yet, there are probably plenty of tourists there who would love to snap me doing something headline-worthy. Sneaking out in the middle of the night to go clubbing solo would definitely make that list.

Instead, I decide to take a selfie to get one last pic of my purple lipstick before I take off all my makeup. A few seconds after I post it to Snapchat, I get a snap from Alfie. My heart flips in my chest, and I open it. It's a pic of him lying on the daybed on the deck, his arm resting behind his head. It's dark, but I can see he's smiling. The caption reads:

So distracted. Your fault.

I decide to have some fun with him. I position myself in front of the mirror, hold my phone up at a flattering angle, wink, and snap the pic. When I look at it closer, I realize my cleavage is showing, and hesitate. Do I look slutty? Is it too much? Does taking selfies like this all the time make me look shallow or conceited?

I sit on the rim of the bathtub and stare at the picture, worrying myself into a shame spiral. I take a deep breath and remind myself of everything Chloe and I talked about.

Rule number three: No Doubts.

Then I go back to the photo and try to see it in a new light, without the noise of other people's potential judgments getting in my way. It's time to turn the volume up on my heart, and down on the crowd.

I like the photo. I think I look good. I refuse to slut-shame myself for it. I add a flirty caption to it: *Time for bed.*

And then I hit send before I second-guess myself again. I tap my heels on the tiles, nervously waiting to see if he replies. When he does, I open it faster than I've opened a snap in my life.

It's him still on the daybed, his shirt lifted slightly, showing off his toned abs. The caption reads:

Two can play at that game.

Ohmygodohmygodohmygodohmygod.

I'm tempted to reply with an even sexier pic, to keep the flirty fun going, but I resist. I may not have had anything to drink tonight, but there's still a chance I could wake up with regrets. I need to get some sleep and see what all this looks like in the light of day.

I turn my phone onto do-not-disturb mode, wipe off my makeup, slip into my pajamas, and hop into bed. I lay there in the darkness, letting the gentle rocking of the yacht soothe me into sleep. It doesn't work. I can't stop thinking about that kiss. Alfie was right. It was amazing. Mind-blowing. Hot. All good kisses are.

A kiss is more than just lips moving and tongues figuring each other out. Yeah, those parts are vital, obviously. But it's so much more. A kiss—a good kiss—is a symphony. A bad kiss is like having your face eaten by a zombie.

What makes a good kiss, though? It depends. I've had symphonies before. And a couple of zombies, too. My first kiss falls into the latter category. It was with a guy at a party that Kassidy's boyfriend threw when I was fifteen. I was so shy about people witnessing my epic awkwardness that I pulled him outside and around the side of the house. When he finally made his move, I laughed from nerves and turned away. Yep, he tried to kiss me and I literally laughed in his face.

When he found the courage to lean in for a second chance, I held back my giggles and spent the next three minutes feeling like our tongues were at war, dueling each other like swordsmen. I'm pretty sure he thought he was Zorro and his tongue was his sword, tracing a hectic Z on the back of my throat repeatedly. To make things worse, neither of us remembered to swallow, so our tongues stirred our saliva together until it dribbled down my chin. There's nothing quite as gross as realizing you don't know if the slobber pooling around your mouth is yours or not. I distinctly remember wanting to hurl.

Once we gave up—err, I mean stopped—we went back inside and he immediately abandoned me to brag to his friends. It occurred to me, as I watched him strut over to his buddies, that he actually thought it was a good kiss. He thought that weird alien battle between our mouths was actually *good*. Meanwhile, I went straight to the bathroom to rinse the dried spittle from my chin and wondered what the hell everyone was raving about. Kissing wasn't fun! Kissing was slimy and puke inducing and embarrassing.

Of course, thanks to a few more test runs with a selection of volunteers of all genders, I would eventually realize that kissing isn't so bad after all. And that brings me to the symphony. A good kiss is made up of many little movements, working together to create one beautiful experience. It's lips, it's tongues, it's hands. It's the heightened tension in the moments leading up to it. It's the way you look at each other, the nervousness you feel, the excitement in your eyes. It's the way your heart races when one of you moves closer. It's the way your breath catches in your throat when it finally happens. It's the way you gasp for air because you can't get enough of each other, or the way your thighs tremble when it gets so heated you don't think you can take much more.

Ugh, I should not have started thinking about Alfie's kiss. Now I'll never get to sleep.

CHAPTER NINETEEN

I wake up with the sunrise, still consumed by that kiss. I mentally scan my emotions for any signs of regret. I should feel at least a slither of regret, right? I'd even settle for a mild sense of weirdness. Something to pull me away from letting that kiss happen again. But all I feel is butterflies. Argh. Come on, heart, give me something I can use!

I'm too annoyed at myself to go back to sleep, so I get dressed and go up to the kitchen to make myself coffee. When I walk outside, the view takes my breath away. Turquoise ocean that blends into the clear sky. Sunshine reflecting off the water, making the whole world glitter. I ignore the voice in the back of my mind telling me I don't deserve this and focus on rule number one: Self Care Comes First.

Other boats dot the water, and I can't help but worry about which ones have cameras on me right now. I lay on the lounge, out of view, and stare up at the sky.

At some point I fall asleep, and when I wake up I hear my friends laughing and chatting, cooking up something that smells delicious. I follow the scent of breakfast and find Chloe, Kass, and Will in the kitchen making bacon and scrambled eggs. They have our album, *Strange Welcome*, playing, and they're singing and dancing around the room.

"Good morning!" Chloe sings.

"Morning!" I beam.

"Want some breakfast?" Kass asks.

"Love some." I help carry the plates to the outdoor dining table and go back inside to make more coffee because my first cup has gone cold.

I'm singing along to our song "All for You" when I feel someone standing behind me. A slow smile spreads across my face. "Good morning, Alfie," I say, keeping my attention on the coffee machine.

"Something smells good," he says, his voice croaky from sleep.

"Breakfast is outside." Goosebumps tingle all over my skin just being in his presence. I'm in so much trouble.

"Nice," he says. I can feel his eyes on me, and it reminds me of the way he looked at me last night. My smile widens.

"Want some coffee?" I ask.

"Sure." He leans against the counter next to me, and I finally glance up at him.

Yep. There's that look again. Big trouble.

"So," he says. "How are you this morning?"

"Fine," I say, my voice barely a whisper.

He smiles. "Good."

We stare at each other longer than two friends should. The coffee machine pings, and I drag my gaze away from him. I move my coffee mug to the side and start preparing his, when he puts a hand on mine. A shiver runs down my spine.

"I got it," he says.

I take my coffee and sit on the kitchen island, watching him.

"Sleep well?" I tease before blowing on my coffee.

He gives me a sideways glance and smirks. "Nope. Did you?"

I shrug. "Not too bad."

Alfie takes a step toward me, resting his hands on the island on either side of me. I look around, feeling like we're breaking so many unspoken rules, but wanting to break so many more.

"What are you doing later?" he asks.

Before I can answer, Ryan emerges from the stairwell, yawning. I push Alfie away and slide off the island. My heart pounds hard in my chest.

"Hey," Ry says through another yawn. He scratches his head, the hair flat on one side from sleeping, then follows the scent of bacon outside.

That was way too close, and yet incredibly exciting. I sit down at the table with my friends, feeling like some sort of secret agent leading a double life.

I'm chewing on a particularly yummy strip of bacon when Alfie joins us. He sits across from me, and I try to ignore his cheeky smirk.

"You look happy, Em," Kass says, putting her arm around me.

I stare at my eggs. "How could anyone not be happy here?"

Will takes a sip of his orange juice. "Did you have fun last night?"

My heart skips a beat, but then I realize he's talking about the party. "Tons! Best party ever."

"Three, two, one!" Charlie shouts. She and Alyssa jump off the yacht, hand in hand. We watch from the lounge, cheering them on.

"My turn!" I say, standing up. I lift my T-shirt over my head and slip out of my denim shorts, standing in just my white bikini. "Who's with me?"

I try not to look at Alfie, even though I really only intended that question for him. I need more time alone with him to figure out what's happening between us. And, okay, yeah, maybe I want to kiss him again.

Kass stands up, finishing her cream soda. "I'll go with you." She shimmies out of her sundress.

"Anyone else?" I ask, this time letting myself glance at Alfie. He's lying back on the cushions, his hat dipped forward so I can't see his eyes.

"Alfie," Kass says. He slides his hat back an inch or two.

"No," he says.

Kass holds a hand out to him. "Come on. Let's cure your fear of heights."

"You don't have to," I say, trying to give him an out. I don't want to pressure him into doing anything that makes him uncomfortable.

"It's totally safe," Kass says. I nudge her.

Alfie looks at Kassidy, then at me, and shakes his head. My heart sinks.

"Fine," he says. "But if I die, I'm coming back to haunt you so bad." He unbuttons his shirt and drops it on the table, wearing only board shorts and a swim binder that matches his pale skin tone.

"Yay!" I grin, trying to convey a hidden message to him with my eyes, one that's flirty and fun and promises more making out. "It'll be worth it."

We climb onto the edge. Charlie and Alyssa are already on the beach, disappearing into the trees. I stand in the middle and link hands with Kass and Alfie. I can feel how nervous he is, his fingers trembling in my own.

Kass turns to shout something at our friends, and Alfie leans in, whispering in my ear, "It's gonna be worth it, huh?"

I give him a sideways glance. "Maybe."

He smiles, but his lips twitch, and I can see he's trying hard to act calm. I squeeze his hand.

"I've got you," I say. He nods.

"Ready?" Kass asks. "Three, two, one. Go!"

We jump, and Kassidy immediately lets go of my hand. Meanwhile, Alfie holds on for dear life. I scream as the wind blows through my hair and the ocean rolls below me. I pinch my nose and squeeze my eyes shut, and then *whoosh!* I'm in it deep. The force of the landing rips our hands apart. The warm, sun-kissed water envelops me, and I let it. I sink lower, opening my eyes to see the rays of sunshine piercing the ocean around me, the tiny bubbles floating up like specks of underwater snowflakes. My legs kick, and I push through to the surface, sucking in the fresh air. I hear Kassidy laughing.

"That was awesome!" she shouts.

Alfie pops up next to her, gasping. His face is hidden behind his hair, and he parts it open like a curtain so he can see.

I swim over to them, smiling. "I can't believe we actually did it!"

"Jesus," he pants. "That was fucking terrifying. Remind me to never do it again."

Kass flicks him with water, starting an all-out splash war.

"Look out below!" Will calls from above. "Cannonball!"

He launches off the yacht, tucking his legs up to his chest. I swim out of the way, but he's too quick. He lands hard, sending waves rippling around him and water splashing into our faces.

"Let's get him," Alfie says.

When Will rises to the surface, we greet him with frantic splashing. He covers his face with his arms and laughs.

"Argh! You assholes!" he says. He disappears under the water, and

I squeal as he swims toward me. I freestyle away as fast as I can, but my own laughter is slowing me down. I feel him tickling my foot and scream.

"I can't swim and laugh at the same time," I say in between giggles.

Alfie takes my hand and pulls me toward him. Will turns his attention to Kassidy, and they erupt in another round of splash wars. I wade in the ocean next to Alfie, trying to get closer without attracting attention. He holds my hand under the water, and it's like my heart has been restarted. Suddenly, I'm very aware of my body, feeling every ripple of the ocean moving against my skin, every goose bump and hair standing up. I glance at Alfie, watching as he laughs with Will and Kassidy, his hair slicked back. All I want to do is kiss him again.

Alfie notices me watching him and winks. Then he leans in, pretending he's looking at something behind us.

"Let's get out of here," he says. He locks eyes with me, like he's waiting for my answer, and I nod.

We sneak away while Kass and Will aren't looking, and swim to the nearby shore. As we walk onto the sand, I can't help but notice how good he looks in his binder and shorts. I've never looked at Alfie this way before, noticing his abs and his arms and his smile. Before last night, he was just dorky, funny, laid-back Alfie, my friend and bandmate. But now, literally overnight, he's become Alfie: Sex Beast and Super Babe. My perception of him changed so fast I've got whiplash, and my mind is racing to catch up to my body and how I feel when I'm around him now.

The moment we're hidden in the trees, he takes my hand and swings me into him. Our mouths merge, tasting of salt water and sunscreen. We wrap around each other like the vines on the palm trees around us. A breeze flows by, rustling the banana leaves. I'm so hot from the sun, and the kiss that it feels like ice on my skin.

But I can't turn off my thoughts. It's like my mind and my body are arguing with each other.

> **Mind:** Whoa now, what's all this?
>
> **Body:** Who cares? Just go with it.
>
> **Mind:** Nope. Nope, nope, nope. I need to understand this.
>
> **Body:** Just. Keep. Kissing!
>
> **Mind:** But why is this happening? What changed?
>
> **Body:** Dunno. All I know is that it feels amazing.
>
> **Mind:** But WHY?
>
> **Body:** Shut up. Kiss him.
>
> **Mind:** But he's our friend.
>
> **Body:** This kiss, though.
>
> **Mind:** But we work together.
>
> **Body:** Those abs, though.
>
> **Mind:** But this is risky.
>
> **Body:** Those eyes, though.
>
> **Mind:** But it's ALFIE.

That does it. I pull away from him and walk deeper onto the island, trying to get myself together. Alfie hurries after me, watching me curiously.

"Everything . . . okay?" he asks.

I laugh nervously, scratching an imaginary itch on my shoulder. "What the shit are we doing, Alfie?"

"Well," he says, shrugging like it's no big deal. "We *were* making out like the world was on fire. And now, we're . . . walking on an island that looks creepily like the one from *Lost*."

I stop and look around, realizing he's right, and I have no idea which way we came from.

"Maybe we should head back to the boat," I say, spinning on my heels. "I don't wanna end up like them."

He laughs, and I try not to notice how it makes his abs tighten.

"I dunno. I'd be okay with being stuck out here for a while." He steps closer, chest to chest, and snakes his arms around my waist. "With you."

And then he gives me that look again, and my mind explodes into a fireball of incomprehensible expletives and nothing else matters except for how good this feels.

I crush my mouth to his, suddenly not caring that this is seriously risky or that I don't know where we are or that our friends could stumble upon us any second.

Alfie's hands run down my back, sliding over my bare skin. I stand on my tiptoes to get better access to his mouth, and he lifts me off the grass. The voice in my head tries to stop me, begs me to listen to it instead of obeying my vagina, but I ignore it.

But then I hear another voice, and it's one I can't ignore.

"Alfie and Em are probably hiding," Will says from a distance. "I bet you a million dollars they're waiting to jump out and scare us right now. Frightsider style."

Alfie chuckles. "Guess again," he mutters to me. He lowers me back to the ground and takes my hand, pulling me farther into the jungle. Our feet slip and slide on the dirt and grass, but we don't slow down. We laugh and pant and run as fast as we can, until we reach a glittering rock pool with a powerful waterfall cascading into it.

"Race you," I say, before bursting into a sprint. I feel him hot on my heels as I leap into the water, feeling like I've just jumped into a picture-perfect postcard. I float onto my back and stare up at the clear blue sky, asking myself the same question I've been asking since the day I first heard a Brightsiders song on the radio: How is this my life?

Alfie stands in the water, spreads his arms out wide, and falls gracefully onto his back, floating alongside me.

"We're like otters," I say.

"Hermione's Patronus," he says matter-of-factly.

"Yeah! You know that when otters float like this, they hold hands so they don't lose each other?" I ask. He doesn't reply, and I wonder if he can hear me. "Alfie?"

I feel his hand take mine, and I know he heard me.

CHAPTER TWENTY

"Did you hear that?" Alfie asks, breaking a long, comfortable silence.

We both stand up in the water, listening intently. Laughter rings out, echoing off the cliff above us.

"I think that's Charlie," I say quietly.

Alfie starts walking out of the water, but I pull him back by the hand.

He cocks his head to the side and smirks. "Still not done with me, huh?"

I shake my head. More laughter bounces around us. He looks at something behind me and nods toward it.

"This way," he says, wading through the water. I follow him, and we swim over to the waterfall. When we reach it, I see a small cave on the other side, just big enough for us to hide in. I hold my breath and go under, feeling the weight of the water hitting the pool as I swim into the cave. When I rise to the surface, I feel like I've entered a magical realm. Sunlight scatters in, reflecting off the cave walls like a kaleidoscope. Other than that, it's dark and cool, and all I can hear is the sound of the thundering water.

Something grabs my waist, and I scream. Alfie pops up in front of me, holding onto my hips and laughing.

"Gotcha," he says. I give him a mock glare and splash him.

He cranes his neck, admiring the cave. "Wow. I bet the acoustics in here would be sweet." And just like that, he starts singing Adele's "Rolling in the Deep." His voice is so strong that I can hear it clearly over the rushing water, and he's right: The acoustics in here are amazing. The words float out of his mouth and off the crevices in the cave walls, creating a sound so good I need to get in on it. I sing along, belting out the emotionally charged lyrics until I feel my own voice vibrating in my heart. When we're done, we look at each other and smile.

Nothing lifts me up like music. Sometimes, when I'm really connected to a song, I feel like I'm floating, like my soul is rising out of my body and into space.

"Remember when we were just starting out," he says, "and we added echoes like that in GarageBand?"

I smile at the memory. "Yeah. And we'd sit in your room all night, eating Ben and Jerry's and testing out all the sound effects."

"What about that song Ry made?" he asks, grinning. "The one that was almost all fart sounds, and then ten seconds of applause."

I laugh hard. All those times spent in Alfie's room with Ryan were once the only bright spots in my day. We'd joke around and play music and watch Netflix, and for a few hours a night I could forget what was waiting for me at home. On good nights, my parents would be passed out by the time I got home. On bad nights, I'd just go right back to Alfie's, where life was normal, and fun, and quiet. I honestly don't know what I would have done without him.

And that's when it hits me: fooling around with Alfie risks losing all that. I lock eyes with him, and his smile fades.

"What?" he asks, peering outside. "Did you hear something?"

"No," I say. "But we should go back."

He frowns and swims closer, his nose just inches away from mine. "But I thought you wanted . . ." He trails off, and I know why. He doesn't know how to finish that sentence. Neither of us do. Neither of us has any idea what we're doing here. And that's dangerous.

"We need to not do this," I say. "It'll just get weird. Or worse."

He watches me for a second, furrowing his brow. "Did I do something wrong?"

I shake my head. "No, nothing. I just don't think it's the smartest idea."

He raises an eyebrow. "Maybe not the smartest," he says. "But it's definitely the funnest." I give him a blank stare, and his face drops.

"Wait, you're serious, aren't you?" he asks. "You really think things will get weird?"

"Yeah. I mean, it's already kinda weird," I say. "Sneaking off from our friends, finding secret hideouts . . ."

"Oh," he says, pushing his hair out of his eyes. "Sure. I get it. Well, if we hurry we can catch up with the others."

"All you gotta do," Kass says, "is hit shuffle on your Most-Played Songs list, and then lip-synch the shit out of it."

We're all sitting in the living area of the yacht after dinner, sharing popcorn and deciding which game to play.

Chloe claps excitedly. "I love this. The only rule is that everyone has to make total losers of themselves."

Kassidy high-fives them. "Yes! Winner gets . . ." She runs to the kitchen island, looking around. She picks something up and smiles. "The last pint of Ben and Jerry's!"

Will leans forward on the couch. "Loser has to jump off the boat nude!"

We all laugh, agreeing to the highly classy terms.

"Okay," Chloe says, glancing around. "Who's going first?"

Ryan throws his hand up. "I volunteer as tribute!"

Kassidy bows and gestures for him to take the room. "May the odds be ever in your favor."

Ryan pushes the coffee table out of the way, turning the room into a dance floor. He takes his phone out, taps the screen, and drops it onto the couch. A song starts playing, and I recognize it immediately as "Pillowtalk" by Zayn Malik. Ryan mouths the words, slowly gyrating and sliding his hands down his body. He's clearly aiming to make this a very sexualized performance, and soon we're all howling with laughter. I'll always be jealous of how easy comedy comes to Ryan. He'll do almost anything to make people laugh, even if it means making a total fool of himself. Half of his tweets are made up of dad jokes or bad puns. I've lost count of the times he's mooned the audience at our concerts, or done cartwheels mid-song to get a cheer from the crowd. It's like he has zero shame.

I take my phone out and start filming for Snapchat. Our fans are going to flip out over this. The song ends, and as a big finale, Ryan tugs his T-shirt off, swings it over his head, and flicks it at me. It lands on my head, and I take it and pretend to cuddle it like I'm holding a kitten. We applaud him, and Will wolf whistles when Ryan flexes his muscles.

"My turn!" Charlie says, springing off the couch. She sets her phone up, and the song from *Dirty Dancing* starts playing. "Oh my God!" she squeals. She dances over to Alyssa and holds her hands out. "Sing with me?"

I swoon as Alyssa stands up and they start serenading each other. They look at each other with so much love, like there's no one else in the room. Alyssa twirls Charlie, then holds her close while they dance, not missing a word with their lip-synching.

I want that kind of love. I want it so much it hurts, like a gaping hole in my chest.

"Are they gonna do the move?" Chloe whispers to me.

Before I can answer, the moment arrives and Charlie leaps into Alyssa's arms. She squeals as Alyssa holds her waist and lifts her over her head, just like Swayze. We all scream in surprise, gawking at them in awe.

"Game over," I say. "They've won for sure!"

Kass throws an arm around me, *tsk*ing. "Emmy, don't give up so easily! Besides, you haven't seen my moves yet."

Charlie and Alyssa bow, then they sink into each other's arms on the couch while Kassidy gets ready to shine.

"Come on," she mumbles to her phone. "Give me something good."

The music gods answer her prayer. Beyoncé's "Single Ladies" begins and she jumps into the air. "Yes!" she shouts, looking up at the ceiling. "Thank you, Queen Bey!"

Halfway through the song, she points at Chloe, who stands up and jumps right into the dance with her, not missing a beat. I have the coolest friends in the world. By the end of the song, we're all videoing the amazingness.

"I feel bad for whoever has to follow that!" Chloe says, flicking their hair back over their shoulder.

Alfie stands up. "Challenge accepted!"

He already has his phone ready, and he dips his head forward and messes up his hair while the song starts up. It's "Need You Tonight" by INXS, and I am not at all surprised that is one of his most-played songs. He is a freak for classic rock: from AC/DC to Guns N' Roses and the Red Hot Chili Peppers, he knows it all. He snaps to the beat with one hand while flipping his wavy hair back seductively to get the full Michael Hutchence effect. It's working.

I take in a deep breath to prepare myself. What happens in the next three minutes could break me.

Gotta stay strong. Need to stay strong. Must stay strong.

Alfie slides across the carpet like he's center stage and has thousands of screaming fans in front of him. I focus on filming it, hoping that putting a screen between us will take my body temperature down a few degrees. It doesn't.

And then he does the moonwalk and grabs his crotch, making us all holler.

"Jesus, Alfie," Charlie says, her eyes practically popping out of her head. Alyssa jokingly covers her girlfriend's eyes.

The song winds down, and Alfie finishes up on his knees, his shirt hanging off of his shoulders, showing all of his tattoos and the straps of his red bralette.

I. Am. Dead.

Why the hell did I have to discover this attraction to him when we were stuck on a boat together for a week?

I keep my gaze down, working on the theory that if I don't look at anyone, they won't see my red cheeks and hungry eyes. I feel like all the dirty thoughts in my mind are livestreaming on my forehead for everyone to see.

Chloe laughs and rolls their eyes. "Okay, chill. We get it, you're hot as fuck. It's Alyssa's turn to rock the mic!"

Alfie sits down next to me, and it doesn't go unnoticed that he neglects to button his shirt back up. Alyssa gets up, hits play, and shakes her arms out. She's an actor, so I'm excited to see her skills shine through. "24K Magic" by Bruno Mars starts, and Alyssa pulls out all her best dance moves. We all start singing, bopping up and down on the couch. She crouches in front of Charlie, busting out the lyrics word for word. Charlie keeps up with her, singing along, closing her eyes at some parts.

"Look at them," I whisper to Chloe. "They're so in sync."

"Right?" Chloe says. "It makes me sick how cute they are together." We stare at them in awe as they wind down the track, and then Will hops up to take his turn. He taps his phone and starts moving as soon as Harry Styles's "Sign of the Times" begins.

Alfie slides closer to me on the couch. "Sorry if I was staring during my song," he whispers. I feel his warm breath on my neck. "I tried not to, but I was nervous and for some reason it helped. I hope it didn't make things weird."

I shake my head. "Nothing's weird. It's cool."

He dips his chin down, looking at me from under his brown lashes. "You sure?"

"Hundred percent," I say with a reassuring smile.

He smiles back, and our gaze lingers. Ryan elbows me in the side, breaking our staring contest.

"Shh," Ryan whispers to me. He gestures to Will, who's lip-synching with his eyes closed. "You're missing it."

"Sorry," I say. I glance at Alfie, and he swipes his thumb and index finger over his lips in the zipping motion. I hold back my laughter.

When the song finishes, everyone looks at me.

That's when I realize it's my turn. I swallow hard. This is going to sound so ridiculous, but I get bad stage fright. I know, I know, I'm in a famous band that has toured the world, and I'm getting stage fright performing in front of my closest friends. It's different onstage: sweating under the lights, high on adrenaline, getting lost in the music, rocking out for thousands of strangers. Plus, I'm never alone up there. I'm always with my friends.

But here, in this intimate setting . . . I'm hesitant. I know these people, and I fear their judgment more than anyone's. I want them to keep liking me. I stand in front of them, my elbows glued to my sides as I open my Most-Played Songs list in iTunes and hit shuffle. Pink's "So What" comes on, and my cheeks warm. I've listened to this song dozens of times already since Jessie and I broke up and I left home.

"Nice," Kass says, nodding. "This couldn't be more on point for you right now."

I push my hair back, close my eyes, and just go with the music. I'm slow at first, but by the chorus I'm giving it my all—head banging, poor attempts at scissor kicking, even rocking the air guitar. I'm so caught up in it that it takes me a second or two to notice when the song is over. I open my eyes, my head spinning and my face burning from going so hard. My friends cheer. Chloe pumps their fist in the air, shouting, "Woo! Woo! Woo! Woo!"

I bask in the applause while I catch my breath, then fall back onto the couch.

CHAPTER TWENTY-ONE

"Okay," Kass says. "Should we vote on the winner?"

Ryan leans back against the cushions, grinning. "I think we all know I won."

I roll my eyes at him, and he winks at me.

"I dunno," Alfie says. "I think we were all too damn good. Maybe we should declare an eight-way tie."

We all agree. We are much too awesome to choose a victor.

"Does that mean we all have to share the ice cream?" Charlie asks.

"Or," Ry says, turning his head slowly, "we all go skinny-dipping."

Chloe is running toward the door before I know what's happening, tearing their clothes off and throwing them on the floor in a trail.

"Holy shit!" Ryan says as he stares after them. "I was only joking!" He looks at all of us. "Wait, what am I saying? I'm in!" And then he's gone.

Alyssa and Charlie grin at each other, having one of their silent conversations. Charlie nods like she's answering a question, then they are up and running outside, too.

"Wait up!" Will says, almost tripping over the coffee table as he runs and pulls his tank top over his head at the same time.

Now it's just me, Kass, and Alfie sitting on the couch, our jaws hanging open. Kassidy turns to me, giggling and giving me a look that says *You wanna?* I dig my fingers into the couch, trying to figure out if I want to do it because it sounds like fun, or because everyone else is doing it. Alfie is unnaturally quiet next to me, and I wonder if he's waiting for me to decide before he answers.

"Maybe I'll just watch," I say, then I realize how that sounds. "Um, in a non-creepy way, I mean."

Kass scrunches her nose up, like she's unsure of what she should do. "Okay, me too."

The three of us walk tentatively out onto the deck, peering over the railing. It's light enough to see our friends in the water, but too dark to see anything else.

Kass smacks the railing. "Fuck it. I'm doing it."

She hurries down the stairs, and I mentally scream for her to come back. I think about asking her to stay, but she'd only ask why, and then what would I say? *Well, I've been having seriously hot make-out sessions with Alfie, and I'm worried I'll do it again if we're left alone together.*

Nope. I think about joining my friends in the water, but then I'll be naked and the answer to resisting temptation is definitely not to remove your clothes right in front of the person tempting you.

"You can go, if you want," Alfie says, breaking our silence. "I was gonna call it a night anyway. So . . . if you weren't going down there because of me, you don't have to."

I tap my foot against the deck. "I wasn't not gonna go because of you." He raises an eyebrow, and I cave. "Okay, maybe it was slightly because of you. But only because of what we talked about today. I'm pretty sure getting naked in front of each other counts as making it weird."

He laughs. "It doesn't have to be weird. Look at those dorks." He gestures at our friends, who are laughing and swimming and having tons of fun without us. "But it's up to you. Like I said, I'm just gonna go to bed."

He rests his elbows on the railing, clasping his hands together like he's praying.

"I don't think I want to," I say, surprising myself. "Also, just to be clear, you are only a tiny factor in that decision. I recently promised myself I'd never do something just because everyone else is doing it. And I think if I went down there, I'd only be doing it so I don't feel left out."

He raises his eyebrow again, but nods. "Ahh, the perils of FOMO. That's very self-aware of you."

I scoff. "It's about time I get at least a dash of awareness."

He nudges my elbow with his. "Don't be so hard on yourself. You're doing fine. I think we've held our own all right, considering how quickly our lives have changed in the last year. We went from being nobodies playing fart noises on my laptop, to having people chase us down the street to get a selfie and playing huge arenas like *that*." He snaps his fingers.

"You say that," I say with a sigh. "But I don't see you getting wasted and making yourself look like an asshole or getting into car accidents. You're just as famous as I am, and yet you're completely well adjusted."

Alfie laughs, but it's strained. "Not even close, Em." He shakes his head, looking thoughtfully out over the waves. "Not even close."

I turn to face him, leaning on the railing. "What, too many supermodels chasing after you? Not getting enough Burberry gigs to pay for your Beverly Hills area code?" I smirk, thinking I'm so freaking funny. But then I see his face, the hurt flashing in his eyes, and I know I've gone too far.

"Shit," I say, putting a hand on his shoulder. "I'm sorry, Alfie. I didn't mean any of that. I know you're going through stuff, too."

He shrugs away from me. "It's fine."

"You know," I say quietly, "you can talk to me about whatever."

"I don't wanna make a big deal of it."

"Come on. You've heard me whine on and on about a million things. It's your turn."

He chuckles. "That is true."

Giggles rise up from the water below. "Hey, Emmy! Alfie!" Kassidy calls. "You coming down or what?"

"Come on!" Will shouts. "Get your sexy naked butts over here!"

I ignore them, keeping my gaze on Alfie. "Do you wanna go inside and talk?"

"We're on vacation. I don't want to bring you down," he says, and it breaks my heart a little.

"Alfie," I say, taking his hand. "I just want to listen. That's all."

His shoulders relax visibly, and he nods. I lead him inside and upstairs to the smaller deck with an elegant fire pit. He sits on the couch quietly while I light the fire and think about what he told me before our show the other night.

I sit next to him, cross my legs, and hug a cushion to my chest. "I'm really sorry," I say. "About the whole supermodels and Burberry gigs remark. It was stupid. Especially after what you told me about your anxiety."

"It's okay," he says.

"That's not all I'm sorry for," I say. "I should have known. We spend nearly every day together. How could I not notice something was going on with you?"

He smirks. "Maybe I'm just a really good actor. I should do what all those other singers eventually do and give Hollywood a shot."

I frown. "That makes me so sad. You don't have to hide things from me. Especially not this."

"I wasn't trying to hide anything," he says. "I just didn't know how to bring it up. And I didn't want anyone to think I was a pussy."

"Hey," I say sternly. "Having anxiety doesn't make you a pussy. Sidebar: Vaginas are, like, super fucking indestructible, so I say be a pussy. A giant one."

That makes him laugh. Not a strained laugh or a small laugh, but a bellowing laugh—the kind that comes from deep in your stomach.

"True story," he says. "And I know, I know. I shouldn't be so worried about looking weak. But I'm not gonna lie, it's hard. I've spent so much time rebelling against everything to do with gender roles, and now I'm also unlearning all the bullshit stigma we've been taught about mental illness. It's like the lies we've been fed never fucking end."

"I feel you," I say. "Obviously, I don't know exactly how you're feeling, but I can relate a little. Things like bi erasure and biphobia and all that shit is why it took me so long to figure out I'm queer, and why it took even longer for me to be ready to come out about it. Fucking society, am I right?"

"Right," he says. "My therapist is big on smashing binaries and the patriarchy and stuff, too, so she's been helping me see a lot of things from a new perspective. Especially when it comes to my mental health."

He leans back on his hands, seeming more comfortable with our conversation, so I decide to dig a little deeper. "When did it start?"

"World tour, second show," he says. "About forty-five minutes before we went on stage, I started sweating and shaking uncontrollably. My arms felt numb and my chest hurt. I for real thought I was having a heart attack. I called in our doctor, who checked me out and told me it was a panic attack. She wanted to cancel the concert. I said no, threw up a few times, and then went out anyway."

"Jesus Christ, Alfie." I find myself sliding closer to him, reaching out for his hands. I try thinking back to that night, but all I remember are my own nerves and excitement and all the fun we had. All the fun I *thought* we had.

He stretches his neck back and lets out a long breath. "I cannot tell you how much of a relief it is just to tell someone."

"Wait," I say. "So no one else knows? What about Ry? Or Sal?"

He shakes his head. "You know Ry: He can't be serious for more than three seconds. He doesn't like talking about this kind of thing, either. Sal would freak, so I've been putting off telling her. I wanted to tell you, but then Jessie came along, and she was always causing drama. And with everything going on with your folks, I didn't want to add to your stress." He rubs his chin. "And I didn't want you to think less of me."

God, that hurts to hear, but I'm glad he's opening up to me. "I would never think less of you. Ever. And I'm really sorry if I made you feel like I didn't have time for you. I always have time. I just didn't have a clue."

I put an arm around his waist and rest my head on his shoulder. "I'm always here if you need me, okay? For anything. If you want to talk or play some music or whatever. Just tell me how to help, and I'll do it."

He pats my hand. "You're doing it right now."

We sit silently for a while, and I become mesmerized by the fire. While I stare into the flames, I replay the last six months in my mind with this new information, wondering how I didn't see that one of my best friends was in pain.

CHAPTER TWENTY-TWO

Alfie and I lay back on the couch, staring up at the stars. The echoes of our friends' laughter float up to meet us, making me smile.

"I'm so tempted to film them skinny-dipping," I say, giggling.

"Ha! Imagine the headlines," Alfie says. He raises his hand to the sky and writes a fake headline. "Brightsiders Caught Having an Orgy in the Ocean."

"Ew," I say, then join in the fun. "Ryan Cho Bares Butt, Causes International Incident."

He laughs, slapping a hand over his eyes. "Ugh, do you ever think that our lives are just one out-of-control headline after another?"

I sit up and point to myself. "Um, have you met me? My entire life is used as clickbait."

"You get it so much worse than me and Ryan do," he says, rolling his eyes. "Ryan parties all the time, but he never gets torn to shreds for it. And I've been around, but no one calls me a skank or even comments on it. Probably because all people see when they look at me is That Genderqueer Kid."

"That's not true," I say. "And if it makes you feel better, I can call you a skank."

He laughs, shaking his head. "How can you just take that shit? You don't sleep around. You've had, like, two relationships since I've known you. And the media would only ever call Jessie your 'bestie.' So how did they get this impression that you're easy?"

I shrug, but it feels good to know I'm not the only one who's confused by it. "But even if I did hook up with a lot of people, so what? That's my business. To be honest, the only real reason I haven't hooked up a lot is because I've never really had the opportunity to do it."

He narrows his eyes at me. "Bullshit."

"I'm serious," I say. "It's like people are afraid of me. Maybe it's the whole fame thing, it freaks people out. I know Jessie had a hard time with it at first. But then she became obsessed with it." I don't want to think about her, so I make a joke. "Or maybe it's because I've got these big guns." I flex my arms, showing off the muscles I've built up from years of smashing the drums. "I've heard queer girls like me find the whole toned-arm thing hot as hell, but guys don't seem as into it. But fuck them douchebags, right?"

"Preach, girl," Alfie says. He holds a hand up, and I slap it with my own. "I definitely find it hot, by the way."

He closes his eyes, his chest rising and falling slowly. All I want to do is kiss him again. Just once more. Maybe it's the stars above us or the glow of the fire, or maybe it's the way Alfie opened up to me, but I find myself regretting the quick decision to stop making out.

His shirt is still unbuttoned at the top. I can see the tattoo of a stag—which he is convinced is his Patronus, despite what Pottermore tells him—on his chest. I drag my eyes away from him and sit up.

Needing a distraction, I pull my phone out of my pocket and go on Snapchat. I watch my story, replaying all the fun from the lip-synching, giggling quietly to myself. But then the video of Alfie plays, and I can't stop myself from watching as he sings. To me. He was right when he said he was staring at me. I didn't notice it at the time because I was too focused on not orgasming in front of everyone, but his eyes are on me the whole time. He mouths the words to "Need You Tonight," looking at me with fire in his eyes. I close the app and slide my phone across the couch, glaring at it like it betrayed me. I rest my elbows on my knees and clutch my head in my hands, fantasizing about our kiss on the island today.

Oh my fucking God, Em. Chill out. Stop acting like a fleshy ball of hormones and think about this. Think with your head, not your vagina.

I start tapping my heel on the floor, trying to get my shit together. I feel Alfie sit up and stretch, and I think about just standing and walking away. At the moment it's the only way I can think of to stop myself from saying something stupid.

"You cool, Em?" he asks sweetly.

I lift my head up, forcing a smile. "Cool. Yeah. Cool. Coolcoolcool."

He smirks and says, "Cool."

Uh-oh. Our eyes have locked on to each other. Sirens are blaring in my mind. If I don't abort this, what happens next will reach catastrophic proportions.

Okay, maybe I'm being a little dramatic. Maybe there's a way this could work. Like a social experiment. Or a rebound thing, to distract myself from the garbage fire back home. Yeah, that's it. That'll work. Won't it?

"Heyyyy?" I say slowly, running my fingers down my hair.

"Mm-hmm?" he says, raising his eyebrows expectantly. He's

biting down on his bottom lip, pinching it between his teeth as he stares at me. Then he drops his gaze, shaking his head slowly, as if he's trying to talk himself out of this like I was a few seconds ago.

"I was thinking," I say. "Seeing as we're here on this yacht this week, in close proximity and whatever, maybe we should just give in to . . . you know, whatever."

His eyes light up, and he leans closer, about to kiss me. I put a hand on his shoulder to hold him back.

"But," I say, holding up a finger. "Only while we're here. This shouldn't come back with us to LA."

He smiles, nods. "Like a vacation fling."

"Exactly," I say. "Maybe we just need to get this—whatever this is—out of our systems. Agreed?" I hold a hand out, and he shakes it.

"Agreed." He waits a moment, smirking down at me. "Can I kiss you now?"

I laugh. "Sure."

He tilts my chin up with his thumb, touching his nose to mine. I close my eyes in anticipation, but what comes is only a restrained brush of his lips, and then he leans back. I open my eyes and look up at him, meeting his gaze. He gives me a half smile, like he was waiting for something and finally found it, and then he gives me what I want.

At first, our kiss starts softly, slowly. It's different from the other two times we've kissed. They were almost accidental, surprising, but this kiss is done with intention, with purpose and expectation and passion. A shiver runs down my neck and my palms sweat against my thighs. I smile against his mouth, because this is what I've wanted since our lips parted under the waterfall.

Alfie kisses like he does everything else in his life: with an intense drive to reach perfection while also letting the moment lead him to new, exciting places.

When he's making music, he gets so heavily in the moment that it consumes him like fire. And right now I feel like he's devoting everything he has to this one kiss, just like he devotes himself to every line in every song, every song on every album, every performance on every tour.

Tonight, here in the middle of the ocean washed with moonlight, the one thing he's devoted to is this kiss.

Matching his heat, I put my whole body into it, like I do when I'm drumming my heart out on stage. Clutching him so tightly that my knuckles whiten. Feeling the moment so intensely that I try to breathe it in, devour every second of it so I don't miss a beat.

Then it builds up, like the kisses we shared before this were just a taste, just the opening notes of a song, and now we're hitting the crescendo. The act of giving ourselves permission to explore each other—however temporarily—has freed us to be as affectionate as we want. And now that there's nothing holding me back; I just want to get closer and closer to him. My fingers find their way to the collar of his shirt, pulling him closer. He runs one hand through my hair, the other down my side and onto the small of my back. I press my chest against his, but I still don't feel close enough, so I kiss him harder.

People always talk about how the whole world supposedly disappears when you're kissing someone. But I'm aware of everything going on around me right now: the sound of the sea lapping against the yacht, the cool breeze tickling my shoulders, the fact that our friends are playing nude Marco Polo in the water below us, completely oblivious to what we're doing up here.

I'm aware of everything going on within me, too. And fuck, is it wonderful. I feel *everything*. Every stroke of his fingers on my back is like flames licking at my skin. The pressure of his lips on mine is like breathing for the first time after being underwater for too long. Feeling the way his back muscles move and clench under my touch is like running my fingers over piano keys until I find the right sound.

After a while, we come up for air, and Alfie falls back onto the couch, slicking his hair back. "Best. Vacation. Ever."

CHAPTER TWENTY-THREE

Will, Ryan, and Alfie are already seated around the breakfast table when I emerge from my room the next morning. Alfie's shaggy hair hangs over his shoulders, his white T-shirt clinging to his body. The body I couldn't stop thinking about all night. We had to stop making out when everyone came in from the water, wanting to play *Guitar Hero* in the games room. I was so exhausted that I went to bed, but the moment my head hit the pillow I was wide awake again.

I suppress a yawn as I sit down next to Alfie and nudge my chair forward, breathing in the smell of pancakes and fruit. Alfie is facing away from me, telling Will some animated story about the time we were chased by fans in Singapore. I figure he hasn't noticed I'm sitting next to him, and I start pouring maple syrup on my pancakes, my stomach rumbling. But when I rest a hand on my lap, he reaches over to find it under the table. He's still talking to Will, still facing away from me, but that one simple gesture has me as gooey as the syrup on my plate. I stuff some pancake in my mouth so the others don't see my giddy grin. It doesn't work, so I reach over to the fruit platter for a strawberry, dip it in the syrup, and take a bite.

Will gasps. "Emmy," he says. Alfie turns to look at me. Will leans over the table, staring at my plate. "Did you just dip your strawberry into maple syrup?"

I glance from Will to Alfie to Ry. "Yeah? Why? What's wrong with that?"

Will scrunches his face up, making his lips disappear under the dark hairs of his beard. "That's so gross!"

I swallow the berry. "It is not. It's amazing." Just to gross him out even more, I pick up another strawberry, smother it in syrup, and eat it.

Will looks horrified. "Oh my God, stop."

I point my strawberry at him, syrup dripping onto my plate. "Hey, don't knock it till you try it, buddy."

"No thanks," he says, shaking his head. "I'll stick to my normal-people food."

"I'll try it," Alfie says, taking a strawberry. He holds it over the glob of syrup on my plate and looks at me. "May I?"

"Go ahead."

He dips it, sniffs it, eats it. And when his eyes light up, I know I've won.

"So good," he says, munching it down like a kid tasting sugar for the first time.

Ryan takes a strawberry and pours maple syrup all over it, then eats it. He makes an orgasmic moaning sound. "Yes. Yes!"

Will's eyebrows shoot up to his hairline. "You're all very strange individuals, do you know that?"

The three of us nod, smiling.

Alfie takes another bite. "Thanks, man. That means a lot."

Ryan laughs, slapping Will on the shoulder. "You should know better than to call us Brightsiders strange, dude. We take it as a compliment."

"You know our album is called *Strange Welcome*, right?" I ask, chuckling.

Will pushes his sunglasses up higher on his nose. "Doesn't that mean, like, when you arrive somewhere and get a strange welcome? I thought it was referring to your fast rise to fame, and how strange Hollywood was to you at first. Like, a culture shock thing."

I shake my head. "It's meant to be kind of like a double meaning thing. That's one way to describe it, but it also means that strange people are welcome with us."

"Ohhh," he says. "I get it."

Ryan cocks his head to the side. "Will, have you even listened to the album?"

He blushes. "I've heard parts of it."

I laugh. "It's okay. I haven't seen the latest season of *Silver Falls*, so we're even."

"I've seen every episode," Ryan says. He starts telling us all about it, but at the same time, Alfie's hand lets go of mine and moves to my thigh. My eyes widen, and I have to pretend to cough so that I don't giggle and swoon and whimper. He's looking at Ryan like he's paying attention, but I can tell from the little smile on his face that his mind is elsewhere, too. His hand moves farther up my thigh, and my mouth goes dry. I pick up my glass of water, but I'm trembling so much I have to use two hands to hold it. I take a sip, and Alfie starts stroking my thigh with his thumb. The water catches in my throat and I spit it back into my glass. Alfie rests his elbow on the table and casually presses his fingers to his lips like he's trying not to laugh.

"Do I smell pancakes?" a voice calls from behind us. Alfie's hand slides off me and we turn around to see Kass walking through the living area toward us.

"Good morning!" I say.

"Morning," she says. She takes a seat next to me and puts an arm around me. "Where did you go last night?"

"Nothing," I say, much too quickly. "I mean, nowhere. Bed. I was tired."

She takes a sip of orange juice. "Well, you missed an awesome game of *Guitar Hero*. Ry won, of course."

I chuckle. "Of course."

Charlie and Alyssa join us next, glowing like they've just spent the last eight hours replacing sleep with sex. They can hardly keep their hands off each other, and it makes my heart ache and swoon at the same time. Then Chloe appears, humming cheerfully as they sit down and complete our circle. I look around at all the smiling faces of my friends, sitting here in the sunshine, the turquoise waters sparkling around us, and I feel the happiest I've felt in a long time.

"I want to capture this moment," I say, reaching for my phone in my pocket, but it's not there. "I left my phone in my room. Be right back." I get up and go inside. "Keep having fun!"

I hurry down the spiral staircase to the lower floor, then run down the hall to my bedroom, finding my phone under my pillow. When I open my door to leave, Alfie is standing there, his hand resting against the wall and a smile on his face that can only mean one thing.

I look behind him to make sure no one is around, then pull him inside and close the door. I push him up against it roughly, and he laughs.

"Easy," he says, smirking. "I'm fragile. Handle with care."

I kiss him, and he kisses me back hard, cupping my face in his hands.

"Mmm," he says, licking his lips. "You taste like maple strawberries."

"So do you," I say before kissing him some more.

Needless to say, I totally forget about taking a photo of our breakfast spread.

The next few days look like this . . .

Breakfast.
Jet skiing.
Making out.
Lunch.
Epic game of Jenga.
Making out.
Dinner.
Lip-synch rematch.
Making out.
Bed.

Breakfast.
Making out.
Binge-watching *Sense8* on Netflix.
Lunch.
Netflix.
Netflix.
Making out.
Dinner.
Netflix.
Making out.
Bed.

Breakfast.
Snorkeling.

Making out.

Lunch.

Obligatory reenactment of Leo and Kate's "King of the World" moment on the bow.

Making out.

Making out.

Making out.

Dinner.

Making out.

Bed.

By the final day, we're experts at stealing glances and know all the best hiding spots on the yacht to fool around. When we're with our friends, we play it cool, and no one suspects a thing. I'm starting to think I might have a future in acting, too. As much as I hate keeping secrets from my friends, I have to admit there's a rush to sneaking around like this.

I'm packing my suitcase to leave when there's a knock on my bedroom door. I skip over to answer it, knowing before I open it that it's Alfie.

"Emmy," he says, tipping the rim of his baseball cap to me.

"Alfie," I say before sneaking him inside.

The sound of my door clicking closed has become our green light, our own Pavlov's dog experiment. Every time we hear the turn of my lock, we start salivating, knowing it's time to make out.

But something's different this time. He's keeping his distance from me, his hands in the back pockets of his skinny jeans. I mirror his body language, not wanting to invade his space if he's suddenly uncomfortable.

"Um," I say, going back to packing to alleviate some of the awkwardness. "What's up?"

He twists his cap backward. "We're going back to LA today."

"Yeah," I say, but it comes out more like a sad sigh.

"I thought, maybe, we should talk?"

Eep. That doesn't sound good. I try to hide my nerves by pretending I'm heavily focused on where to place my makeup bag in my case. "Go for it."

Alfie walks over to my bed. "Mind if I sit?" I nod, watching him as he drops onto the bed and stares out the window.

"What's up?" Dammit. I already asked that.

He stretches back on my bed, resting his head on his arms. His T-shirt slides up, and I try not to stare at the exposed skin of his hips.

"We agreed to keep this . . . us . . . whatever this is, here," he says. "Like, what happens on the yacht stays on the yacht."

"We did," I say. I fold the same pair of shorts for the third time, but he doesn't seem to notice.

"Once we get back to LA, no more make-out sessions."

"That's what we agreed."

He nods. "So, we'll stick to that."

I can't tell if he's asking me or telling me. "Yeah. Yeah?"

"Yeah."

I narrow my eyes at him like it will somehow allow me to read his mind. It doesn't work, and he just keeps staring blankly at the ceiling.

"We'll reel it in," he says. "Go back to normal. Friends without benefits. Netflix but no chill. No more doing the no-pants dance."

That makes me laugh. "Well, to be fair, we didn't do the 'no-pants dance.'"

He waggles his eyebrows at me. "There's still time. We're not in LA yet."

All the blood rushes to my cheeks. "We should be tapering off of each other, not going back for more."

He rolls his eyes jokingly. "Fine. Guess I'll just have to keep imagining it."

"*Keep* imagining it?" Lord, he is not making this easy.

He flashes a cheeky grin. "Oops. I've said too much." He stands up quickly, feigning embarrassment. "I must go."

He's about to walk past me when I reach out and take his hand. His stops, locks eyes with me, and crushes his mouth to mine.

I savor his taste, the feel of his body pressed against mine, the way he makes me moan. Because after today, it's all over. Done and dusted. Mission accomplished. That's all, folks. The end. *Fin.*

It doesn't matter how much fun it's been, we agreed that what happens on the yacht stays on the yacht. So what if just the thought of not being able to touch him or kiss him again makes me feel sick to my stomach? Who cares that I might have replaced one bad binging habit with another? What does it matter if I'm drunk on Alfie? None of it matters. It's one thing to fool around in secret corners of a yacht, where we have some privacy. But we have all eyes on us in LA, and if even one paparazzo catches the scent of this fling, we'll be eaten alive. People will say I cheated on Jessie with Alfie even though I didn't. They'll call me greedy and sex obsessed and a liar. I'll be slut-shamed and used as "proof" by bigots that bisexuals can't be trusted. I'll be branded a bad bisexual.

And that's just me! Who knows what lies they'll spin about Alfie.

Nope. I can't let that happen.

The second our plane lands on LA soil, things have to go back to normal.

It all ends here.

CHAPTER TWENTY-FOUR

We leave the terminal at LAX to be greeted by dozens of
paparazzi. I'm prepared: baseball cap pulled low, oversize sunglasses
on, head down. Neutral. Just stay neutral. As usual, they flock to me
like bees to a hive.

"*Emmy! Emmy! Look over here!*"

"*How's it feel to be out of the closet?*"

"*People say you're just going through a phase? What do you think?*"

"*Smile! Come on, Emmy, smile!*"

"*Any comment on the leaked tape?*"

"*Where's Jessie? Did you dump her for Alfie?*"

"*Hey, Alfie, how does it feel to not be the only gay in the band?*"

I cringe at the barrage of problematic questions. The way the pap
phrased that last one—"the only gay"—especially doesn't sit well with
me. It feels icky. And I feel bad for Alfie. It sucks enough that they're
already trying to erase my bisexuality and saying it's "just a phase,"

but Alfie has been out as pansexual and genderqueer since before we were famous. Only now, he's dealing with invalidation and misgendering on a global level. I don't know how he doesn't snap at them after all this time.

I step in front of Alfie so he's not in any pictures and shove a hand in front of the nearest lens. "Give us some space."

Suddenly, a fresh batch of photographers notice us as we approach the exit, and they rush us. We're surrounded. Ry, Will, and Alfie quickly move in front, trying to forge a path through. Chloe, Kass, Charlie, Alyssa, and I huddle together close behind them, shielding our eyes from the constant flashes of light.

Chloe takes my hand, and Kassidy clutches the back of my jacket. I can hear Kass's panicked whimpers as we're knocked back and forth by the mass of men with cameras around us. This isn't the life she chose. She's not used to being bombarded like this. Hell, I've been doing it for a year, and I'm still shaken whenever it happens. But it's not fair that she has to deal with this just to spend time with me.

"I have to get to my flight back to Boston," she says in my ear, her voice frantic. She gives me a quick hug. "I'm gonna make a run for it. I'll text you!"

"Love you," I say.

"You too." Then she's gone, shoving her way through the crowd and bolting through the airport like she's escaping a pack of wolves.

Finally, we break through the wall of people and run to our waiting SUV.

"Next time," Ry puffs once we're safely inside, "we need to hire more security. We're too famous to go incognito now."

Charlie stares at the lenses pushed against the windows, frowning. "Too famous is right. This is legit terrifying." Someone smacks their hand on the window, making us all jump.

"Back off, mate!" Charlie yells, her Australian accent thicker than usual.

As the car pulls away from the curb, I worry about how many paparazzi are waiting for us outside Chloe's house.

I distract myself by going through photos on my phone. Pictures from Hawaii that already feel like they were taken so long ago. Then I look through all the screenshots of tweets, comments, and Tumblr messages I got from supportive fans, congratulating me on coming out. I've never seen so many rainbow heart emojis in my life. Before I know it, I'm smiling again.

We pull up to Alfie's house and he says his good-byes, and just before he gets out of the car, I catch his gaze. His eyes sparkle with that same intensity from Hawaii, and it sends a shiver down my back.

When we drive away, I get a text.

> **ALFIE:** thanks for making this trip so memorable ;)
>
> **EM:** My pleasure.
>
> **ALFIE:** mine too.
>
> **EM:** Thank YOU for helping to organize it. Best birthday ever.
>
> **ALFIE:** no problem.

———————

That night in bed, I'm overcome with fantasies about Alfie. I relive our kisses in my head, imagine what it might have felt like to go further. I can't help myself. It does not bode well that I haven't even been back in LA for a whole day and I'm already craving him again. I'm so restless that I turn to writing music to ease some of my tension, and end up with new song.

We're in the city of glitz and glam . . .

. . . and our names are up in lights.

The stars are blazing . . .

. . . I wanna see you in between my sheets . . .

Come on over and flirt with me,

roll around in the dirt with me,

came from nowhere, now we're on Sunset . . .

Come so far, baby, we're stars . . .

. . . I'll be their scandalous girl, their clickbait queen,

. . . just a little fun, that's what we said.

Hmm. Writing that was a mistake. Now I'm even hotter under the collar. Then, like some sort of sign from the sex gods, I get a text from Alfie.

> **ALFIE:** bored.
>
> **EM:** Same.
>
> **ALFIE:** miss Hawaii already.
>
> **EM:** Same.
>
> **ALFIE:** let's go back.

EM: I'm in.

ALFIE: we could just pretend we're back on the yacht.

EM: How?

ALFIE: I could come over and show you. ;)

Oh man. This is not helping my restlessness at all.

EM: Bad idea.

EM: Tempting.

EM: But still bad.

EM: Dangerous.

EM: Risky.

ALFIE: danger is my middle name.

EM: You don't have a middle name.

ALFIE: I do now. I just gave myself one. Alfie Danger Jones.

EM: 😑

ALFIE: you said you're tempted.

EM: Did not.

ALFIE: you did. I have receipts.

He sends me a screenshot of my earlier text.

EM: Okay, fine. I'm tempted. So what?

ALFIE: so, I'm tempting to you, huh?

EM: Not as tempting as I am to you 😏

ALFIE: probably true.

He types for a while, and I lie in bed staring at the screen, biting my bottom lip so hard it hurts.

> **ALFIE:** I know we promised no more making out . . .
>
> **EM:** . . . We did.
>
> **ALFIE:** but maybe we can work around it.
>
> **EM:** I'm listening . . .
>
> **ALFIE:** I propose a new rule: sexy snaps are allowed. Thoughts?
>
> **EM:** Hmmm . . .
>
> **ALFIE:** ?
>
> **EM:** I might need to see a sample before I cosign this.

It only takes him a second to send me a snap. My jaw falls open when I see it: Alfie posing in front of his bathroom mirror, wearing only an oversize Rolling Stones T-shirt that's riddled with holes.

> **ALFIE:** remember, that's just a sample. You gotta say yes before the real fun starts.
>
> **EM:** Yes.
>
> **ALFIE:** that was fast!
>
> **EM:** I'm not shy.
>
> **ALFIE:** prove it.

I drop my phone next to me and bury my face in my pillow, squealing. I can't believe we're doing this. I can't believe *I'm* doing this. I roll out of bed and race into my en suite with my phone. I'm in my unicorn onesie that I got when the band was in Tokyo. It's baby blue with a pale pink tail and a fluffy mane on the hood, topped with a gold, plushy horn. I undo the snap buttons and slide it slightly off of one shoulder. After taking a minute or two to find the best lighting and pose, I take a photo and send it to Alfie.

> **ALFIE:** jesus. permission to screenshot?
>
> **EM:** NO!
>
> **ALFIE:** okay.
>
> **ALFIE:** I like this new rule.
>
> **EM:** Me too.

We stay up late, sending more flirty snaps to each other. When I finally fall asleep, my dreams are filled with Alfie and his kisses.

CHAPTER TWENTY-FIVE

Chloe is spending the day in their office space downtown, filming a series of vids for their channel, so I have the whole house to myself. I'm not going anywhere, but the urge to dress up strikes, so I paint glitter into my hair and do my makeup all fancy.

Then I hook up my phone to the ceiling speakers and dance through the house, letting my faves fill me with their genius. First it's Beyoncé, then Gaga and Adele, who are later joined by classics like Alanis Morissette, Joan Jett, Tina Turner, and Janis Joplin. Even though my relationship with my parents is rocky to say the least, music is the one thing we have in common. I'll always be grateful that they introduced me to a wide variety of sounds. My dad was obsessed with bands like the Rolling Stones, Nirvana, and Green Day, while Mom never went a day without singing along to Bikini Kill's "Rebel Girl" or Alanis Morissette's "You Oughta Know." Alfie and I were the only kids in school who knew the words to Blink 182's "All the Small Things," and for that I'll always be proud.

Inspired by my idols, I get back to working on some new music. Once I have enough of "ILY" written, I invite Alfie and Ry over to hear it.

> **EM:** New song alert! Come to Chloe's so we can test it out?
>
> **ALFIE:** Be there in ten.
>
> **RYAN:** Can't. Busy. Sorry.

Alfie shows up at the door with his guitar in one hand and an In-N-Out bag in the other.

"In-N-Out?" I ask as he steps inside.

"We always get the munchies during a writing sesh," he explains. I follow him into the kitchen, grinning like a goofball. Just being in the same room as him now suddenly makes me feel like I'm about to burst out of my skin. He's different around me, too. He's flirty, more energized, and every now and then I catch him focusing on me like I'm a song he's trying to memorize.

And yet we keep dancing around each other, avoiding any conversation about what's happening between us. Probably because neither of us has any idea what we're doing. I sure don't. All I know for sure is that I don't want it to end. God, I wish we were still in Hawaii. No rules applied there. I could walk up to him and ask him to kiss me, and he would do it. And it would be totally cool.

But we're not in Hawaii anymore. The vacation is over, and so is all the fun we had. I quietly curse myself for coming up with the bright idea of putting a geographical perimeter around our kisses.

We sit at the kitchen island and eat while we take turns guessing what Ryan is doing.

"Working on his memoirs," Alfie says, taking a bite of his burger.

"Working on his guns," I say, flexing my arm muscles and pretending to kiss them.

Alfie laughs, but then he gasps. "What if he's seeing another band?"

"Oh my god!" I say. "I bet it's a prettier band, too. A band with a harp and a double bass and a saxophone."

"You think he's cheating on us with an orchestra?" he asks, trying to hold back his laughter.

I nod, smirking. "A big one, too. I bet he's with the whole strings section right now."

His eyes widen. "No, Emmy! Not the strings section." He drops his burger and covers his eyes with his hands, pretending to cry. "Anything but the strings section!"

"Face it, Alfie," I say, sighing. "We've lost him to the Los Angeles Philharmonic. He's probably making sweet, sweet music with them right now."

Alfie drapes himself across Chloe's marble counter, howling with laughter and fake tears. I have a half-eaten fry in my mouth but can't swallow it because I'm laughing so hard. I throw him a napkin, and he dabs at his eyes.

"How dare he," he says. "Asshole."

"Stop," I say, clutching my stomach. "Stop making me laugh. I can't breathe."

He holds his palms up innocently, but the expression on his face is anything but innocent. I wipe my eyes again, and when I look up at him he's got two French fries tucked in front of his gums, hanging out of his mouth like walrus teeth. I crack up again.

"You're such a loser," I say. He throws a fry at me, but I dodge it.

He takes a sip of his Coke, letting me finally catch my breath.

"You know," Alfie says, looking deep in thought. "I've hardly heard from Ry at all since we got back to LA. Have you?"

I think back. "Not really."

His forehead wrinkles in concern. "You think he's okay?"

"Yeah," I say. "He had the time of his life in Hawaii. I've never seen him so happy."

"I thought he'd be itching to get back to work," he says. "We haven't had a jam session since before the Pride show."

"Oh!" I jump off the bar stool and run over to my guitar. "That's what my song's about. You ready to hear it?"

He wipes the salt off his hands. "Go for it."

I settle the guitar strap on my shoulder and take in a deep breath. "Remember," I say. "I just finished this, and it needs to be work-shopped, like a lot. It's called 'ILY,' as in *I love you.*"

He nods, and I start playing. I close my eyes as the lyrics pour out of me, filling the house with my voice.

Cover me in love, cover me in ink . . .

. . . cover me in kisses till we're so in sync . . .

. . . I love who I love who I love who I love . . .

. . . I am who I am who I am who I am . . .

I can't wait to finish this track and sing it in front of a crowd. I know that whenever I sing it I'll think of the night I came out and be filled with pride.

When it's over, I open my eyes and look at Alfie for his reaction. A slow smile spreads across his face, and he claps. "I love it," he says. "And I think all those people who were at that concert are going to lose their shit when they hear it."

I'm beaming. "I hope so." I put my guitar back on the stand.

"They will, for sure," Alfie says. "It's like a love song to our fans." He walks around the island and gives me a bear hug. His oversized hoodie is soft on my cheek, and I breathe in his cologne.

"God, you smell good," I blurt out. I squeeze my eyes shut, embarrassed.

"Thanks," he says into my neck, giving me goosebumps. "So do you."

Our hug lingers. My heart thumps harder. My mouth goes dry. I don't want to let him go.

"I have a song, too," he says, releasing me. "Interested?"

"Sure," I say. He picks up his guitar and goes into the living area to sit on the couch. I follow and sit on the coffee table across from him.

He plucks a few strings and clears his throat. "I've been working on it since Hawaii. It's called 'Where There's Smoke.' It's about . . ." He trails off, looking me in the eyes. "You know what? I think I'll just let it speak for itself."

He starts playing, and I lean forward, ready to listen.

Skin burned . . .

    . . . from your touch.

        . . . little taste . . .

    . . . new addiction . . .

       Where there's smoke . . .

           . . . . . there's fire.

Skin hot like a chili pepper . . .

     . . . eyes like truth or dare . . .

     What fools we were . . .

. . . to think that we . . .

. . . could leave it there . . .

. . . by the sea.

The last note fades into silence. When Alfie opens his eyes, they're full of heat. I feel my pulse in my fingers, my tongue, my lips. No one's ever written a song about me before. The lyrics were so drenched with desire that I can practically see the hunger on his face. There's a tightness in my chest, like my own hunger is devouring my heart, eating me up from the inside.

His song was a question for me, and I know the perfect way to answer it. I reach out and grab his guitar, using it to pull him closer, and then I crush my mouth to his. He kisses me back right away, like he's been waiting for this ever since we stepped foot off that yacht.

I rest a hand on the guitar and lean over him, kissing him harder. He sinks into the couch, tilting his chin up and taking my face in his hands. My hand slips off the guitar, dragging down the strings.

"Wait," he says. He kisses me once more, then lifts the strap from around his neck and puts the guitar on the coffee table behind me, freeing up the space between us. Then he takes my hands and pulls me onto the couch. I notice something on his mouth and suppress my laughter. He raises an eyebrow.

"What?" he asks, touching his face.

"I got glitter on you." I dab some of it off his mouth with my thumb and show him.

He smiles, the glitter sparkling along his bottom lip. "How does it look?" He bats his eyelashes and pouts.

My eyes narrow. "Hot. As usual."

"Maybe it can be my new thing." He flicks his hair back theatrically.

I punch him lightly on the shoulder. "Hey, jerk. Glitter is *my* thing."

He frowns and rubs his shoulder. "All right, chill," he says as he pokes me in the stomach. "If you don't want me to wear your second-hand glitter, stop kissing me."

I smirk. "Says the kid who literally wrote a song about how much he wants to kiss me again."

He sees my smirk and raises me a smug grin. "Please, that song could be about anyone."

Determined to win this game of flirty banter, I stand up from the couch and start walking away. "Fair enough," I say. "I'll just go sprinkle my glitter somewhere else, then."

He groans and catches hold of my wrist as I walk by, then looks up at me with pleading eyes. "Stay."

My heart melts. I lean over him, kissing him upside down. Glitter falls from my hair into his like a tiny, sparkly avalanche. He rolls over and kneels on the couch so we're at eye level, then wraps his arms around my waist and pulls me in until we're chest to chest.

"Okay, so maybe that song *was* about you," he says, giving me that same look from the first night we kissed on the yacht.

"Me? I had no idea," I say sarcastically.

He sighs. "It's true. It's you who's *hot as a chili pepper.*"

"*Eyes like truth or dare?*" I ask.

He smiles. "You like that line, huh? That's one of my faves, too."

"I love it," I say. "And I love the chorus, too."

He starts singing. "*What fools we were / To think that we / Could leave it there / By the sea.*"

I shake my head slowly. "What fools we were."

He nudges my nose with his, and my lips tingle with expectation.

"So," he says quietly, his voice low. "Looks like this is happening. Again."

I nod. "Looks like." I drape my arms over his shoulders. His hands feel so good on my waist.

He gives me a half smile. "Making out never hurt anyone, right? What's a little fun between friends?"

"Right," I say. "There's no shame in it. We're both single. It's nothing serious."

He brushes his mouth over mine. "Right. Just a little fun."

"Just a little," I whisper.

And then he kisses me, and I start to wonder if I might be falling for him.

Just a little.

CHAPTER TWENTY-SIX

The next day, I wake up in bed alone.

"Alfie?" I whisper, not wanting Chloe to hear. No answer. I sit up and stretch. "Hey, Alfie?" I say a little louder. Still nothing. He must have gone home. I don't know how to feel about that. I run my fingers over the glitter scattered over my sheets, wondering if I even have a right to be upset that he left. We're not a couple. We didn't even have sex. We just played music and made out. A lot. I didn't ask him to stay, but when I fell asleep with him spooning me, I hoped he would.

Random pieces of paper are scattered around the room. Some are crumpled up into balls and others are highlighted and scrawled on with notes. We workshopped "ILY" all night. It still needs some more fine-tuning, but what we have so far is a pretty cool punk-rock anthem of gratitude for all the Brightsiders in the world. A few more late nights like this and it'll be perfect, but right now it has good bones, and for that I'm proud.

The time on my phone says 1:45, and considering we didn't go to sleep until sunrise, I'm not surprised.

A knock on the front door interrupts my thoughts, and I race downstairs and open it with a smile, hoping to see Alfie.

"Hey," Chloe says, smiling. "Forgot my key."

"And where have you been all night?" I tease, raising an eyebrow.

They walk past me, avoiding all eye contact. "I may have . . . accidentally . . . kinda sorta . . ." They pause to clear their throat. "Slept with Paris last night."

My jaw drops. Chloe tries to make a run for it to the stairs, and I chase after them.

"Oh no way," I call. "You can't just spring that on me and run away!"

They start to laugh and sit on a lower step, letting their hair fall over their eyes. "Don't judge me."

I sit next to them and drape an arm over their shoulders. "I would never. But you gotta give me something here."

"I made a mistake," they say, their head falling back over my arm. "She's supposed to be in New York! But she was at Bar 161 last night, and the second I saw her I knew I was in trouble." They let out a long sigh. "It was wild, though. Like, hot as fuck. But it cannot happen again."

Paris is Chloe's kryptonite. I don't blame them for going all weak in the knees around her; Paris is a Victoria's Secret model who is fluent in four languages and speaks with a British accent. I mean, come on. But all she and Chloe did when they were together was fight and have sex. I lost count of all the times I received distraught texts from Chloe, telling me about the latest argument they'd had with Paris. Eventually, it became too much and Chloe ended it, but it broke their heart.

"Em," they say, "if you ever see me and Paris in the same room, you gotta get me the hell out of there. No matter how much I want to hook up with her again. Okay?"

I nod. "I got you."

"Uggghhhhh," Chloe moans. "Maybe we need a new rule: Just. Say. No."

We both start laughing, and I'm relieved to see they're not letting this upset them too much.

"Hey," I say, pulling them in closer, "if it helps, I'm pretty sure I've broken all of our other rules at least once already."

They laugh some more. "That does help. I guess we can't expect to have it down instantly. As Paris would say, *It's a journey, you know?*" Chloe does their impression of Paris, raising their voice an octave or two. "*Live, laugh, love!*"

We laugh so hard that tears run down our cheeks. Chloe leans forward, slapping a hand on their thigh, but then stops suddenly when they look at me.

"What?" I ask, swiping my fingers under my nose. "Do I have something on my face?"

Chloe narrows their eyes and grins. "Not on your face, no." They point to my neck. "Is that a hickey?"

I slap my hands over my throat. "What? No."

They squeal, trying to pry my hands away. "It fucking is! Don't lie, Emmy. I know what a hickey looks like."

"Shut up." I run over to the mirror in the hallway and inspect the damage. Chloe's right; there's a splotchy purple mark just under my jawline.

Chloe stands behind me, smirking at me in the mirror and folding their arms. "Tell me everything."

Shit. Shitshitshitshitshit. "Um," I mumble.

They hug me from behind, giggling. "Whose handiwork is that?"

My cheeks burn red. "No one."

They groan impatiently. "Oh lord, please don't tell me it was Jessie. I swear to God, Em."

"No!" I say. "It wasn't her, don't worry." But hearing her name jolts me a little. It hasn't even been two weeks since we broke up, but she's hardly entered my mind since. Huh. Maybe I wasn't as in love with her as I thought.

Chloe starts typing on their phone.

"What are you doing?" I ask.

They grin. "Texting Kass. She's gonna love this."

I make a move for their phone, but they dodge out of the way, holding it up over their head. Damn them and their long legs.

"Stop it!" I whine. "Staaahhhhhhp!" I fight them for it, wrestling them to the floor while we laugh and scream and swear.

Just then, Alfie walks through the front door with two Starbucks coffees in his hands. He stops like a deer in headlights when he sees us rolling around on the floor.

"What's . . . happening?" he asks.

"Sent!" Chloe sings, waving their phone in my face. They see Alfie and give him a lazy wave. "Hey! What are you doing here?"

"Umm," he says, his gaze darting between me and Chloe.

"I asked Alfie to come over," I say as we climb to our feet, "so we could workshop some new songs."

Chloe nods, fixing their hair in the mirror. "Cool."

Alfie acts casual, carrying the coffees past us and into the kitchen. We follow and sit at the island.

"Check out Em's hickey," Chloe teases, pulling my hair out of the way so he can see it.

He smirks. "Impressive."

"She won't tell me who gave it to her, though," they say, then elbow me in the side. "Very suspect."

Alfie nods. "Very." We give each other knowing looks.

"Thanks for the coffee," I say, taking a sip.

He holds his cup up like he's giving a toast. "That really is one impressive hickey. That mystery biter must be pretty talented."

I give him the finger.

"Fiiiiine," Chloe says. "If you're not gonna share, I'm going to take a shower. I'll text the gang later and tell them to come here before we go to the party."

"Cool," I say.

Alfie furrows his brow after Chloe disappears upstairs. "Party?"

"The Halloween party," I say. "It's tonight, remember?"

He slaps his forehead with his hand. "Shit! I was supposed to pick up my costume yesterday. I gotta go."

He collects his keys and his coffee and says good-bye. On his way out of the kitchen, he leans in and gives me a passionate, unexpected kiss that takes my breath away. I stare after him wide-eyed as he walks down the hall. He looks at me over his shoulder, giving me a cute wink before heading out the door.

I run upstairs for a shower, and as the hot water runs down my skin, I can't get Alfie off my mind. I feel like my world has turned on its axis, and now I can't get my balance. Last night, I could have sworn I was falling in love. But now, in the light of day, I'm not so sure. My heart is yo-yoing inside me, the string getting twisted around my ribs, tying my insides in knots. I can't be in love with him. Loving him like that makes everything suddenly so complicated, and what we're doing is just meant to be fun.

Maybe I'm overthinking this. Maybe my relationship with Jessie ended so badly that I'm desperate to fall in love, because that means I've moved on. And if I've moved on then Jessie can't hurt me anymore.

I rest my head on the cool tiles of the shower wall, frustrated with myself. My mind is spinning in circles, searching for something stable to hold on to. I just want not to hurt anymore, and Alfie has never hurt me.

CHAPTER TWENTY-SEVEN

I may have gone a tad overboard with the hairspray. But every hair on my black wig is in place, perfectly quiffed, so it's worth a little suffocation. I pop the collar on my jacket and run my contouring brush over my jawline one more time. I've spent over an hour trying to create the perfect Travolta chin dimple.

When I finally walk down the stairs, ready to show off my Halloween costume, the first thing I see is Alfie. Dressed as an angel.

"Oh, fuck off!" I blurt out.

He holds his arms up. "What?" he asks with a half smile.

"An angel?" I ask. "Really?"

His costume doesn't get much simpler: white skinny jeans with rips over the thighs and knees, glittery gold ankle boots, a white lace bra, and white, feathery angel wings. A gold halo sits atop his mess of brown hair like a flower crown.

"I can pass as an angel for one night," he says. He looks at my outfit and raises an eyebrow. "Gender-bent Danny Zuko, right?"

I spin around to show him the T-Birds graphic on the back of my jacket, flipping my collar up again for that extra *Grease* vibe. "That's my name, don't wear it out." My Danny Zuko impression needs work, but I have all night to perfect it.

"Ooh," Alfie says. "Tell me about it, stud!"

Chloe struts toward me, dressed as Prince in his famous *Purple Rain* outfit. "How do I look?" they ask. "And you can only answer in Prince titles."

"Baby, you're a star," I say, taking a photo of them on my phone.

Chloe pulls me in for a hug. "I knew I was friends with you nerds for a reason."

"Um," Alfie says, scratching his chin. "Oh! Nothing compares to you."

"Is my rainbow straight?" Charlie asks when she walks into the room. I turn to her, and my jaw drops. She has turned herself into the Snapchat unicorn-rainbow-vomit filter, painting rainbow lines down from her bottom lip, over her chin, and down her neck. She continued the stream by painting it all down her white tank top. A unicorn horn sits atop her head.

"Nah," Chloe says, giggling. "There's nothing straight about you, honey."

Charlie bounces on her heels nervously. "No, seriously. Is it okay?"

"It's fine!" I say.

She pouts. "I was going for iconic."

"It's iconic."

"Thanks!" she says.

"Hey, Em," Chloe says, pointing to my neck. "Are you going to cover that hickey up?"

"Nah," I say. "It's part of the costume now. A hickey from Kenickie. I'm dressed as my headcanon version of Danny Zuko, where he's hopelessly devoted to Kenickie."

Charlie frowns, crinkling her rainbow. "Who does Sandy end up with?"

"Frenchy, of course. And Rizzo becomes the first female president and saves the world."

Ryan comes out of Chloe's guest bathroom dressed as Jon Snow, his cape flowing behind him majestically. "Halloween is coming."

"You know nothing, Jon Snow," Charlie says.

"Hold up," Chloe says before adjusting Ryan's wig for him. "Perfect."

Charlie searches her Blizzard backpack and pulls out a selfie stick. "Let's get a group selfie."

We all huddle together, posing as our characters while Charlie holds out the selfie stick and takes photos. "Everybody say 'pumpkin spice latte'!"

Our limo joins the line, inching toward the entrance to the red carpet. My fingers shake from nerves. This is my first big media event since the day the breakup tape was leaked. The others step out before me, and I take a second to check my wig and just breathe. When I step out, paparazzi and reporters and fans push one another out of the way to see who can get closest to us.

I have a love/hate relationship with red carpets. On the one hand, it's tons of fun getting glammed up for the cameras and star spotting on the carpet. On the other, getting yelled at by men to smile and show some skin while a million lights go off in my face is disorienting, to say the least. But I do get to see fans, and that always gives me life.

Step and pose and smile and pause and step and pose and smile and pause. Repeat until someone who actually knows what they're doing tells you to move along so someone more famous can have their photo taken.

While we're posing for photos, Alfie leans in and mutters in my ear. "Just FYI, you look incredibly hot in that costume."

I do my best to not move a muscle so the cameras don't capture something in my face that I don't want them to see. But that's hard to do when someone like Alfie is whispering sweet nothings in your ear.

Neutral, Em. Stay neutral.

"Your ass looks amazing in those jeans," he whispers. I swallow hard, my smile quivering.

"Alfie!" one of the paps yells. "Look straight at us, pal! Just look straight!"

"Sorry," Alfie says, waving. "It's impossible for me to ever look straight." He sticks his tongue out and waggles his eyebrows.

We're hustled off the carpet and into the party. On the way in, I take him by his elbow, stand on my tiptoes, and say in his ear, "Are you *trying* to turn us into a scandal?"

He flashes a half smile and puts his lips right against my ear. "I wish I could kiss you right now."

I play it cool even though I feel like I'm melting into a puddle. "Later. Try to control yourself until then." And then I wink and walk away, because looking at him is making my heart ask questions that my mind doesn't want to hear.

If this were a month ago, now would be the time I'd head to the bar. Instead, I focus on a round table covered with food in the center of the room. There are cupcakes that look like brains and pumpkins and spiders, doughnuts with vampire teeth in the holes, and cookies that look like tombstones. I take a doughnut and three cake pops made to look like eyeballs.

"Baby!" a voice calls, and Charlie runs over to a table where Alyssa is sitting with their friends Taylor and Jamie. I follow her over to say hi.

"Your costumes are so adorable," I say as I take a seat.

To match Charlie, Alyssa is dressed as the golden-butterfly-crown Snapchat filter. Tay is dressed as Queen Firestone from the famous book and movie series, and her boyfriend Jamie is some kind of anime-looking character whom I don't recognize.

"Naruto," he says when I ask him.

"You make an awesome Danny Zuko," Tay says.

"Thanks! Your Queen Firestone is pretty on point, too."

She beams, and Jamie puts an arm around her. "Tay came runner-up in a Queen Firestone cosplay contest at SupaCon last year," he says.

Tay blushes faster than I've ever seen anyone blush in my life. "Wow," I say. "That's so cool." Pharrell's "Happy" starts playing, and they all freak out. They hurry over to the dance floor, dragging me with them, and I swing my hips while munching on my last cake pop.

"Hey, look who it is!" a guy on stage says into the microphone. "Is that Emmy King?"

A spotlight glides over the crowd, stopping on me. People in the crowd turn to look at me, then mutter to each other. I try to tell myself they're all saying nice things.

"Are all the Brightsiders here?" the guy asks. Before I can answer, he holds his hand above his eyes to shield from the light and scans the crowd. "Hey, Alfie! Ryan! Why don't you three come up here and play us a song?"

I start walking toward the stage, knowing that we can never resist a request to rock out. Alfie runs ahead of me, leaping onto the stage and taking the microphone. Ryan and I jump up and take our places onstage. I sit behind the drums, already feeling at home. I'm my most confident when I'm sitting at a drum set. It's the one place where I have complete control; I know exactly what I'm doing. I know every beat I need to hit and when I need to hit it. And I'm damn good at it, too. My name may be King, but this is the only place where I actually feel like a king.

Alfie turns around to talk to me and Ry. "'All For You'?"

Ryan nods, and I give them the thumbs-up.

I hear my friends screaming our names and see famous faces scrambling for their phones to capture this surprise performance. There's nothing like the feeling you get when people you've admired all your life think you're cool. How is this my life? I'm in the same room as my idols, and they think I'm cool. This is wild.

I shrug my T-Birds jacket off and roll the sleeves of my T-shirt up higher. Chloe wolf whistles from the crowd and shouts something about my arms. Alfie glances back at me, and I give him a nod to let him know I'm ready. It's time to go into beast mode.

I slam my drumsticks together. "A one, a two, a one two three four!"

CHAPTER TWENTY-EIGHT

"Hey, Em," **Alfie says to me** while Ry plays his guitar solo. "Let's do 'ILY' next."

I'm so taken aback that I almost miss a beat. "Huh? No way! It's not ready!"

He grins. "Sure it is."

My mouth goes dry. "Well, I'm not ready!"

"Sure you are."

Nope. Nope, nope, nope. "But Ry doesn't even know it."

That gives him pause. He goes back to the mic to end the song. And then he jumps right back over with another comeback. "Let's do an acoustic version, then. We have enough verses and chords for that. You on the mic, me on the guitar, baby."

Oh lord. He called me baby. And he's looking at me like he really believes I can do this. He doesn't have a single doubt in his mind about me or what I can do. That reminds me of one of the rules Chloe and I created: No Doubts.

"Yes," I blurt out. "Okay. Let's do it."

He beams at me. "Wild!"

The song fades out, and Alfie updates Ry on what we're doing while I settle myself in front of the microphone. I spot Sal dressed as Wonder Woman in the crowd and wave. She waves back, but is clearly perplexed why I'm sitting front and center. God, I hope she doesn't flip out. Doubts start to fill my head, but I shake them off.

No doubts. No doubts. I want to do this. No doubts.

I look to Alfie and nod once he's ready with his guitar, and the moment he starts playing I feel like this is exactly where I'm meant to be.

"This is something new we just wrote for our fans," I say. The nerves melt away and the latest version of the lyrics pour out of me.

I'm going for the win, I'm going for gold . . .

. . . I wear my heart on my sleeve 'cause I'm just that bold,

. . . oh yeah, I'm here and I'm queer and I won't slow down . . .

. . . we're here and we're queer, white, black, and brown.

The next two minutes and twenty-two seconds go by in a blur. When Alfie plucks the final string, there's a moment of silence. My heart stops. Fuck. They hated it. I find Sal in the crowd; she's moved right up to the front of the stage. But she's not scowling at me. She's smiling. And then she starts to clap. In a flash, the whole party is cheering. I hear people asking one another if that was a new single, and others saying they didn't even know I could sing.

I turn to Alfie, who's clapping for me with everyone else. He winks, and I almost fall off the barstool I'm seated on. We get up and make our way off the stage so the regular band can keep playing, and Sal grabs me by the arm.

"Emmy!" she says. "Where has that been hiding?"

I give her a quizzical look. "Literally nowhere. I've been begging you to let me do a song for ages!"

She waves it off like she doesn't remember. "Okay, honey, we're getting you and that song in the studio ASAP. I'll make some calls tonight." And then she's gone, her phone up against her ear as she moves through the party.

Alfie spins me around to face him and pretends to drop a microphone. "Boom!"

I throw my arms around him and hug him close. "Thank you for believing in me."

He squeezes me around my waist. "Always have, always will."

When I find Chloe after our impromptu concert, they've already downed some champagne and greet me with ear-piercing screams. After congratulating me and gushing over how much they love "ILY," Charlie walks over and they start debating over the best costumes at the party. Chloe seems determined to convince Charlie that the girl dressed as Winifred Sanderson from *Hocus Pocus* is the best. Charlie is on the side of the girl dressed as Ms. Marvel. I stay out of the line of fire and eat some more cake.

The DJ plays "Disturbia" by Rihanna, and I sing along to it while I look around the party. The waiters and waitresses are painted gray, like they've stepped out of an old black-and-white movie. Skeletons hang from the rusted, dirty chandeliers. The walls are covered with cobwebs, fake blood, and creepy Victorian-era portraits that watch our every move. The deep red lighting is interrupted every few minutes by a subtle flash of white imitation lightning, and jack-o'-lanterns glow on all the tables.

A werewolf on roller skates zips past me, and as I'm watching it roll through the crowd, I spot Levi and Nate, two guys from a band called Lost & Found that we opened for back when we were just starting out in LA.

I finish my last cake pop, slip the plastic vampire teeth from my donut into my pocket, and leave Charlie and Chloe to their battle.

"Emmy!" Nate says when he sees me. I'm secretly thrilled that he remembers me, because I had the most embarrassing crush on him when we worked together.

"Hey, guys," I say. "Having fun?"

"I guess," Levi says, shrugging. He's been in LA a lot longer than I have, so he's probably been to hundreds of these extravagant Hollywood parties, but I hope I'm never that obnoxiously bored by it.

"Buy you a drink?" Nate asks.

I smile but shake my head. "No, thanks. I'm not drinking."

He looks at me like I'm speaking gibberish. "But it's a party."

"I noticed that," I say, feeling self-conscious and a little irritated at his condescending tone.

"Come on, my treat."

I narrow my eyes at him. "The drinks are free."

Levi puts an arm around me, and I flinch. "Let the man get you a drink, Em. He's just trying to be nice."

"I'm not drinking," I say again, this time louder. "And it would be *nice* if you both respected that."

Ignoring me, Levi waves a waiter over and leans in. "Can you bring over another one of these?" He points to his drink, then looks at me. "And Emmy will have . . . ?"

They look at me, waiting for me to order a drink. So I do.

"I'll have a Coke," I say. The waiter nods and walks away to get our drinks. The guys roll their eyes at each other.

"So boring," Nate says, removing his arm from my shoulder. "All

I've heard about you lately is how much of a party girl you are, and you're not even having one drink!"

I slide my clenched fists into the pockets of my jacket, trying to channel some Danny Zuko attitude. "I guess I just realized that at some point you have to grow up and not let your life revolve around the next drink."

I don't smile to lighten the blow. I don't add the words *sorry* or *no offense* or *just kidding*. I don't coat my anger with a pound of sugar like I usually would.

Levi scoffs. "Translation: You're no fun."

"Seriously, Emmy," Nate says, giving me the side-eye. "One drink isn't going to hurt you. Join the fun! Have a drink, then maybe we can find you a girl to make out with."

Levi leans in, his breath stinking of booze. "Only if we can watch, though."

Bile rises in my throat. "I'm sure your legions of fans would be so proud if they found out you're trying get an underage girl drunk so you can exploit and objectify her based on her sexuality."

"That's not what we were doing," Nate says, but I can tell by the scared look in his eyes that he knows I'm right.

Levi opens his mouth to say something but instead takes another swig of his drink. The waiter arrives with my Coke, and I take a sip.

"Have a good night, boys," I say before walking away with my chin held high.

I find Ryan and Alfie sitting in a booth and join them.

"Those guys are jerkoffs," I say to them, gesturing to Levi and Nate. "I can't believe how hard I used to try to impress them."

Ry stares at them, nodding. "Yeah. I tried talking to them before, and they made a crack about *Strange Welcome* being 'okay, for a teen band.'"

Alfie rolls his eyes. "Dicks."

Ry notices my drink and nods toward it. "What are you drinking?".

"Chill. It's just Coke."

He winks at me. "Just wanna make sure you're all good."

"I'm all good," I say.

Alfie raises his Red Bull, and we clink our drinks together.

"Where's your halo?" I ask him, noticing it's not on top of his head anymore.

He pouts. "I lost it."

Ryan and I laugh.

"Well," Ry says. "Typical."

Alfie smirks. I feel his foot nudging mine under the table, and I take a long gulp of Coke to cool myself down.

"How'd you lose it?" Ry asks, oblivious to the game of footsie going on beside him.

"Someone just yanked it off my head and ran," he says.

Ryan shakes his head. "It'll be on eBay tomorrow. Alfie Jones's Halo: five thousand dollars."

Alfie waves to someone on the other side of the room. "Be right back," he says, then gets up to leave. Ryan and I watch him cross the dance floor toward a group of unbelievably tall, thin, symmetrical people.

"Models," Ryan says with a smirk.

"You can join them if you want," I joke. "I won't be offended. Or I could be your wingwoman like I was on tour."

He laughs but waves a hand at me. "Nah, I'm good." He turns toward me in the booth and leans in. "I'm actually seeing someone."

I push his arm. "Shut up! Who?"

Even in the dark party glow, I can see his cheeks turning a shade darker. "You can't tell anyone. It's still super new, and nothing's official, so I don't wanna jinx it by telling everyone."

I put a hand on my heart. "I won't tell a soul."

His gaze drops to the table, then he smiles. "It's Will."

My jaw drops. "Will. Wait, Will? Like, *Will*?"

"Shh!" he says, even though I was practically whispering. "Yes. Will. Tall, nerdy, and handsome Will. TV star Will. Beefcake Will."

I don't know what to say. I've known Ryan for years, we've shared classrooms and tour buses and hotel rooms and stadium stages together, and yet I've only ever seen him date girls.

"You're not saying anything," he says, narrowing his eyes.

"I—" I start, then grin. "That's awesome, Ry! Sorry, I'm just surprised. But yay! I love Will. He's a babe!"

He blushes again. "Yeah, he is."

"So," I say. "Are you bi? Or pan? Or you're not labelling it? Sorry, you don't have to answer that if you don't want to. I'm just excited."

He thinks for a moment, scratching the back of his neck. "I'm still figuring that out. I mean, you think *you're* surprised, but it *really* surprised me. I'd never felt like this with a guy before. I thought I was totally, fully, one hundred percent straight. Until Hawaii."

"Hawaii?"

He chuckles. "Yeah. We hooked up on the yacht. We've been low-key dating ever since."

I laugh, thinking how funny it is that we both started secret, surprise flings, hiding in hallways on the yacht. I'm tempted to tell him about Alfie and I, but quickly decide against it. I don't want him to freak out.

"Alfie and I have been wondering where you kept disappearing to," I say instead, slapping his knee.

"Yeah, sorry," he says.

I shake my head. "All good, man. Gotta follow your heart. Even when it leads you to unexpected places."

"Thanks." He looks away, then back at me. "I hope my parents are as happy for me as you are."

"You don't think they will be?"

He shrugs. "I think they will be. One of my cousins is gay and came out about five years ago. The family was shocked at first, and some of my relatives were real assholes about it."

I slide closer, wanting to comfort him. "How did your parents react?"

"Well, they weren't assholes. But they weren't super supportive, either." He's quiet for a moment, then seems to shake himself out of it. "They seem cool with him now, though?"

He says it like it's a question, then adds, "I want to tell them about Will, but I never, ever talk to them about dating anyone. It's just too awkward."

"But they know you've dated," I say. "Even if you don't tell them, they'd see it online and in magazines."

Someone calls Ryan's name and he waves back absentmindedly. "Yeah. They *know*, but we don't actually talk about it. But I want to tell them before it gets leaked or something."

I frown. "You shouldn't have to come out before you're ready though, dude."

His shoulders visibly relax. "I'm in the general vicinity of ready. I'm just not one hundred percent there yet." He smiles, and so do I.

"You've got time," I say. "And if you tell them and it doesn't go the way you want it to go, I'm here. We're family, Ry."

I give him a big hug, and then we sit in the booth arm in arm for a few minutes, people-watching. I spot Sal floating from one corner of the room to the other, schmoozing people in her Wonder Woman costume. Alfie is waving his arms in the air as he talks to his model friends, and they're hanging on his every word.

"How does he do that?" I ask Ryan.

"Do what?"

"Look at him," I point to Alfie. "He's surrounded by some of the most beautiful people in the world, and they're literally looking at him with stars in their eyes. They're totally mesmerized by his spark. They love him."

Ryan laughs. "He's Alfie." He shrugs as he says it, like that's enough of an explanation.

I watch Alfie some more, smiling when he smiles, laughing when he laughs, even though I don't know what he's saying. And I realize I'm just like them. I'm looking at him with stars in my eyes. I'm totally mesmerized by his spark.

I love him.

Shit.

CHAPTER TWENTY-NINE

"I gotta go," I say to Ry. I spring up from the booth, my gaze darting around the room, looking for the nearest exit.

"You okay, Em?" he asks, concern all over his face.

I give him the most reassuring smile I can muster. "Yeah, I'm fine. I think I'm just gonna go, though." I fake a yawn. "I'm super tired."

He stands up. "I'll walk you out."

"Thanks."

We walk through the crowd, and I steal a glance at Alfie again, testing myself. He locks eyes with me, and my heart stops. He smiles at me, and my knees grow weak. He waves, and suddenly I'm smiling. He keeps talking, and I keep walking. I need to get some air, collect my thoughts, straighten myself out, because something must be seriously off with me.

Just as Ryan and I walk out the door, Will walks in wearing a Thor costume. I feel Ryan stop breathing.

"Hey, you two!" Will says, flashing his trademark smile.

"Hi," Ryan says, his eyes lighting up like fireworks. If I weren't freaking the fuck out, I'd swoon.

"You're not leaving, are you?" Will asks, looking only at Ryan.

"I am," I say. "Ryan was just being a gentleman and walking me out." I turn to Ry and give him a hug. "Go get him," I whisper in his ear, and he squeezes me tight.

"Bye!" I say, before leaving them to bask in each other's cuteness.

Security hustles me past the cameras and into a car. I give the driver Chloe's address and lean back, rolling down the window. I breathe in the night air, taking in this city and its awesomeness. Los Angeles on Halloween is perfect for when you need a distraction from your rebellious heart and imploding mind.

We pull up at a set of lights. The same set of lights where Jessie and I got into that accident.

"Hey!" someone calls from the car next to me. "Danny Zuko!"

I give them a casual chin nod and quickly roll the window up. I don't want them to recognize me. Not here. I close my eyes until the car starts moving again. We pass Grauman's Chinese Theatre, where people dressed as Buzz Lightyear and Zorro pose for photos with tourists for cash. All the famous names beneath their feet, engraved in stars. One day my name will be alongside them. I catch a glimpse of the Hollywood sign, peeking out between buildings and smog. I pull out my phone and take a picture for Snapchat, adding the caption: *Happy Halloween, Hollywood xo.*

It doesn't take long for my worries to catch up with me, and I start beating myself up for letting myself feel the way I feel about Alfie. How could I let this happen? Why didn't I see this coming? Alfie obviously is dealing with this better than I am. He was having a blast chatting up all those supermodels. He's not stuck in traffic on Halloween, drenched in hairspray and self-pity.

By the time we reach Chloe's house, I'm sick of my own thoughts. I walk into the dark, empty house, feeling tired and lonely and like my heart is betraying me in the worst possible way.

An hour later, I'm still awake. I can't seem to turn my brain off. It's strange being in Chloe's house late at night by myself—every now and then I hear a sound, and my heart leaps into my throat.

As screwed up as it sounds, I need noise to sleep. I grew up in a house where music was blared until the early hours of the morning. My lullabies were shouting matches between my parents, chairs scraping along floors, and doors slamming. It was only ever quiet when they were both passed out or when my dad was stewing on something, getting angrier and angrier until he exploded. I'm used to the sounds of drunken bickering and beer cans opening, but here, in this big, dark, empty house, all I can hear is the sound of the pool filter bubbling downstairs.

The silence becomes too much, and I turn on the TV. Flicking channels, I find a horror movie marathon playing Charlie's movie *The Rising*. I snap her a pic of me watching it, then check my feed to see if my friends are all still having fun without me. All their stories are filled with dancing and laughing and filters and posing with celebrities. I try not to be jealous. I try to remind myself that I made the best decision for me tonight. I did good.

I watch Alfie's snaps, and I find myself smiling. And then I do what no one should ever do when they're feeling sorry for themselves late at night: I turn to Google to find answers to my romantic life.

Is it bad to fall in love with your best friend?

How do you know if someone loves you back?

Do friends-to-lovers relationships work?

I read in-depth articles and top-ten lists, and I even take a quiz or two. After an hour of trying to turn the internet into my own personal Mirror of Erised, I give up. I know how I feel: I'm in love with Alfie Jones. So, basically, I'm screwed.

I rub my temples and groan. "Congratulations, Emmy. You played yourself."

I hear a noise from outside and sit up. This place is too quiet. I wish Alfie were here with me. I go back into Snapchat and take a selfie of my face half hidden under the blanket. I caption it with: *Can't sleep*, and send it to him.

I make myself close the app so I don't send anything else, and try to focus on the movie. Charlie's running through the streets, fighting gross zombies. My phone pings, and I see a notification saying Alfie replayed my snap. A second later, he sends me one back. I grin like an idiot as I open it. It's a selfie of him pouting his lips, with one hand mussing up his hair. The red lighting of the club makes him look like a devil even though he's dressed as an angel. His caption reads: *Miss me?*

I obey my stupid, stupid heart and reply.

EM: Not even a little.

ALFIE: Liar.

I send back the wink emoji. I am having too much fun right now.

ALFIE: these cake pops are the best.

EM: RIGHT?! I had like ten of them.

ALFIE: guess what they brought out after you ditched.

EM: what???

ALFIE: unicorn cupcakes.

EM: DAMMIT FML.

He sends me a snap of him eating one. It even has a tiny edible horn.

EM: I regret everything.

ALFIE: want me to bring you some?

He sure knows the way to my heart. My stomach somersaults inside me. Go with Your Gut, Em. Go with your gut.

EM: Yes.

My heart feels three times its size, and I can't wipe the smile from my face as I squeal into my pillow. Tingles run down the back of my neck. I calculate the minutes it will take for him to get here. A voice in my head tries to talk me out of this, but it's drowned out by the thump-thump-thump in my chest.

I'm waiting at the door when he arrives, standing on my tip-toes to watch for his car through the window. He pulls into the driveway, jumps out of the car, and leaps up the steps to the door. I don't even give him a chance to knock. He doesn't even give me a chance to say hi. He scoops me up into his arms, kissing me hard.

"I really didn't want to be alone in this house," I say when he puts me down. "I'm not used to the quiet, and Chloe is still partying." He takes my hand, and I lead him up the stairs. I realize how much I love the feel of his fingers linked with mine.

"I stole cupcakes for you," he says, gesturing to his backpack.

Yep. I love him. "Thank you. You've saved me from a lifetime of regret."

"I'd never be able to live with myself if I denied you delicious baked goods."

"*The Rising* is on," I add. "We can watch Charlie kick some undead ass while we overload on sugar."

He chuckles. "Whatever you want."

We go into my room and crawl into bed. He lays an arm out over my pillow for me to lie on, and I snuggle into his chest. I'm instantly reminded of all the nights I ran away to his house when I was a kid. Hearing him breathing, knowing he was there, was all I needed to feel safe. He hands me a cupcake, and I stare lovingly at it before devouring it.

Soon, my breathing begins to slow. My eyelids grow heavy. In my sleepy daze, one thought bubbles up from my chest and into my mind . . .

I'm in love with Alfie Jones.

We're both asleep before the credits roll.

CHAPTER THIRTY

The next day, Chloe and I are driving through Los Angeles to our fave Sunday brunch spot. We're being tailed by paparazzi, so Chloe takes a couple of wrong turns and circles around until we lose them. We're stopped at a traffic light when I notice a newsstand on the corner, the shelves lined with at least five different magazines with me on the cover. But one of them makes my heart stop.

I clutch Chloe's forearm, lost for words.

"Em?" they say. "What?"

"My parents" is all I can manage to spit out. I point to the newsstand. Chloe follows my line of sight, their eyes narrowing when they see it.

"You've got to be fucking kidding me," they say as they quickly pull the car over to the curb. With shaking hands, I open the door and step out. As I walk over to the stand, everything feels like it's moving in slow motion. This can't be real. They couldn't have done this.

On the cover of a tabloid magazine are my mom and dad, their faces sullen and sad. They're on our couch at home, although the place looks much tidier than usual. Dad has his arm around Mom, and her head is resting on his shoulder. I've never once seen them embrace like that. And then there's the headline:

EMMY KING'S PARENTS TELL ALL: HOW THEY TRIED TO SAVE THEIR DAUGHTER AND THEIR PLEAS FOR HER TO SEEK HELP

I reach out to take it off the shelf, but Chloe swats my hand away.

"Don't do it, babe," they say, holding my hand instead.

"I have to see what's in it." I tug my hand out of their grip and pick up the magazine, flipping it open to the four-page spread. "Oh, God," I moan. I'm immediately hit with photos of my parents, hamming it up like the fame-seekers they are. Mom's hair is perfectly styled into loose waves, and she's wearing a beige turtleneck sweater that she probably borrowed from a friend. Dad is clean-shaven, his hair brushed back and his button-down shirt tucked into jeans. These people aren't my parents. They're cardboard cutouts, stand-ins, fakers who orchestrated this so that they look like the good guys. My parents are hard liquor, but the people smiling at me from these glossy pages are virgin cocktails.

Chloe shakes their head. "Those pull quotes are just plain wrong."

I scan the paragraphs.

"We did the best we could, and it still wasn't enough."

"It kills me to see my baby girl like this."

"She's out of control."

"I'm trying my best not to blame myself, but a mother always cares."

Lies. All of it. Made-up stories about how they caught me doing drugs, how they begged me to go to rehab but I refused, how they're worried I'm going to end up dead or in jail. But the biggest lie of all is them acting like they care.

I throw the magazine to the ground like the piece of trash it is.

"Don't worry," Chloe says to the guy behind the register. "She'll pay for it."

"Yeah." I scoop up every copy into my arms. "I'll pay for these, too." Then I dump them all on the ground and stomp on them like the Hulk. I don't even care how childish I look. I pull out my phone and FaceTime my mom. When she answers, I point the phone at the pile of pages on the sidewalk.

"This is what I think of your tell-all bullshit!" I scream, then stomp on the covers some more. People have started to stop on the street and watch. I don't care.

Mom sighs through the phone. "Classic Emmy. Such a drama queen."

"How could you?" I ask, finally stopping so I can yell at her. "How could you do that to me? There isn't a shred of truth in any of it!"

Mom laughs. She actually fucking laughs. "You sound so shrill, darling."

"Because you lied about me in a national magazine!" I scream.

"Of course we lied," she says casually. "They would never have paid so generously for the truth."

My cheeks burn from anger. I feel like my head is going to explode. "Well," I say, "I hope it was worth it, because I'm done. I'm never talking to either of you ever again."

She rolls her eyes. "I've heard that before."

"I mean it," I say. "You've gained some fame, but you've lost your daughter. And I'll make sure no magazine or TV show or freaking stranger on the street ever gives you a dime to lie about me again. I'm taking legal action. Get a fucking lawyer. And don't ever contact me again."

I end the call, then pay the cashier for the trampled magazines before picking them up and carrying them over to the nearest recycling bin. Chloe holds it open so I can stuff every copy into it.

"It's not worth it. *They're* not worth it." Chlo says as they pull me into a hug, and I just want to stay in their arms forever. I know in my heart that Chloe's right. Reading this trash is only going to break my heart even more.

A car screeches up to the curb behind us, and paparazzi leap out. Before I even know what's happening, they're blocking our way back to Chloe's car.

"What kind of daughter abandons her parents?"

"Emmy, are you going to rehab?"

"Did you know your parents were doing a cover story?"

"Have you spoken to them today?"

"Sorry, folks," I say bitterly. "You missed the show." I point to the handful of people still filming me. "But those guys got it all. Make sure you pay them well."

Chloe and I climb into the car and lock the doors. I lift my knees up to my chest and bury my head in my hands. I want to disappear. Chloe turns the car around and heads back the way we came, back to their house. It's not safe for me to be outside today.

By the time we walk through Chloe's front door, my rage has turned into defiance.

"How dare they?" I say as we sit on the daybed by their pool. Chloe is just as furious as I am.

"You should sue them," they say as they slam their fist on the cushion. "They're trying to profit off your fame. There's got to be something you can do. This is defamation. Or slander. Or something. Right?"

"I'm already emailing Sal." My thumbs slide over the screen of my phone as I type her an email, asking for her help. "She'll know what to do."

The moment the email swooshes off into the ether, I get a text.

ALFIE: how fucking dare they?

EM: I'm on it. Asked Sal to take legal action.

ALFIE: good girl. you don't deserve this.

ALFIE: are you okay?

EM: Numb. Mad as hell. But not surprised.

ALFIE: you want me and Ry to come over?

EM: Thanks, but Chlo is here.

ALFIE: ok. if you need anything.

EM: Thanks xo

My phone starts buzzing in my hand. Kass is FaceTiming me.

"Hey," I say.

I can see that she's still in bed. Her hair is a mess, and mascara clumps under her eyes. She must have had a big night.

"What the hell is wrong with them?" Her voice is so loud it makes me wince. "I am so sorry, Em. I cannot fucking believe they did this."

"Unfortunately," I say with a sigh, "I can totally believe it."

She sits up in her bed. "You are never allowed to talk to them again. You hear me? You've given them enough second chances. I forbid it."

She rambles on for a while like this before I manage to get a word in.

"Kass!" I say. "I get it. And I agree with you. One hundred percent. I already called Mom and told her that I'm done."

She wipes a hand down her face like she's relieved. "Okay. Good. You don't need them. You've got me."

"Hey," Chloe says, putting their arm around me and poking their head into the shot. "And me, too. I'll always have your back. Both of you."

I put a hand on their knee and squeeze. "I'd totally fight for you two. Like, claws-out, gloves-on fight."

They both laugh. Chloe curls their fingers into a claw, their long shiny nails looking sharp as knives. "Roar!"

Just then, my phone buzzes with an email from Sal.

> Emmy,
>
> I contacted our lawyers the moment I saw the cover this morning. We're on it. Don't worry, we'll make sure this won't ever happen again.
>
> Hope you're okay, love. I'm here if you need me.
>
> Sal

Sal comes across as uncaring sometimes, but when one of her people is under attack, she's there. Like a mama bear, she shows up ready to take down the threat.

I have some pretty stellar people in my corner.

CHAPTER THIRTY-ONE

I snuggle under a blanket on the Brightsiders' private jet, shaking with nerves. We're on our way to New York. Sal hooked us up with a gig on *Good Morning America* to celebrate the surprise release of the track. In just two hours, "ILY" will be out in the world.

"Do you think they'll like it?" I ask Ryan, who's just woken up.

He gives me a thoughtful smile. "Em, they are going to adore it. I can feel it."

I wriggle excitedly in my chair. "Ahh! I can't stand this suspense! I just want them to hear it now!"

Our crew are scattered throughout the plane: Zach and our glam squad of stylists, Sal and a few other people from our management, and our security team.

The past few days flew by in a blur of rehearsals and long sessions in the studio that ran late into the night. It's been a welcome distraction from the media vultures circling around me right now.

After video of my freak-out at the newsstand went viral, and people heard my mom admit my parents' lies on the phone with me, the narrative turned in my favor. But all this has made gossip blogs even more thirsty for stories, and the number of paparazzi stalking me has increased dramatically. While all that has been happening around me, my feelings for Alfie have been wreaking havoc within me. In a word, it's been intense. Which is why I've hardly left the recording studio in three days.

Sal wants to drop "ILY" on our fans the minute it's ready. Alfie, Ryan, and I have worked closely with our team at the studio to make sure it debuts at midnight tonight. I've only left the recording studio for a few hours at a time to sleep and shower. I should be exhausted, but I've never felt more alive. This is the work I was meant to do.

Alfie stretches his long legs out next to me. I'm so painfully aware of every move his body makes. Of every word he says. It's like my heart is trapped in one of those escape rooms and Alfie holds all the clues I need to set myself free.

Wow, that makes me feel pathetic. I really need to get some sleep.

I haven't been able to keep my eyes shut since we left LA, so I've filled pages of my notebook with subpar sketches of the Empire State Building, bagels, coffee cups, and city skylines. I'm absent-mindedly tracing my pen in a spiral on a cluttered page when I get an idea. Our publicist asked us to prepare blasts to send out to our followers to announce the song drop, and these cute doodles could be perfect. I turn to a new page and write *ILY* in the center in big, thin letters. Underneath, I add, *Surprise! New single out now!* and decorate the blank space with unicorns, rainbows, hearts, and stars.

Soon, the plane lands and we get in our convoy of black SUVs to go to the hotel. I check the time on my phone every minute, counting down until my baby song is released.

"Five more minutes!" Sal calls as we wait in the lobby of the hotel for everyone to check in. Phones are chiming with texts and emails as the people here communicate with our people back in LA, making sure the links are ready for us to tweet out. I slip on my headphones to listen to "ILY" one more time to make sure it's flawless.

The time comes, and Sal hits send on the press release to all the media outlets. "Go, superstars!" she says, beaming. "Blast it!"

I post my sketch to Snapchat, Twitter, Tumblr, Instagram, and everywhere else, along with a link to the single on iTunes. My phone blows up. Likes, retweets, shares, screenshots, comments . . . they come in so fast I can't keep up.

Sal buys everyone a round of drinks to celebrate, although pretty much everyone opts for water because we have an early call time for *Good Morning America*. My fingers tap-tap-tap on my screen, replying to excited tweets from all our Brightsiders fans.

"The best part," Alfie says, grinning at his phone, "is that this is just the beginning. Imagine what the response will be tomorrow!"

"Right?" Ryan adds. "It's gonna be out of control after the show in the morning!"

"Wild!" Alfie says. They high-five each other, and then Alfie holds his hand up to high-five me, too. I want to take hold of his hand and never let it go.

"I think it's bedtime for me," I say, yawning. I bid good night to our whole crew and make my way up to my room. I don't know how I'm going to get a wink of sleep tonight. Nervousness has held its hand out to Excitement and they are doing a fancy waltz in my stomach.

The first thing I notice when I walk into my room is the generously stocked minibar. I sit on the edge of my bed and stare at it, tapping my feet on the floor. It's like I can hear the devil on my shoulder, telling me that just one drink would ease my nerves. Just one of those teeny tiny bottles of booze would help me get some sleep. And sleep is vital when you have such an important show in the morning. A show that could make or break your career.

The angel on my other shoulder chimes in, reminding me of all the times just one drink has led to three then five then ten until I blacked out. I drag my gaze away from the minibar and pry myself off my bed. I'd rather be sleep-deprived than hungover. I've come so far: almost six weeks without a drop of alcohol. Giving in now would mean I have a bigger problem that I thought. I'm not my parents. I'm just a normal eighteen-year-old girl who binged a few times too many. I'm not my parents.

If Mom and Dad were here, they would have cleaned out the minibar already. They'd be dialing room service for refills or heading down to the hotel bar to keep the party going.

That's not me.

I slip on my unicorn onesie and hop into bed, choosing to binge on social media instead. My cute little drawing has amassed thirty thousand likes on Instagram. Whoa. I jump on Twitter and scroll through all the tweets in the now-trending #ILYOUTNOW and fan-started ILY ALEMRY—the ship name they use for Alfie, me, and Ryan. I've already been retweeted over ten thousand times and "ILY" is shooting up the charts. Double whoa.

I tug the deliciously soft hotel covers higher and snuggle under it, watching the tweets flow in as I cry happy tears. Some of our die-hard Brightsiders have sent me videos and snaps of themselves singing along to the song, and I cry even harder with every one I watch.

After hours of soaking up the love, I take a teary selfie and post it with the last two lines of "ILY":

Look at you, I hope you know,
Look at you, I love you so.
I add, *Thanks for the love, kids xoxo*

Then I roll over and try to get a little sleep. But not a minute has passed when my phone lights up with a text.

> **ALFIE:** you're still up.

I stare at it, chewing on the inside of my mouth, trying to stop myself from grinning. I can't be in love with him.

> **EM:** I am.
>
> **ALFIE:** I can't sleep.
>
> **EM:** Same.
>
> **ALFIE:** you want to go for a walk or something?
>
> **EM:** Ok. Meet you in the hall.

I slip on the complimentary hotel slippers, pull my unicorn hood over my head, grab my room keycard, and step out into the hall. Alfie is strolling toward me from his room, wearing leggings and his Gryffindor house sweater.

"I forgot you're a Gryffindor," I say, narrowing my eyes at him.

He *tsk*s at me, shaking his head. "And you call yourself a Slytherin." He flicks the fluffy horn on my hood. "Or are you a unicorn now?"

I lift my chin up. "I'm not exclusively Slytherin or unicorn. I can be both."

He giggles. "Believe me, I get that."

It takes me a second to realize he's referring to being genderqueer, and I giggle with him.

We wander around the hotel, hand in hand, comparing all our favorite responses to "ILY" so far.

I'm confused and euphoric and afraid and hopeful all at the same time. We meander down the hall, our hands swinging between us. I want this hotel hallway to stretch on for miles just so I can feel my hand in his a little while longer.

"Have you ever been to the roof of this place?" he asks.

I shake my head. He turns us around and leads me over to the elevator.

"You'll love it," he says as the doors open and we step inside. "When we stopped here on our tour, I wasn't on my anxiety meds yet so I didn't sleep much. So I hung out in the rooftop lounge writing songs while everyone else slept."

Hearing that makes me want to hug him forever.

We rise up three floors to the roof, then walk through a dimly lit and empty restaurant and out the glass door to a terrace. The cold November air greets us, prickling my cheeks and making me realize just how thin my onesie is. I tug on Alfie's hand to go back inside.

"It's freezing," I say, my teeth already chattering. "And I think this floor is closed. I don't think we're allowed to be up here so late."

He grins. "What's the point in being famous if we can't break a rule every now and then?"

I shiver visibly, and he lets go of my hand and takes me by the shoulders, guiding me back inside. "Wait here," he says before going back outside and disappearing behind a timber screen covered in vines. A minute later, he pops his head out from behind the screen and waves me over.

When I reach him, he's standing by an outdoor fireplace in a secluded corner of the terrace. He holds a blanket over his arm and gestures to a hanging egg chair.

"Your chariot awaits," he says.

I hesitate, my arms hugging my torso as an icy breeze washes over me. My whole body shivers, and I gravitate toward the chair in front of the fire like a moth to a flame. The chair swings slightly as I climb into it and get comfy, then Alfie slides in next to me, wrapping the blanket over us. Between the heat from the fire, the heat from our two bodies under the blanket, and the heat that's been brewing between us since Hawaii, I shift from freezing to overheated in less than a minute.

I'm so self-conscious that I don't even let myself breathe too much, as if any sudden movements might scare him away like a startled rabbit. I don't know how to act around him now.

LED lights sparkle from within the vines creeping above the fireplace and the screen behind us, replicating the night sky. I start counting them to take my mind off my frantic heartbeat and my close proximity to Alfie. I don't even make it to ten before I become intensely aware of his arm pressed against mine, our hips and thighs touching and our feet dangling next to each other out of the chair. Alfie starts humming Ryan's song "And by the Way," his fingers tapping his chest to the beat.

"Are you excited about your first gig as lead?" he asks.

An uncontrollable smile forms on my face. "Very. But I'm nervous, too. I almost thought about having a drink back in my room, just to calm me down enough to sleep."

He turns to look at me, but I can't meet his eyes. I'm too scared of what I'll see.

"I'm glad you didn't," he says. "If you ever feel that way, you know you can always text or call me."

"Thanks," I say. "I'll keep that in mind. You are the resident expert on resisting the temptations of alcohol."

He gives me a cute salute and pairs it with an even cuter wink. "Major Sobriety, here for duty."

I chuckle and pull the blanket up higher. "How do you do it? All the parties we go to, all the nights we spend around people drinking, how do you just say no every single time?"

He shrugs. "It wasn't easy at first, but now everyone knows I don't drink, so they don't even try it anymore."

"But how?" I ask again. "Like, I've seen how people offer you free drinks all the time. It doesn't even faze you. You're always just like, 'Nah, I'm good.' And if someone pressures you, you're like, 'Nah. I don't drink.' And people just accept it. Whenever I try saying that to people, they look at me as if I'm an alien or something."

"I get those looks, too," he says. "But people get over it. And if they don't, then they're not people whose opinions matter to me anyway. Like, why would I want to impress someone who judges people for choosing not to drink?"

Oh my God. That's exactly what I used to do. I was so worried about impressing people, I never asked myself if they impressed me. And people who give me shit for being sober? Why would I want to impress them? Why would I want to be friends with people like that?

I slap a hand to my forehead and let it sit there, hiding my eyes.

"Em?" he asks.

"I tried so hard to get people to like me by drinking or going clubbing or saying yes when I really wanted to say no . . . I never thought to ask myself *if I like them*. God, I've been so desperate that I literally have been craving the approval of people I might not even want to be friends with! Ugh. UGH. UGGHHHHH!"

Alfie searches for my other hand under the blanket and squeezes it. "Everyone does stuff like that every now and then. Remember when we were touring with Lost and Found? I spent that whole tour trying to look cool for them." He pauses, taking in a deep breath. "I got drunk with Nate and Levi one night. Like, really drunk. They starting giving me shit about our fans. Just making fun of them like they weren't real fans or some crap like that, just because they're mostly teenage girls. I started mouthing off; I don't even remember what I said. Something about their heads being so far up their asses that they can't tell that all they do is talk shit."

I snort with laughter, but I can tell he didn't mean it to be funny.

"One of them," he continues, "I can't remember which one, pushed me. He said, 'You dress like a man but I bet you still hit like a girl.' So I took a swing at him, but I was so drunk I basically just punched air, and when he dodged it he fell on his face. It made so much noise in my hotel room that the tour manager came up and started screaming at us. He threatened to kick the Brightsiders off the tour. I was terrified that I'd ruined our one shot to make it big. I haven't touched alcohol since."

I turn to him, my jaw hanging open. "Jesus Christ, Alfie! Those fucking assholes. Why didn't you tell us?"

"I didn't want you or Ry to get mad at me."

He stares straight ahead at the fireplace, his head hanging slightly, like he's ashamed of himself. It's such a sad sight to see.

"Oh, Alfie," I say, frowning. "We would never be mad at you for standing up for yourself. If I was there I would've taken a swing at him, too. So that's why you never drink?"

He thoughtfully traces his fingers over his chin. "Part of it."

"What's the other part?"

He gives me a sideways glance. "I don't know if you want to hear it."

I turn to face him, showing him he has my full attention. "I do."

"Hmm," he says. "Well, it's because of your parents. But I really, really don't think you wanna hear the full story."

My heart starts racing. I'm not sure I want to hear it, either, but I have to know. "Alfie, I said I want to hear it. I can handle it."

He purses his lips, then nods. "One night, maybe when we were thirteen or fourteen, you rode your bike over. Your parents were trying to sort things out, remember? They hadn't partied or even touched alcohol for a month and one week, so you hadn't needed to sleep at my house in a while. You'd been so happy at school, so excited and proud of them. And they'd started spending more time with you. Then, one night, I heard you tapping on my window, and my heart sank because I knew that meant they were partying again. You didn't say anything when I opened the window, but there was a big thunderstorm that night—you were soaked and shaking like a leaf. I gave you a pair of pajamas, then you crawled into the bottom bunk without a word."

"I remember that storm," I say quietly. "The damage it caused was on the news the next day. Trees fell down in my street, and wires were all over the road." I remember riding my bike through it, too, lightning cutting through the clouds, thunder so loud it shook my bones. Hail stinging my cheeks and my knuckles as I clutched my slippery handlebars.

"Yeah," he says. "It was bad. I climbed into my bed and just lay there for a while, thinking about how bad it must have been at your house for you to choose going out in that storm rather than staying there. You must have thought I was asleep, because you started crying. And you didn't stop. I stayed up all night listening to you cry, debating whether or not I should climb down and hug you or get you tissues or at least ask if you were okay, but I'd never seen you cry before and I didn't want you to feel embarrassed. I didn't know how to make things better, and I didn't want to make things worse, so I just lay there, frozen, too scared to even move in case you knew I was awake." He swallows hard. "That's when I promised myself I'd never be like your parents. I'd never get so bad that I hurt the people I loved. I'd never make anyone so afraid that they'd rather trek through hail and lightning than be under the same roof as me. Staying sober is one way that I keep that promise. That night with Nate and Levi was the only slip-up, and it just made me more determined."

My eyes are closed. I'm sweating, and it's not from the fire but from the simple memory of that night. Mom and Dad threw a huge-ass party, inviting not only friends and neighbors but random people they'd met at bars that day. I stayed up in my room, heartbroken that it was happening again. The music from downstairs was so loud it made the walls vibrate. I got so mad at Mom and Dad that I ran downstairs and kicked one of the speakers into the swimming pool. All their friends cheered—they thought it was hilarious. Mom was so embarrassed, and Dad was furious. They came upstairs and screamed at me for twenty minutes, saying how disrespectful and ungrateful I was. They said I was so boring and useless that they needed to throw parties to keep their sanity. Then they went back to the party and I sat alone in my room. The beat of the music rattled my windows again and again, drowning out my sobs. I had to get out of there, so I snuck out and rode away as fast as I could.

My stomach hurts, my shoulders are tense, and I have a lump in my throat the size of a golf ball. That's how powerful trauma can be. Years later, one memory can take you back like no time has passed.

"Emmy," Alfie whispers. "Are you okay?"

I nod, but a stray tear trickles down my cheek, betraying me. Alfie lets out a sad sigh.

"I'm so sorry," he says, wiping the tear away with his thumb. "I shouldn't have told you that."

I shake my head. "No. It's okay. I'm glad you did. But I'm sorry my parents had such an effect on you. I swear, it's like everything they touch turns to shit."

"That's not your fault," he says. "Their shit is not your shit. Cutting them out of your life was the best decision you ever made, Em. All you ever did was try to save them, to get them help, paying off all their debts. You did more than most people would. But you can't save people who don't want to be saved."

I can't stop my bottom lip from quivering. "I know. Thanks, Alfie." I honestly don't know what I would have done without Alfie back then.

Actually, when I think about it, I don't know what I'd do without him now, either.

CHAPTER THIRTY-TWO

Alfie and I lie next to each other, holding hands while the fire crackles in front of us. I feel my eyes getting heavy, my head slipping gently onto his shoulder. After a while, he pulls me in closer and presses his lips to my forehead. Our eyes lock, our noses only an inch or two away from each other. Clouds of mist from the cold leave our lips and dissolve in the heat between us. His gaze flickers to my mouth. A zap of electricity runs down my spine.

He leans in closer, and I swear I can hear his heart pounding. Or maybe that's just mine.

His gaze falls to my mouth again. I chew nervously on my bottom lip, and he sucks in a sudden breath. Did I do that? I test it again, this time tracing my tongue lightly over my lip. He clenches his jaw, his eyes darkening. I suppress my smile and do it once more, this time letting my tongue linger along my mouth.

"Emmy," he mumbles, his voice low. He says my name like it's a question, and I know what he's asking.

I make eye contact with him and nod. Then I lift my chin up higher, kissing him softly on his chin. He sighs and crushes his mouth to mine, so hard that I feel the air jolted from my lungs.

"I've missed you the last few days," he whispers. He doesn't give me a chance to reply, so I show him how much I've missed him by biting his bottom lip. He gasps, then kisses me with even more desperation.

There's a voice in my head warning me against this, reminding me of all the reasons why we shouldn't be doing this.

He's your friend.

You work together.

You're in love with him.

Your heart is going to get broken.

This is just going to make things weird.

You have a show in a few hours.

You can't keep lying to your friends.

Secrets have a way of coming out.

He's a Gryffindor.

I squeeze my eyes shut tighter, trying to drive the thoughts out of my mind. Alfie brushes his lips over my chin, my jawline, down my neck. All those worries fade away with every touch of his lips to my skin. The chair sways on its chains as Alfie leans over me, our chests pressed against each other. I thread my fingers through his hair while he starts undoing the buttons of my onesie. He's moving too slowly, and there are too many buttons, so I push his hands away and do it myself. He smirks and leans in to kiss me, but just as he does I look down to inspect a button stuck on a loose thread, forgetting about the fluffy horn on my hood.

"Ow, fuck!" Alfie grunts, clutching his eye. He lies back in the chair, grimacing.

I gasp. "Oh my God. What happened?"

He starts laughing, still rubbing his eye. "Your damn unicorn horn thingy poked me in the eye."

"I'm so sorry," I say, but my laughter breaks through my attempt to sympathize.

He blinks a few times, then rolls back over to me. I'm hyper aware that my bare breasts are hanging out of my onesie, and I watch as his gaze moves down from my eyes to my chest. I swallow nervously, wondering why he's staring so long. Do my boobs look weird? I know one is bigger than the other, but I didn't think it was that noticeable. Maybe they're too lopsided or too small or my nipples are too big or they're just not as round as other boobs he's seen. I realize I'm not breathing, and I take in a shaky breath that makes my breasts wobble slightly, only making me even more self-conscious.

"You're so gorgeous," he says, his voice cracking a little. My mouth curves into a smile, and I close the gap between us, kissing him hard. He wraps his arms around my waist and pulls me into him, and I get such a rush from feeling the soft material of his sweater pressing against my bare skin.

His hand slips under my onesie, resting on my ribs. I keep kissing him, but all my focus is on his hand, like every other part of my body is numb except for that one spot, which is sizzling under the warmth of his palm. His fingers twitch higher, and my heart leaps into my throat. My skin tingles in anticipation. His hand moves a little higher. Oh my God oh my God oh my God. Alfie is about to touch my boob. ALFIE. HAND. BOOB. MINE.

He slides his hand higher, his thumb cupping the underside of my breast. Just one more swift movement and he'll be there, and I think I'll explode.

It happens. He makes the final move, his fingers tracing lightly over my nipple and the palm of his hand resting on my breast. YES. Dingdingdingdingding! I feel like a slot machine hitting the jackpot, lights flashing and music blaring to alert the whole casino that WE HAVE A WINNER! We have officially, finally, slid into second base, and it's just as amazing as I imagined it would be.

Of course, I've made it to second base before, but, just like that first kiss with someone new, it never stops being a thrill. I'm honestly surprised it took this long to get here with Alfie. I always had this impression that he could charm his way into someone's pants within seconds of meeting them. But maybe that's just the rock-star image he projects to the world.

I lean in closer, pressing myself farther into his hand, and he squeezes. I bite his bottom lip again, and he moans. But then, out of nowhere, he stops kissing me back. His hand pulls off of me, and he leans back, sticking his head up like he's listening for something.

"Do you hear that?" he whispers.

Whistling. Someone nearby is whistling. And it's getting closer.

"Shit!" I say, scrambling to do up the million buttons on my onesie. Alfie starts helping, taking on the top buttons while I hurry with the rest. A light turns on inside the restaurant, illuminating the little alcove where we're hiding. Alfie edges himself out of the chair and peers around the screen.

"Oh no," he says. "The restaurant is opening. They must be getting ready for the breakfast rush."

I feel the blood drain from my face. "Shut up. Please tell me you're joking."

He shakes his head. "I only see one person in there so far, but we need to leave before anyone else shows up."

I scramble to do up the last button and then push out of the chair. Alfie takes my hand as I peer over his shoulder, spotting a guy in a black T-shirt putting a red apron on. He sings to himself as he turns on coffee machines and other equipment behind the counter. We wait until his back is turned, then make a run for it.

I hold my hood over my face as I run, but just as we're about to walk through the door from the terrace, another guy in a matching apron walks in. I jump out of sight, pulling Alfie with me, and we hide against the cold brick wall like we're secret agents on a mission.

"Did you hear the new song from the Brightsiders?" one of the guys asks. We must have left the door open ajar; we can hear everything they say.

Alfie and I glance at each other.

"What?" the other guy says. "What new song?"

"You haven't heard?! It's called 'ILY,' and it's dedicated to their fans. When I heard it I was like, dead! I've already listened to it, like, a hundred times this morning. Here . . ."

A couple seconds later, our song starts playing. Alfie and I try not to giggle too loudly. I poke my head out and see the guys leaning over the back counter, bobbing their heads to the tune.

"If we go now," I whisper, "they won't see us. But we gotta be super fast."

Alfie nods, and then we go for the door. My slippers sweep across the hardwood floor as we hurry around tables hand in hand. By the time the third verse starts playing, we've made it out unseen.

Our laughter bounces off the walls in the elevator. Alfie walks me back to my room, where we idle for a moment, watching each other curiously. I wonder if he wants to come inside, and by the look on his face I can tell he's wondering the same thing about me.

I slide my keycard into my door and push it open. Alfie stands in the hall while I linger in the doorway. He opens his mouth to say something, but I interrupt him by taking his hand and pulling him into my room. In the seconds it takes for my door to swing closed, we've locked lips and started shuffling toward my bed.

"Shit," Alfie says, staring at something behind me. "Is that the time?"

I glance over my shoulder at the clock on my bedside table. It's 5:30 a.m. We're supposed to be heading to the studio in fifteen minutes for makeup and a quick rehearsal. I drop my head against his shoulder and groan.

"Nooooo," I whine.

His chest shakes against me as he chuckles. "To be continued . . ."

CHAPTER THIRTY-THREE

The stage is set. My earpiece is in. The crowd is amped up and sounds surprisingly large considering the early time and bitingly cold temperature. Alfie, Ry, and I are waiting to go out there, standing side by side at the door.

"Five minutes," the floor manager says, pointing at us. We nod.

My teeth chatter from nerves. Fingers tremble. Heart races. I stretch my neck and shake out my arms and legs. I've been humming "ILY" on repeat ever since we left the hotel, going over the lyrics in my mind. Alfie lets out a shaky breath, and I turn to see his chest rising and falling rapidly.

"Be right back," he says before disappearing into a nearby bathroom. My heart sinks for him—I know he's trying not to puke in there right now, and I feel helpless.

"Two minutes!" the floor manager calls.

Sal struts toward us. "Where's Alfie?"

"I'll get him," I say. I hurry into the bathroom, my heels clicking against the concrete. "Alfie?"

"I'm good," he says. He walks out of a stall, his face a little paler than usual. "Didn't blow chunks, so I consider that a win."

"I'm here," I say. "Whatever you need. I'm here."

He smiles weakly. I want to rub his back or give him a big cuddle, but I don't want to make him feel self-conscious or even more anxious. He washes his hands and dries them on a paper towel, his shoulders so tense they're halfway up to his ears.

"I just need to get out there," he says. "Once I'm onstage, I'll be fine." It sounds like he's saying that more for his benefit than mine, so I just nod. He stares at me in the reflection of the mirror, tracing his eyes down my body. "You look fucking amazing, by the way."

I beam at him. "Thank you! And back at ya."

This outfit is one of my new faves: a bright blue minidress covered in hot pink lips, and matching pink heels to complete the look. Not only does the dress hug my curves in a flattering way, it matches one of my most-loved lines from "ILY": *cover me in kisses till we're so in sync*. It's definitely not suited for the chilly weather outside, but it looks rocking and I'll only be onstage for three songs, so it's worth the potential frostbite.

Alfie is wearing a slightly more sensible outfit: a purple striped blouse (unbuttoned just enough to get the fans going), tucked into black skinny jeans and paired with glittery silver ankle boots.

I push my breasts up to reach peak cleavage, and he raises an eyebrow.

"That is not helping my anxious heart," he says, his voice dropping an octave. His hands find my hips, and I lean in to him.

"Alfie! Emmy!" Sal screams. "You're on!"

We run into the hallway so fast we almost trip over each other.

Ry waves us over just in time. The double doors open, and we're greeted by hundreds of ear-piercing screams. Cameramen are stationed all around the stage and in the crowd, filming our every move. I wave and smile and blow kisses as we climb the stairs onto the stage. I'm so alive with adrenaline that I don't even feel the cold.

Ry and Alfie pick up their guitars. One of our backup crew takes my place behind the drums. And then, for the first time—finally, FINALLY—I step up to the mic. I'm center stage. All eyes are on me.

This is what I've been waiting for.

"Hello, New York!" I yell. "We are the Brightsiders, and this is our new song that we wrote just for you. It's called 'ILY,' and we do." I make a heart with my hands, and the band starts playing me in.

I clutch the microphone, and the words leap out of me like I've done this a thousand times before. Because in my dreams, I have.

In between riffs and verses, I raise my hands over my head and clap. The audience does the same. I glance over at my two bandmates. Alfie's fingers run over his guitar, his hair hangs over his eyes, his hips thrust to the music. Ry winks at me and sticks his tongue out, looking like such a rock star. And I sing my song.

"We wave our rainbows in the air,

We sprinkle glitter from here to there,

We fight for our rights, speak our truth,

We are the future, we are the youth . . ."

When I hit the final chorus, dozens of hands rise up from the crowd. All of them have colorful hearts drawn on them with glitter paint. I keep singing as more and more rainbow hands reach for the sky. Pink hearts, blue hearts, purple, red, yellow, green. Soon, almost everyone in the audience is holding their hand in the air, their painted hands sparkling in the early morning sun. I glance at Alfie, then at Ry, who both look as surprised as I feel. Hands stay raised for the rest of the song, some perfectly still, others swaying to the music. They raise their voices, too, the lyrics bouncing back at me.

By the time the last line echoes off the buildings around us, I've wiped countless tears from my eyes—thank God for waterproof mascara. I didn't expect to see so many people in the audience singing along. They knew every word. They sang it like they felt it as deeply as I did when I first wrote it.

"Thank you so much!" I say into the mic. "We love you all."

They keep their hands raised. I have no idea what's happening, but it looks beautiful and I'm loving it. A member of the crew hurries onto the stage and hands me a handwritten note.

> *Dear Emmy,*
>
> *The hearts we have drawn on our hands are for you. We know you're going through a hard time. When we heard about your Good Morning America appearance, all your online fans worked hard to spread the word and make sure everyone showed up with a heart on their hand for you. We want to show you how much you mean to us.*
>
> *We want you to know that we will always support you, love you, and fight for you. No matter what.*
>
> *Thank you for coming out. Thank you for your voice. Thank you for being you.*
>
> *All the love,*
> *@Brightsiderjane, @EmmyStan99,*
> *and all of your fans*

I bite the inside of my mouth to stop myself from bursting into tears. Even with all the lies swirling about me today, all the clickbait headlines and rumors, the fans remain by my side. They still have my back. They still love me. And my music means something to them.

I'm the luckiest girl in the whole damn world.

"Oh my God," I croak into the microphone, the note trembling in my hands. "Thank you. You have no idea how much this means to me. How much *all of you* mean to me. You give me life."

Alfie cocks his head to the side, and I hand him the note. Ry slides next to him to read it, too. Then they both swoon a little and hug me. My heart swells enough to envelop the whole city.

We have ten minutes of *Good Morning America* segments and commercials before we go live again. I stand in the middle of the stage with Ry and Alfie on either side of me, our arms around one another while fans snap pics.

My nerves are still going strong, so I grip onto the back of Alfie's shirt, trying to keep myself grounded. He must sense my tension, because he leans in to say something in my ear.

"Don't worry," he says. "You rocked it. I knew you would." My smile grows wider.

We take some time to pose for selfies and meet the loyal fans who've braved the cold just to see us.

When we get the signal, we step back onto the stage, and I take my seat behind the drums while Ry moves to the front with his guitar. When we're live again, Alfie takes the lead and we launch into everyone's fave: "All for You."

After our set, we do a quick interview with the hosts about "ILY." To my relief, they actually listened to Sal and didn't ask me any questions about my relationships or rumors or scandals. Once we're done, we spend an hour posing for photos with fans outside, and then jump in the car to go back to the hotel.

Ry and I are already buckling our seatbelts when Alfie sees a little girl wearing a Hermione Granger T-shirt. I swoon a little as he kneels to be eye level with her.

"Hello there," he says, giving her a warm smile. She freezes like an adorable little statue.

"Are you Alfie?" she asks, her hands clasped together.

"I am," he says. Her eyes light up. "What's your name?"

"Um, Kimberly." She looks up at her mother, who's grinning at her and holding her phone up, snapping pictures.

"Hi, Kimberly," Alfie says. "I like your T-shirt. Is Hermione your favorite?"

She looks down at her shirt and nods.

"She's my favorite, too."

Kimberly smiles and takes a hesitant step forward. "Hermione is your favorite?"

"Of course! She's the smartest and the toughest, don't you think?" She nods.

"Hey, Kimberly," Alfie says. "Can I have a photo with you?"

Her cheeks turn beet red, but she nods. Alfie holds his arms out and she hurries forward, standing in front of him and turning to face her mother, who captures the moment on her phone.

Kimberly glances at the car I'm in, and I immediately undo my seatbelt and slide out to join the photo. Ryan does the same.

"Thank you so much," her mother says, beaming. "You're Kimmy's favorite band. She idolizes you."

We hug Kimberly and make funny faces at the camera with her. Soon her nerves seem to have faded and she's giggling with us.

It's moments like these that make me love being famous. It comes with a lot of pressure and pitfalls, but seeing the sparkle in this little girl's eyes washes all that away. Days like this make it all worthwhile.

CHAPTER THIRTY-FOUR

"You're sure about this, yeah?" Alfie asks as we wait in the reception area of a tattoo parlor.

"Sure I'm sure," I say. "I've wanted a tattoo for years. Now that I'm eighteen, I can finally do it. And I want to remember this moment in my life."

He leans on the counter, pushing his sunglasses onto his head and making his long hair puff out like a lion's mane. "What moment would that be?"

"Singing my first solo, duh! And . . . I want to always remember all the love our fans have been showing me since I came out. All the hearts on their hands. I want it on my skin." I flip open a book of tattoo examples and study the options, but I already know what I'm getting. "So I can look at it whenever I'm sad and remember how loved I am."

Alfie gives me a half smile. "So you know what you're getting?"

I nod and pull out my phone. "I'll text it to you." I tap it in and hit send, and a second later he's sliding his screen open.

He furrows his brow. "Heart emojis?"

"Not just *any* heart emojis," I say. "I want a line of heart emojis—red, yellow, green, blue, and purple—to create a rainbow of hearts, just like the ones on people's hands at the show."

"Oh," he says, nodding. "Like a Pride tat. I love it."

"Yep. I'm out and proud, and now I'm going to literally wear my hearts on my sleeve."

He laughs. "Awesome."

The super-cool-looking tattoo artist, Georgie, beckons me over. Her arms, chest, and neck are covered in colorful tattoos of pinup girls, mermaids, and flowers. "I'm ready for you," she says, her thick blond hair pulled to one side in a braid.

My heart flutters nervously as I walk behind the counter and take a seat at her table. Alfie pulls up a chair next to me, sitting on it backward and resting his chin on the back.

"It's so sweet of you to be here for moral support," Georgie says to Alfie as she prepares the space on my wrist.

Alfie smiles. "Someone's gotta do it. She acts tough, but she gets squeamish."

Georgie looks at me from under her long lashes and winks. "I've got you, girl. You're safe in my hands."

I chuckle. "I trust you."

Alfie does a little cough, like he's trying to get my attention. I glance at him, but he's not looking at me. He's just staring at my arm, watching Georgie stencil the hearts onto me. He looks so serious.

Oh my Lady Gaga. I think he's jealous that she was flirting with me. I suppress my smile, trying not to look too smug at him sitting there being all Sulky McSulkypants.

Trying to break through the silence, I open Snapchat and start filming my arm.

"Guess what I'm getting?" I ask my followers. I lift my phone so Georgie is in the shot, and she smiles, her red lipstick shining. "This is Georgie, and we're getting ready to do some tattooing!"

I quickly move the phone to get Alfie in the shot, and he perks up instantly—ever the performer. He sticks his tongue out and does the rock-and-roll horns sign with both his hands. The timer ends, and I choose the most flattering filter, then add the snap to my story.

"Okay," Georgia says. "Ready?"

I swallow hard. "Let's do this."

The moment the needle touches my skin, I tense up. It feels like a thousand bees are stinging me. I bite down on my bottom lip to stop myself from whimpering and remind myself that this will all be over soon, and it's going to look so damn good when it is. At first, I make myself watch as she outlines the hearts, but it makes the pain so much more real, so I look away. I focus on Georgie's lips, on the concentration in her face, on how flawless her makeup is. But I can still see the needle in my peripheral vision, so I turn to Alfie.

"Distract me," I plead.

Obviously seeing the pain in my face, he acts fast. In a flash, he's pulling up Charlie's latest YouTube video, and we watch it together. It's a tutorial on how to create Pokémon-themed nails, and watching her paint the tiny Pikachu on her thumbnail distracts me from the pain.

"Man, I wanna do that!" Alfie says, squinting at the screen.

"Same!" I say.

The pain increases as Georgie starts adding color to the red heart. I suck in a long, deep breath.

Alfie puts a hand on my shoulder, and my skin tingles.

"You good, Em?" he asks, concern all over his face.

I breathe out. "Good."

"Almost done with the first heart, babe," Georgie says. I nod, but I can't bring myself to look at it yet.

"Let's do another snap," Alfie says, prying my phone from my tense hand.

He starts filming, and I force a smile, trying to act like I'm totally not in agony.

"How's it going, Em?" Alfie teases.

I give him a thumbs-up. "So good. I can't even"—Georgie starts coloring in the yellow heart, and I squeeze my eyes shut—"feel it."

Alfie and Georgie laugh, and Alfie switches the camera to himself so viewers can see him. "She's dying," he jokes. "So much pain right now."

"Shut up!" I cry. I want to punch him in the arm, but any sudden movements will ruin my tattoo, so I make a mental note to punch him later.

He locks my phone and hangs his head, his shoulders shaking from his laughter. I narrow my eyes at him, but before I can tell him to shut up again I feel another shot of fire in my wrist.

"Ow," I whine. "Fuck, this hurts so much." I gesture to Alfie's arms, covered with tats of every color and size. "I honestly don't know how you've sat through this so many times."

"Hey," he says, flexing his arm muscles, "I'm Alfie Jones. I don't feel pain." His voice is low, and he scrunches his face up like he's angry.

Georgie and I exchange eye rolls and laugh.

"I call bullshit," I say.

He rests his arms back on the chair. "Okay, I may have maybe almost cried a little when I got my first tat." He looks for it on his right forearm, then points to it. It's the David Bowie lightning bolt, with stars and planets around it. "It hurt bad. All that color killed."

Georgie admires it in between coloring. "Bowie, right?"

He nods.

"Alfie's a Bowie stan," I explain. "He sang 'Rebel Rebel' at a school concert once. No one else had even heard of Bowie."

"They knew all about him once I was done." Alfie laughs at the memory. "Mom was up all night trying to make that red jumpsuit."

"That's so cute," Georgie says. She starts coloring the last heart, and I cringe.

My bones feel like they're vibrating, but in a sharp, stinging kind of way. I squeeze my eyes shut and take in another deep breath.

"Em?" Alfie says.

I just nod, keeping my eyes closed.

"We're so close, honey," Georgie says softly. "You're doing so good."

"Mm-hmm," I mumble. "Either I seriously underestimated how much this would hurt, or I overestimated my pain threshold."

Suddenly, music starts playing. It's "Rebel Rebel." I open my eyes to see Alfie standing up, playing air guitar. He slips his sunglasses down over his eyes and starts mouthing the words, flipping his hair back and forth as he rocks out. He skids and kicks and spins his way around the parlor, entertaining the other people getting tattoos. Even Georgie can't resist, lifting the needle off of me so she can turn in her chair and watch his performance.

By the end of the song, everyone in the store is watching and laughing and clapping for Alfie, and he's beaming. There it is, that spark. We can all see it: like an aura of golden light or a neon star above him, you know it's there. He flicks the hair out of his face and struts back to his chair, swinging his leg over it and sitting down like nothing happened.

Then he tilts his sunglasses lower on his nose so I can see his eyes, and smiles. "Feel better?"

"Much better."

A few minutes later, Georgie wipes excess ink off my wrist. "Aaand you're done!"

I let out a relieved sigh. "Thank god. And thank *you*, Georgie!"

She smiles. "My pleasure! What do you think?"

I lift my wrist closer so I can see every tiny detail. There they are, my rainbow hearts. They look exactly like the emojis, complete with the shading and highlighting.

"Oh. My. God!" I say. "It's perfection. Seriously, it's even better than I imagined."

Georgie claps her hands. "Yay! I'm so glad you like it."

"I love it." I hold my wrist out to Alfie. "How awesome is it?"

He looks at it and smiles. "Wow, I love it. Maybe I should get one."

Georgie and I do a double take.

"Seriously?" I ask, getting excited.

He shrugs. "Yeah. I'm queer as hell, too. I wanna wear it loud and proud just like you."

A slow smile grows on my face. "Do it."

Georgie nods. "I'll get everything ready!"

I start snapping photos of my beautiful new Pride tattoo, bursting to share it with the world. I post it on Snapchat, Instagram, Twitter, and Tumblr, with a heartfelt caption:

Got my first tattoo today! I'm out and proud and literally wearing my hearts on my sleeve! I honestly can't thank you all enough for the love and support you've shown me. Thank you for sticking with me through everything, and thank you for embracing me for who I am. I decided on this design after seeing all those beautiful painted hearts on your hands, and all the rainbow heart emojis I see in my mentions. I want you to know that I love and embrace you for who you are, and you deserve all the happiness in the world. Em xo

"Where should I get it?" Alfie asks. He rotates his wrist and pouts. "Doubt there's enough space on my arms. I want it to really stand out, and it'll just get lost there."

"What about your chest?" Georgie asks.

In a second, Alfie is slipping his shirt off, wearing only a strappy bralette and tight jeans. I quickly look away. I don't want to look like

I'm obsessed with him, even though I totally am. We're in a public place, and one rumor about me drooling over Alfie in a tattoo parlor would spread like wildfire.

"Well, then," Georgie says with a smile. "Love your body confidence!"

"Confidence is a work in progress," he replies thoughtfully. "Right, Em?"

For some reason, I can't find my voice.

"Em?" Alfie says, waving a hand in front of my face.

Shit. I was staring. "Yeah, yep. What?" I stumble over my words.

He smirks, like he knows he's got me flustered and he is *loving* it. "Can you snap this for me?"

"Oh," I say as I take his phone. "Sure."

I take a photo of Alfie giving a thumbs-up as Georgie stencils the design onto his chest, just under his left collarbone.

"Got it," I say.

I hit post, then sit back and smile as rainbow hearts are inked over Alfie's real heart.

CHAPTER THIRTY-FIVE

"Why did no one tell me that tattoos hurt more *after* they're done?" My wrist feels like it's been gnawed on by the sun. I go to touch it, but Alfie pulls my hand away.

"Don't touch it," he says, chuckling. "Pain is part of the healing process."

I stare at him. "That's deep." I say it like a joke, but the more I think about it, the truer it feels. I take Alfie's hand under the table.

We're sitting in the private room of Nobu in downtown Manhattan. Sal told us to meet her here because she has something big to tell us. I'm a bundle of nerves.

"S'up, kids?" Ry says as he walks through the door. Alfie and I let go of each other's hands so fast I get whiplash. Sal walks in right behind him.

"Hey, superstars!" she says. "I have to tell you something that is amazing on another level."

She and Ry sit down across from us, and I can tell by the pearly white smile on her face that it's good news.

"'ILY' just hit number one on iTunes!" she says in high-pitched excitement.

I gasp. "Are you serious?!"

She claps for us. "Congratulations! That makes it your third chart-topping single, and the fastest one of your titles to hit number one. You've just broken your own record!"

We all stand up and hug Sal, celebrating our victory.

"That's not all," she says, pursing her lips. "I just got off the phone with the people from the Grammys. They want you to perform 'ILY' and another new song at the show. I already said yes."

"Whaaaaaaat?!" I yell. "No way!"

"We're performing at the Grammys!" Alfie says.

"Oh, also," Sal says casually. "You're nominated for some little thing called Album of the Year."

"WHAT?!" we all scream, not caring that the whole restaurant can probably hear us.

Sal beams at us. "You are now a Grammy-nominated band. Congratulations!"

Alfie's hands fly up to his mouth.

Ryan falls back in his chair, repeating the words *oh my god* over and over.

My heart is about to burst out of my chest and start dancing on the table in front of us.

Sal puts her hands on her hips. "I knew you'd like that. I'm so proud of you. And this is just the beginning for us. Next up: world domination!"

We all sit back in our chairs, Ry, Alfie, and I just staring at one another in shock.

"Is this real?" Ry asks quietly. "I feel like it was just yesterday we were sitting at the back of English class, uploading our first vid to YouTube."

I nod slowly. "It's all happened so fast."

"I can't believe we've made it," Alfie whispers, like he's afraid that if someone hears us they're going to realize we're not as great as everyone thinks and take our success away.

"You made it," Sal repeats. "And you deserve every bit of it."

After dinner, a waiter walks in carrying a huge cake. He places it on the table in front of us and Sal thanks him.

"I figured we can't celebrate without cake," she says, laughing.

It's the biggest cake I've seen in my life—and I've seen a lot of cakes. But the coolest thing about it is that the cover of the "ILY" single is printed on top of it like a photo.

"This looks too good to eat," Ry says.

Alfie smirks. "But you will."

Ry nods. "Well, it's cake. I kinda don't have a choice."

"But first!" I hold my index finger up with one hand while reaching for my phone with the other. "Instagram." We all stand over the cake, snapping photos to share its beauty with the world.

"Okay," Sal says, laughing. "Let's eat! We've got a plane back to LA waiting for us."

Ry shoots off a quick text. "I'm telling everyone to meet us at Bar 161 tonight. This news needs to be celebrated."

That night, we strut through the paparazzi, past the velvet-roped entrance and into Bar 161. Ry booked the entire VIP lounge, where our friends are already waiting for us, cheering and clapping. I've never been inside this VIP room before, and it's like walking inside a disco ball.

"Whoa," Ry says as he looks around the room. "I feel like we just walked into the lair of a James Bond villain."

The walls are made of rose gold mirrors; the booths and tables are metallic gold; the floor is lined with shimmery gold tiles. There's a very obvious theme here, and I'm digging it. In here, I feel like *I'm* made of gold.

I never really felt worthy of VIP rooms before. But I've been through enough heartache lately to know that good things need to be celebrated.

Chloe wraps their arms around me, and we let our hug linger. "Proud of you, Em."

"Thanks, Chlo," I say, tearing up a little. When we finally let go of one another, we join the others.

I slide into the booth next to Alyssa, and Alfie slides in next to me.

"Congrats on the Grammy nom!" Alyssa says as she puts an arm around me. "Also, you rocked it on *Good Morning America*, Em."

Charlie, sitting on her other side, leans over to touch my thigh. "Totally rocked it! And you looked so damn hot! That dress was a stunner!"

"Thank you so much!" My cheeks burn. "I froze my tits off, but it was worth it." We laugh, and I feel Alfie's hand rest on top of mine on the seat. He's talking excitedly about our Grammy nomination with Taylor and Jamie, and I keep talking to Charlie and Alyssa, but just feeling his hand on mine sets off fireworks in my belly.

Soon, we all venture out onto the dance floor to rock out. I'm not worried about the paparazzi waiting for us outside. I'm not worried about people in the bar snapping sneaky photos of me. For the first time, I think I'm adjusting to life in the spotlight. I don't even feel the urge to drink. I look around at my friends, the people I love most in the world, and seeing them having fun fills me with such happiness I could explode. These people are my family.

"Em!" Chloe says into my ear. "I'm going to order some more fries. Come with?"

"Sure," I say. As I slide past Alfie, I bend strategically so he can see down my shirt. His jaw clenches, and I raise an eyebrow at him suggestively.

Chloe and I link arms, then walk to the bar and wait to be served. My phone vibrates, and I check it to see a text.

ALFIE: meet me in the James Bond room.

I glance back at the dance floor. Alfie's watching me, and he's got that look in his eyes. The same one from the night when he first kissed me, the heat emanating off of him and hitting me right in the gut. He walks my way, his gaze still locked on me. I can't take my eyes off him as he strides over. The back of his hand brushes against my butt as he walks straight past me. I visibly shiver, and Chloe gives me a weird look.

"What can I get you?" the bartender asks.

I try to answer, but my mouth is as dry as the Sahara desert, so Chloe orders instead. Physically, I may be standing at the bar, but I'm just a shell. My brain, my heart, and my ovaries are already chasing Alfie.

"Gotta pee," I say to Chloe, then step away from the bar and hurry to catch up with Alfie. I look over my shoulder as I walk down the long hallway to the VIP room, making sure nobody is watching. A hand takes mine and pulls me through the golden door, and I smile before I even see his face because I know it's him.

He locks the door and pins me against it, peppering kisses down my neck. "What took you so long?"

"I wanted to make you wait."

He sticks his bottom lip out into a pout. "You're mean."

"You're sexy."

He smiles. "You're forgiven."

I run my hands through his hair and pull him in closer, kissing him slowly. He snakes his arms around my back and lifts me up, carrying me over to the booth and resting me on the table. His fingers run over my knee and up my thigh. I feel my body temperature rise with every inch of skin he covers, until he reaches the hem of my skirt. His hand lingers there, and I want it to move higher, so I slide my tongue into his mouth, hoping it will prompt him to keep going. It does. His fingers tremble against my thigh as he pushes my skirt up a little, and then a little bit more.

BANG. The door explodes open, and Ryan jumps into the room.

"Frightsi—!" he yells, holding his phone up at us. "What the fuck?!"

I scream and tug my skirt down. Alfie pulls Ryan in and slams the door closed behind him.

"Alfie," Ry says, his forehead wrinkled in confusion. "Emmy?"

"I thought the door was locked!" is all I can think to say.

Alfie jiggles the handle and drags a hand down his face. "The lock's broken. Fuck!"

Ryan is frozen, standing there staring at me with his jaw hanging open.

Alfie holds Ry at arm's length. "Ry, don't freak out."

Ryan shrugs Alfie's hands away. "Oh, trust me, I'm freaking out. Of all the things in the world to freak out about, this is definitely in the top three. I mean. What? How? When? What? WHAT?!"

I stand up and tug my skirt down again, feeling painfully self-conscious. I notice Ry's phone still in his hand and start to panic.

"Ry," I say, trying to sound calm. "Did you . . . snap that?"

Ryan still looks like he's in shock, but he gets himself together long enough to check his phone. I hear the recording of his voice replaying over and over on Snapchat, saying, *Frightsi— What the fuck?!*

Alfie clutches his head. "Ry, man, please tell me you didn't post it."

He shakes his head. "No. It didn't post yet."

Alfie and I both step forward, waving our hands at him.

"Please don't do it," Alfie says.

Ry looks hurt. "Do you really think I would do that? If this got out, it would blow up our whole lives. But apparently that's something you don't understand."

Neither of us says anything. We just stand there sheepishly.

"Ryan," Alfie says, "we're just messing around. It's no big deal."

I nod even though it hurts to hear that. Ryan doesn't look convinced.

"That's supposed to make this better?" he says. "Look, it's one thing if we were all just friends hanging out. *But we're in a band.* This has disaster written all over it, seriously. What if one of you gets hurt? What if you get together and then break up? What does that mean for the Brightsiders? Have you even thought about any of this?"

Ry just said all of my worst fears out loud, but Alfie just laughs. He actually laughs.

"Dude, of course we have," he says. "Don't worry, this is just a little thing we've been doing. I'm sure we'll both get sick of each other soon and move on—to people outside the band next time. And we are not getting together. It's just a physical thing, right, Em?" He turns to look at me, an amused smile on his lips.

Oh, God, this was such a mistake. My heart crumbles, sucking up all the oxygen from my lungs like a sinkhole.

But I nod. Of course I nod. What else can I do?

Ryan glances between us, his eyes still narrowed with suspicion. The three-second video of us making out replays again and again like a cruel reminder of how quickly everything can turn sour. Three seconds. That's all it took to ruin everything.

Ry deletes the snap from his phone. Alfie and I sigh with relief, but he's not done. "If whatever this is"—he waves his hands between me and Alfie—"actually doesn't mean anything, then it needs to stop. It's not worth risking our futures for. Especially when there are literally thousands of people in this town who would love to make out with either of you." He drags a hand down his face. "I swear to God, you're so lucky it was me who busted you and not Sal, she'd kill the both of you. This kind of shit is exactly what has destroyed bands before."

"Okay, Ry," I say. "We get it. We fucked up." *I* fucked up. Classic Emmy.

"Promise me this is done," Ry says, his eyes pleading with us. I feel terrible for putting him in this position.

Without waiting a single second, Alfie takes his hand and shakes it. "Promise."

Ryan nods, then holds his hand out to me. "Emmy?"

I want to beg him not to make me do it. But they're both staring at me, both waiting for me to give my answer. If I say yes, I'll be saving the band and all three of our careers. If I say no, I'll be laying my bloodied heart on these golden tiles for Alfie to stomp on with his damn glittery boots. Why was it so easy for him to shake Ry's hand, so easy for him to just give me up, like I'm nothing to him?

I'm nothing to him.

I'm nothing.

I reach out and shake Ryan's hand. "Promise."

CHAPTER THIRTY-SIX

Ryan leaves us in the VIP room so we, as he put it, "can clean ourselves up." All we do is stand there, facing each other while masterfully avoiding actually looking at each other.

"Um," Alfie says, rubbing the back of his neck. "I guess . . . it was fun while it lasted. But Ry's right. Right?"

"Totally." My voice cracks, and I clear my throat. "He was right. Someone could really get hurt." I feel tears threatening to spill over. I pull my phone out and pretend I'm reading a text.

"Emmy," he says softly. "Are you okay?"

I nod. Fake a smile. Nod again. Alfie puts a hand on the small of my back, and it almost kills me.

"Hey," he says. "It's cool. He deleted the video."

I scoff. "I'm not even worried about that, to be honest."

"You're worried about Ry?" he asks. "You know him, he doesn't hold grudges. Yeah, he's pissed now, but by the time we leave tonight we'll all be buds again."

"I know that."

His hand drops to his side. "Oh. Then what's wrong?"

How can someone so smart be so damn clueless? I look up at him, suddenly furious.

"You're what's wrong!" I shout.

He steps back slightly, frowning. I ignore the pain in his eyes and start saying my piece.

"How little do I mean to you if you can just drop me with the shake of a hand? You didn't even need to think about it. You just gave me up"—I snap my fingers—"like *that*."

"Wait," he says, holding his palms up. "That's what you're pissed about?"

"Hell yes, I'm pissed about that! I'm pissed that it was so easy for you to give me up, like I'm nothing. Like I'm not worth holding on to. Like I'm not worth fighting for even just a little bit."

He furrows his brow. "You wanted me to fight Ryan?"

I clench my hands into fists and groan. "No. But I didn't think it would be so easy for you to end this."

He's getting mad now. His jaw clenches and unclenches. "What was I supposed to do? He had video of us!"

I roll my eyes. "Alfie, be real. As if he would actually post a video like that. He even said it himself."

Alfie throws his arms into the air. "Fine. But he busted us. And he was right; our careers aren't worth risking over some easy fun."

Those last two words fly out of his mouth like bullets, hitting me straight in the heart.

Easy fun. Easy fun. Easy fun. The words ripple through me like shockwaves.

"Easy fun?" I ask. I try to sound ferocious, but it sounds more like a squeak. I'm like a lion who can only meow. "So I'm just easy fun."

He pushes his hands through his hair. "That's not what I said."

"Yeah," I say. "It is."

"Well, it's not what I meant."

I blink back tears. "Whatever."

"*You're* not easy fun," he says. "This"—he gestures to us—"was easy fun."

I hold my hands up to silence him. "Just stop. Repeating it isn't making it sound any better."

He squeezes his bottom lip between his fingers, studying me. Then he shoves his hands in his jeans pockets. "I don't get it. I thought you wanted easy fun?"

"I . . ." I clench my jaw. This is too hard. He just doesn't get it. He obviously doesn't feel what I'm feeling.

"Emmy," he pleads. "Talk to me."

I lose it. "I wouldn't gamble everything we've worked hard for over 'easy fun.'" I make air quotes with my fingers. "But maybe I'd gamble it all for you."

He sucks in a quick breath. "Hold up. What are you saying?"

"I'm saying . . ." I trail off, staring at his surprised expression. He looks horrified. What the hell am I doing? I wouldn't really risk my entire career over him, would I? I push out an exasperated sigh. "Fuck it. I'm done."

I storm out, only to do a 180 and storm right back in a moment later. Alfie is leaning on a table, his head hanging low.

"Fuck it again," I say. "I'm saying that I lo—"

Someone bursts into the room, hitting me in the back with the door.

"Ow!" I cry out. "Motherfucking asshole!" I hunch over, rubbing my back. I can already tell it's going to leave a nasty bruise.

"Shit!" Jessie says, bending down to look at me. "I'm so sorry, babe. You good?"

I straighten up, blinking at her like I've seen a ghost. What fresh hell is this? Have I been cursed? I glance behind her, almost expecting my parents to walk into the room, because that's the only thing that could make tonight worse than it already is. Then I notice the glass of bourbon in her hand.

"Jesus, Jessie," Alfie scolds her. "You almost knocked her out. What the hell are you doing here, anyway?"

"Fuck you!" she yells. "The only reason I came in here was because I saw Ryan walk out looking like he was ready to smash something. I wanted to see what made him so ragey. I should've figured it was you."

She watches us for a minute, her lips pressing into a hard line. Alfie and I stay silent, the tension so thick it's suffocating me.

"I fucking knew it," Jessie finally says. She gets right in my face. "You and him are together, aren't you?"

I glance over her shoulder at Alfie, then shake my head. "Nope. That has been made abundantly clear."

"Bullshit," she says. "Tell me the truth."

Alfie tries to step between us. "She doesn't have to tell you anything."

"Get out of my face," Jessie says, waving her glass around. "I can tell she's been crying. And I know it's over you. Get away from her, you dick."

Alfie scoffs. "Oh, you're coming in here, acting all heroic after all the shit you put her through? All the times you made her cry, *I* was the one who was there while you were out partying with her credit card."

That's when Jessie snaps. She throws her drink in Alfie's face, soaking him.

"Jessie!" I yell.

Alfie gasps, his shoulders and arms tensed. "What the actual *fuck*?!" He pushes his hair back, drops of bourbon flicking onto us.

"Jessie," I say, tugging on her elbow. "Get out."

She turns to me, her eyes wide. "You're taking his side?"

"I'm not taking anyone's side!" I feel like I'm about to burst into tears, so I get the hell out of there.

When I find Chloe, they're holding their phone in front of them, pretending to be texting even though their gaze is trained on something across the bar. I follow Chloe's line of sight to see Paris making out with a gorgeous woman with killer cleavage.

"Jesus," I say, rolling my eyes. "This night is turning to shit so fast." I tug on Chloe's hand. "Come on, let's go home. I think we're done here."

They stay put. "No. I can't leave because of her. If I avoided places because my ex-girlfriends might be there, half of LA would be off limits." Chloe laughs, but then they notice the tears on my cheeks and gasp.

"Honey!" they say. "What happened?"

I swallow the lump in my throat. "I'm fine." My voice cracks, and all my focus is going to holding back more tears. "But hey, I promised you I'd help you escape if you were ever in a room with Paris again, so let's make a run for it before you're pulled in by her sex fumes." I force a smile, but I know they can see right through my tough-girl act.

"More like sex *rays*," they say, laughing. I smile, appreciative of their attempt to cheer me up.

Chloe glances at Paris, then back at me, and nods. Then they take my hand and start leading me out the back exit of the bar.

CHAPTER THIRTY-SEVEN

I'm awake before my alarm goes off. I spent half the night lying here, staring at the ceiling, trying to come up with a reason to skip the recording session today. I spent the other half beating myself up for letting myself start something with Alfie that was destined to burn me. I don't know when it happened—maybe it was when he held my hand under the table in Hawaii, maybe it was when he sang about my truth-or-dare eyes, or maybe it's been there since the first night I rode my bike to his house in the middle of the night when I was twelve years old.

Whenever it happened, there's no denying it anymore. I'm in love with Alfie Jones.

But he's not in love with me.

By six a.m., I can't stand it anymore. I get up and go downstairs for an early-morning swim in Chloe's infinity pool, hoping exercise will burn off some of my nerves. I do a couple of laps and then roll onto my back, floating, but I stop when it reminds me of that day on the island when Alfie and I floated in the lake. He took my hand when I told him about sea otters holding on so they don't lose each other. Maybe that was when I started to fall.

I lift myself out of the pool and shake the water off, trying to shake the memories off, too. It doesn't matter that he held my hand, because now he's let it go. He's been one of my closest friends for years, has stuck by me through all the shit, has known me better than anyone. He's one of the few people in my life who has never doubted me. And now it's all ruined.

My heart cracks at the thought of never being with Alfie again, of never kissing his lips or touching his skin or running my hands through his hair. But I need to suck it up and endure the pain. I need to push through this even though it's destroying me.

I wrap my towel around me, go upstairs, and step into the shower, trying again to come up with an excuse to bail. I watch the water swirl into the drain at my feet. I feel like I'm swirling into an abyss, too. The last thing I want to do today is lock myself in a recording studio with Alfie. I wish I could run away, just get on a plane and get the hell out of LA, out of the US, out of this freaking hemisphere. But ghosting on Alfie today would also mean flaking on Ry, and I can't do that to him. I've already hurt him enough.

Ry has been like a brother to me for years. Once he looked at us the way he did, like we had betrayed him, it was all over. I never want to see that look on his face again. I can't let him down again.

When I begrudgingly arrive at the studio, Alfie and Ry are already jamming together. I smile like I'm not broken, say hello like his name doesn't burn my throat, sit down like every step I took to get here didn't feel like walking on hot coals.

I've had trouble sticking to my other rules lately, but this one is too important to bend or break—my career depends on me showing up, no matter how much it hurts.

"So Sal wants us to do an acoustic version of 'ILY,' right?" I ask, pretending I don't notice all the tension in the room.

"Yeah," Ryan says flatly as he looks over the set list. "Let's aim to do 'Where There's Smoke' and 'And by the Way,' too."

I nod, repressing my urge to scream NO and sink to the floor in a puddle of tears. Alfie sits on the office chair across from me, staring into the booth. Ry snaps his fingers in front of his face.

"Yo," he says. "You with us, Alfie?"

"Yeah," he says. His voice is croaky and tired.

"Are you okay?" I ask without thinking.

His eyes widen a little, like he's surprised I'm talking to him. "Never better." I've never heard a more sarcastic comment in my life. It makes me shrink in my chair.

"Jeez," I mutter. "Sorry I asked."

"Let's just get this done," Ryan says.

The urge to dissolve into tears returns with a vengeance, and I have to excuse myself from the room.

I hide in the bathroom for a few minutes, dabbing my eyes with toilet paper and trying to talk myself into going back out there. Gotta move. Gotta go back in.

I show up, back in the studio. My heart races, my palms sweat, but I show up.

Ryan greets me with a smile that I know means he wants to move on from last night. "Ready to get to work?"

"Ready as I'll ever be."

We dive into the music for hours. It hurts to play these songs over and over again, to pour over every word, every verse, every beat until it's right. But still, I sing along, I slam the beat out of my drums, I let the music vibrate through my bones even though it's killing me. This is the soundtrack to my pulverized heart.

This is what I showed up for, this is what the people who love our songs are waiting for, and I'll be damned if I don't give it 100 percent.

When we record "Where There's Smoke," all I can see is the fire in Alfie's eyes when he sang it to me that night on the couch. When we record "And by the Way," Ryan's lyrics have a whole new meaning to me. I feel the arrow in my own heart, and it's carved with Alfie's name.

The only song that doesn't ache to play is "ILY." The memory of our fans that night is the only thing keeping me going, and I clutch it like my life depends on it.

Alfie and I only talk to each other when it's about the songs, and even though Ryan attempts to crack jokes and lighten the mood, it doesn't work.

I check the time on my phone. Two p.m. I need a caffeine hit if I'm going to make it through this. I leave the room and lean against the wall in the hallway, just trying to breathe. There's a wall between me and Alfie, and I don't know how to climb over it. I grab a Red Bull from the vending machine, chug half of it, and prepare to go back in.

Gotta show up.

"I was just telling Alfie about a new song I wrote," Ry says when I go back in. "Wanna hear it?"

"Go for it," I say as I take a seat on the couch. Alfie sits nearby, on the arm of it, even though there's plenty of space free by my side. I pretend I don't notice the distance he's putting between us. He's probably worried I'll pounce on him like a horny tiger or be drawn in to his pheromones like a zombie to brains. I take another sip of Red Bull and mentally roll my eyes. He's so full of himself.

Ryan goes into the booth with his guitar and slides the headphones over his ears. He starts strumming, and then his velvet voice fills the room.

I think you're flirtin' with that grin . . .

. . . I think I'm flirtin', too.

You won my heart . . .

. . . when you held my hand.

When you call me around . . .

. . . I can't get there fast enough . . .

. . . you wait for me at the door . . .

. . . arms open when I show up.

It's all new, this feelin' and me . . .

. . . never felt this, about anyone.

"Thoughts?" he asks when he comes back into the room. I can't answer him, because I'm choking on my own pathetic tears.

"Wild," Alfie says, and for the first time today, I see his smile.

Ry looks to me for my opinion, and all I can do is nod.

"Are you crying?" he asks. Alfie whips his head around to look at me, and I swear I see a hint of pain in his eyes when he notices the tears in mine.

"It's just that good," I croak. "I just . . . I feel it, you know?" I avoid Alfie's gaze.

I know that song is about Ry and Will, but I can't help but notice the parallels between their relationship and mine with Alfie. Same beginnings, but very different endings.

"Same," Alfie says. He turns to face the booth again. "I feel it, too."

My heart perks up like someone called its name. He feels it, too? Does he mean the song? The lyrics? Or does he mean . . . he feels what I feel about him?

"You do?" I blurt out. My cheeks burn from embarrassment.

Alfie shrugs. "Of course. The tune is on fire."

Oh. That's what he meant. Not the lyrics. Not me.

Not me.

CHAPTER THIRTY-EIGHT

"This is a really bad idea," I say to Chloe as we walk into Bar 161 for the second night in a row.

They link arms with me and pat my hand. "I told you, Paris is in New York. I'll be fine. But you can go back to my place if you don't wanna be here."

I scan the bar and groan when I see Alfie sitting at the booth with our friends. I don't want to be here, but my only other option is to sit alone at Chlo's all night, and that sounds even worse. At least here I can't hear myself think. I don't know what it says about me that I can't bear to be alone in an empty, quiet house. Am I so used to being surrounded by chaos that peace and quiet scares me? Whoa. That is not a rabbit hole I want to slide down right now.

I bring my attention back to Chlo. I can continue my existential crises later.

We slide into the booth next to our friends, and I end up across from Alfie. When I dare to meet his gaze, he looks away, brushing his hair back. As he lifts his arm, I notice a new tattoo near his left elbow. He must have gotten it once we were finished at the studio this afternoon.

"New ink?" Alyssa asks, noticing it, too.

He stretches his arm out. "Yeah. Got it done today."

Charlie leans forward, squinting. "What's it say?"

He glances at me. "*Only fools.*"

Alyssa stares at it, furrowing her brow. "Isn't that from an Elvis song?"

Alfie doesn't say anything. He drops his arm under the table, out of view, and tugs on his sleeve.

Chloe takes a sip of their drink and absentmindedly pokes the ice with the straw. "Yeah, it is. Great song, too. Why'd you get that?"

"Does it matter?" is all he says. Chloe narrows their eyes at him.

"What's with the attitude?" Chloe asks.

All I can do is watch, but my insides are twisting and turning over and over. Everyone is staring at Alfie, and I can't handle it anymore, so I get out my phone and pretend not to be paying attention.

"Nothing," he says, his voice strained. "What's with the twenty questions about my tattoo?"

"Alfie," Chloe says, a surprised expression on their face, "chill. You always love telling us about your new ink. Why are you acting so salty?"

He clenches his jaw and stares out over the bar. "I'm not acting salty. And the tattoo doesn't mean anything." He locks eyes with me then, and I hold my breath. "It means nothing."

Silence falls over our table, even though the rest of the bar is buzzing with music and conversation. I'm fuming. It's taking all my strength not to scream. I want to yell at him, to take him by his T-shirt and ask him what the fuck that tattoo is supposed to mean. Is it a dig at me? Is it some strange way of getting my attention? Or is this his way of carving the date of death on the tombstone of our friendship?

"Um," Charlie says, holding her palms up in the air. "Am I missing something here? I'm so lost right now."

Chloe stares at Alfie. "Same."

Finally, I find my voice. "I need a water."

The next thirty seconds are filled with awkward glances and quiet discomfort as I climb out of the booth. I linger for a moment, wanting to say something to him. I rest my palms on the table and lower my head until Alfie looks at me.

"Nice tat," I say, trying to keep my words steady. "Real nice." I roll my eyes and push away from the table, his sad expression the last thing I see before I disappear into the crowd.

I push through the busy dance floor and pull up a seat all the way on the other side of the bar, out of view from my friends. Someone sits next to me and nudges me with their elbow.

"Hey," Jessie says.

I groan internally.

"Soooo," she says when I don't say hello. "I'm sorry about slamming the door into you last night. Is your back okay?"

She rubs my back, and I wince away even though it doesn't hurt that much. "I'll be fine. I know it was an accident. I was about to royally fuck myself over anyway, so you kinda saved me."

"Seriously?" She pushes my shoulder. "What were you about to do?"

I sigh. "It doesn't matter. I didn't do it."

Jessie calls out to the bartender and orders a tequila. I roll my eyes, thinking there's no way he's going to serve her, but then I remember she was drinking here last night, too. A moment later, the bartender places two shots in front of us, along with lime slices and salt. I cringe. She pushes one in front of me.

"No, thanks," I say to her. "How are you even getting served? I thought the cops took your fake ID."

She shrugs. "They did. But me and Paulie go way back." She waves at the bartender, and he grins at her. "And he owes me for the time I got him tickets to Yeezy's sold-out show."

I remember that. She went behind my back and harassed people on my management team until one of them wrangled tickets for her.

Wow. Why was I with this girl? And why the hell am I sitting next to her at a bar right now?

"Come on," she says, nudging the glass closer to me.

"Fuck off," I say.

She picks it up and waves it in front of me like she's trying to hypnotize me.

"One won't hurt," she says.

I fully intend to swat her hand away, but somehow I end up just staring at the shot, trying to talk myself out of taking it. I don't know if it's the thumping music or the drunk people pressing up against me or the drip-drip-drip of my heart as it drains of all hope, but I cannot come up with one good reason not to drink this shot. The devil and angel squabble on my shoulders.

Six weeks sober.

Six weeks of roller-coaster heartbreak.

You've come so far.

Yes, you've come far. One drink won't hurt that.

Think of your career.

Exactly, you should be able to celebrate your career. Just one drink.

One drink could be enough to ruin everything.

One drink could be enough to wash all the pain away.

I look at Jessie, and she must see the hesitancy on my face because she groans.

"Em," she says, putting an arm around my shoulders, "it's just one drink. And I already paid for it." She slides it closer to me again. "Come on. I'm not doing it unless you do it with me."

"Maybe we shouldn't do it, then?" I suggest. But then I glance over the bar and see Alfie. He sees me with a shot and Jessie's arm around me. Then he shakes his head, like he's disappointed, and that just makes me so mad that I sprinkle salt on my hand, lick it, then pick up the shot glass and tip the tequila into my mouth just to spite him. My throat burns. I bite down on the lime, and my eyes water. And I do it all while staring him down.

"Woohoo!" Jessie calls. "Emmy King is back, baby!"

I keep glaring at Alfie, and just to prove to him that I don't need his love or his pity, I snatch Jessie's shot from her hand and drink that, too.

"Whoa!" Jessie says. "Okay! Two more, please, Paulie!"

I tear my gaze away from Alfie and back to the bar, picking up the next shot as the bartender pours it. I tip it back and slam the empty glass onto the bar.

"Yes!" I scream, already feeling a little woozy. "Two more, please, barkeep! The King doth hath returned!"

Jessie laughs. "Here we go, girl."

Soon I've lost count of how many drinks I've had, and I'm giggling uncontrollably as Jessie tells some story about a girl she hooked up with last night.

"I'm glad to know you've moved right on to the next," I say.

"What can I say?" she asks, lifting her arms into the air. "I got game."

We laugh some more, and then she leans in closer. "So, hey, what was that uncool thing you were about to do when I hit you with the door last night?"

I roll my eyes. "Lord. You do not wanna know. Trust me."

"Sure I do! Come on. We're all friends here." She gestures to everyone at the bar, all of them strangers.

I sigh and drop my face into my hands. "I was about to tell Alfie I'm in love with him. Can you believe that shit?"

"I knew I was right!" She throws her head back in laughter and slams her hand on the bar.

I wag a finger in her face. "Nope. Nope. I swear to God, it started after we broke up."

She rolls her eyes. "Whatever, girl. We should go grab some cheeseburgers."

I start to shake my head, but it makes me dizzy. "Nah. Paps outside. Can't leave till I'm sober."

"Ha! Not possible." She runs her fingers down my arm. "Come on, you can fake it. Neutral, remember?"

"Thy musteth take shelter in this here dungeon of inebriation." I concentrate, trying to focus my vision on her. "If I get caught like this, I'll be in big trouble. BIG. Capital B."

Jessie laughs. "You know what else has a capital B?"

"Boobies?"

Her gaze falls to my cleavage, and she bites her bottom lip. "Well, that, too. But that's not what I had in mind. Maybe for dessert."

"What starts with B?" I ask.

"Burgers!" She squeezes my cheeks, and I shake her off.

"Nooooo," I say. "You go. I'll stay here."

Jessie looks away, and I follow her gaze to see Alfie still sitting in the booth with our friends. He's laughing with Chloe about something, and it hurts to see him so together while I'm drowning at the bar. Jessie's hand is back on my cheek again, turning me to face her.

"I'm not leaving you here with him," she says, glaring at him over my shoulder. "He obviously screwed you over."

"Pfffft," I say. I try to roll my eyes, but I just end up throwing my head back in a weird, uncoordinated way. "You're acting like he's dangerous. He's not. He's harmless. And sweet. And sexy. And such a good kisser. And . . . And . . ." A wail spills out of me. "Why doesn't he loooooove meeeee?"

Other people at the bar give me sideways glances. Jessie puts an arm around me, and even though I'm drunk, I'm very aware of how uncomfortable it makes me. I don't want her to touch me, but I know if I tell her to stop she'll just get mad.

Wow. That's not good. I'd rather let her hang an arm around me and be uncomfortable than speak up and make her mad. Memories of us when we were together run through my mind, all the other times I felt uncomfortable or belittled or invalidated by her but didn't say anything out of fear of making her angry. All the times she doubted me or didn't trust me. All the times she hurt me but then I was the one who apologized. I didn't see it as an abusive relationship at the time, but now . . .

God. I'm gonna puke. But I burst into tears instead.

"For real, Em," Jessie says. "You are being so pathetic right now."

Hearing that only makes me cry harder.

"Stop," she says, finally pulling her arm away. "Don't be such a little bitch. You've got the whole world in the palm of your hand, and you're crying over some douchebag. Do you know how many people would kill to have your life? Do you know what *I* would do to have your life?"

I sniff back more tears. "Just because I'm having a shitty night doesn't mean I'm not grateful for everything I have." I want to say more, but the words get stuck in my throat.

"Shut the fuck up," she says, looking at me like she's disgusted. She downs another shot and wipes her mouth with the back of her hand. "You think you're the only one who's got a broken heart? Stop being so selfish."

She slides another shot over to me, and I wave it off, my stomach lurching just at the sight of it. She shakes her head.

"Fine," she says. "I'll have it. But you're paying for it."

Suddenly I feel just as small as I did when we were together. I reach into my bag and fish out my purse, handing my credit card over to the bartender. I just want to get away from her as fast as I can.

"She's paying for the whole night, all our drinks," Jessie tells Paul. He looks to me for confirmation, and I nod. Just pay and leave, Emmy. Then I watch as Jessie does my shot and sucks on a lime.

The bartender hands me back my card and I slip it into my purse.

"I'm gonna go," I say.

She slams her fist on the bar, and I jump.

"You're gonna leave me again?" she says. "Fine. See if I care. Run off to Alfie and spend your whole life waiting for him to love you. But he won't ever love you like I do. No one will."

My bottom lip quivers. "That's not true."

"It is!" she yells. "*No one* will ever love you like I do!" Everyone within a few yards of us goes quiet, listening to our public meltdown. I see more than a couple of phones turn toward us. People are filming. Like this is entertainment. Jessie glances at the people videoing us, and I wait for her to snap at them, but she doesn't. Instead, she smirks, then glares at me.

I may be drunk, but I'm still smart enough to see what's happening here; she's trying to make a scene. She's trying to punish me by airing all our private business in public. My chest tightens in fear.

Chloe appears next to me. "Everything okay, folks?"

All I want to do is fall into their arms and cry.

Jessie snorts. "Yeah, everything's fucking amazing." She says it loud enough for nearby cameras to pick up, and I wince.

Chlo puts an arm around me. "Em, what's wrong?"

Jessie pushes them off of me. "Why don't you go ask Casanova over there?" She points to Alfie, and everyone turns to look at him.

Chloe doesn't fight back, but I can tell by the look on their face that they're furious. "Excuse me?"

Jessie flicks her hand, ushering them away. "You're excused."

A wave of nausea washes over me. I throw up in my mouth and my hands fly up to cover it, then I swallow it back down.

"Shit," Chloe says, helping me off the barstool. "Time for a bathroom break."

We leave Jess at the bar and weave through the crowd, acting as neutral as possible. Some people put their phones away, but others don't seem to care if I know they're filming me.

The second Chloe opens the door to the bathroom, I run into the closest cubicle and barf hard. Chloe closes the cubicle door behind them and holds my hair back. Once I'm all puked out, I close the toilet lid and sit on it, crying uncontrollably.

Chloe crouches in front of me, looking at me with worried eyes. "Emmy, dude. Please tell me what's going on."

In between choking gasps for air, I tell them they were right about Jessie all along. Then I tell them the whole messy story about me and Alfie. They squeeze in next to me on the toilet, hugging me and listening for what feels like an eternity.

"And . . . ," I say after I've finally let it all out, "now I'm in love with him. But he's . . . he's not."

Chloe stays quiet for a while, holding me as I run out of tears. People float in and out of the bathroom, doing their business around us, no doubt hearing snippets of my drama-filled monologue. But I'm too drunk, tired, and heartbroken to care anymore.

"I'm so sorry," Chlo says, sighing. "I don't even know what else to say."

"You don't have to say anything."

"How about this," they say. "I'll order us a Lyft, and we'll go back to my place, order a pizza, and watch a Leo movie. Or we can binge *Bob's Burgers* or something. I think we both need a break from the world for a few hours."

For the first time all night, I smile. "That sounds like exactly what I need."

CHAPTER THIRTY-NINE

When we walk back into the bar, our friends are on the dance floor.

"I'll text them to say we've left when we get in the car," Chloe says. "Let's go out the back exit. If the paps see you like this, there'll be a circus."

We duck into the back of the bar, but not before Jessie spots us.

"Hey," she calls after us. "Emmy, wait up!"

I try to stop and wait for her, but Chloe keeps ushering me forward.

"She's sick," they say to Jessie. "I'm taking her home."

Jessie snatches me by the elbow. "I'm not done talking to her yet."

"Ow, Jess," I say, pulling out of her grip.

She takes my hand instead. "Em, I can't believe you were just going to leave. I've been sitting at the bar waiting for you for, like, an hour. I was worried."

"Sorry," I say, training my gaze on the floor.

Chloe sighs. "Em, you don't have to apologize." They turn to Jessie. "If you were really worried, you could have just come into the bathroom to check on her."

"Hey," I mutter. "Please, no more fighting. I can't handle it."

Charlie runs over to us, grinning. "Hey! Why are you all hiding back here?"

Chloe gestures to me. "Em's not well. I'm taking her home. Jessie was just saying good-bye."

The tone of Chloe's voice alerts Charlie to the tension around us, and she nods.

"Hey, Jess," she says with a sweet smile. "You wanna go dance or something?" I love her for trying to diffuse the situation.

Out of nowhere, Jessie pushes Charlie into the wall. "Fuck you! I said I'm not done talking to her yet!"

"Hey!" I yell, stepping in between Jessie and Charlie. "Don't you dare lay a finger on my friends, you hear me?"

Just when I thought things couldn't possibly get any worse, Alfie marches toward us, with the rest of our friends following on his heels.

"Did I just see you push my girlfriend?" Alyssa asks Jess. She's pissed, and I don't blame her.

Charlie puts a hand on her shoulder. "I'm fine."

Alyssa backs off, but then Alfie gets in Jessie's face. "You need to leave."

Chloe puts their arm around me and steers me toward the door. "Everyone just needs to chill. I'm taking Emmy home before this *really* gets out of control."

They open the door into the back parking lot and *FLASH*, cameras surround us.

"Emmy! Chloe! Em! Emmy! Chloe! Chlo! Hey, Emmy!" they all shout at once, hurting my ears. Chloe pulls me closer, and I hold my hand over my eyes to shield them from the lights.

"Emmy!" another voice calls, and this one I recognize. Jessie has followed us outside.

Chloe and I try to walk faster, but there are too many photographers in between us and our ride.

I feel Jessie push me from behind, and I stumble onto the concrete, scraping my knees. Chloe tries to help me up, but the paparazzi are getting in their face, too.

"Security!" Chloe calls while paparazzi holler and snap pictures of us.

"What the fuck?" another voice yells. Alfie. "Don't touch her!"

"Back off, Alfie," Jessie spits. "Go entertain your fangirls somewhere else."

Alfie storms past her and wraps an arm around my waist, lifting me to my feet. Security appears then, trying to keep the cameras at bay while I try desperately not to cry. Chloe runs ahead of us to wave down our ride.

"Are you okay?" Alfie asks, lifting my chin so he can look into my eyes. All I do is look at him, and he seems to know the answer. "Come on. Let's get out of here."

"Emmy!" Jessie calls. "I love you! After everything I've done for you, you're just gonna leave me like this?"

Hearing that makes me so angry that I turn around and march right up to her. Paparazzi be damned.

"After everything *you've* done?" I growl. "Like what? Spend my money? Constantly talk down to me? Embarrass me in front of my friends? Pressure me into doing things I never wanted to do? Is that what you mean?"

Paps circle us like vultures, provoking us, taunting us, screaming at us to fight and kiss and scratch each other's eyes out. Some of them even meow and hiss, and it only heightens my rage.

Then, spurred on by the crowd, Jessie takes my hand and pulls me into her, trying to kiss me. I dodge it and wrestle my hand from her grip, staring at her in shock.

"Seriously?" I say, so surprised that I'm almost laughing. "Nope. Not happening. I can't believe I was ever with you."

She looks around us, frowning at the cameras like we're in our own soap opera or reality TV show. "But," she says, pouting, "I love you."

I narrow my eyes at her. "That might be true. But would you love me if I weren't famous? Would you still want to be with me if I lost all my money and no one knew my name? Would you stay by my side even if I couldn't get your name to trend?"

Her mouth hangs open, but she doesn't say anything. Her silence answers my questions. Chloe reaches for my hand, and I take it, letting them and Alfie take me away.

"You never loved me, either!" she screams from behind us. "How could you love me if you were fucking Alfie the whole time we were together?"

*Ooooooh*s and *whoooooo*as ripple through the growing crowd.

"That's right!" she adds. "She cheated on me with Alfie! She's a fucking whore! Your little girls worship a slut! She's bad for them! She's bad for the world, that ho!"

Alfie groans. "I can't listen to this anymore." He turns around, ignoring Chloe's calls for him to leave it alone, and gets in Jessie's face.

"Get out of here!" Alfie yells. "Emmy doesn't love you anymore, so just move on. Stop trying to mooch off her accomplishments and go find your own life to live. I'm so goddamn sick of you abusing her like this. Stop torturing her."

It's not just paparazzi documenting this epic blowup now: People have spilled out from the bar to see what all the commotion is. Everywhere I look, people are holding their phones up, staring at us in disbelief, whispering to each other while they livestream the drama.

I can't breathe. I can't stay neutral. I can't stop my tears.

"Hey," Jessie says smugly, "you're the one torturing her now."

Alfie rolls his eyes. "Stop with the lies, Jessie. You're embarrassing yourself."

Jessie looks past him, straight at me, and smiles. "You wanna tell him, or should I?"

"Jessie," I say, giving her a pleading look. "Please. Just stop."

Alfie looks at me, then back at Jessie, then back at me. "Tell me what?"

"Yeah!" a pap yells. "Tell him what?" They all chime in.

"What do you need to tell him, Emmy?"

"Tell him!"

"Be honest, honey!"

"Speak your mind!"

I wave Alfie over. "Can we please just go? Please?"

Alfie starts walking toward me, and I breathe a sigh of relief. I just want to go home.

"Alfie," Jessie calls in a sing-song voice. "Emmy is in love with you."

Alfie stops walking. Even with the lights flashing in his face, he barely even blinks. He's standing a few feet away, in between Jessie and me, still as a statue. He's staring at me, but I can't read his expression.

"She's lying," he says. "Right?" He steps toward me. "Emmy. Right?"

I pinch my eyebrows together, wondering why he's acting so surprised.

"It's . . . ," I start, then take in a deep breath. "Of course I'm in love with you. What else would you expect from a fuckup like me?"

Alfie just stands there, shocked, while the crowd converges around us. We start getting shoved around as the paparazzi fight for the chance to get the best photo.

My heartbreak is going to make a lot of these people very rich tomorrow.

"We gotta go," Chloe says. Alfie still doesn't move, so Chloe and I elbow our way through the mob, leaving him and Jessie on the other side. I look behind me, searching for his face.

I can't see him through the blinking lights, can't hear Jessie anymore over the people screaming in my ears, asking me questions about my heart, my body, my bed.

Finally, we break through the wall of people and jump into the Lyft waiting for us. Chloe gives the driver their address, and we speed away. I catch a glimpse of Alfie storming back into the bar, while Jessie continues screaming into the void. I don't talk to Chloe the whole drive home. I'm too busy crying.

CHAPTER FORTY

I hate how badly I want to text Alfie.

I'm lying in bed, in that weird state of mind that means I'm too tired to stay awake but too awake to fall asleep. Chloe is fast asleep beside me, not wanting to leave me alone in my wasted, distraught state.

I hate how much I miss having his arms around me. I hate that he's not spooning me right now, that I'm not falling asleep to the sound of his breathing.

Jessie texts me for the eleventh time in an hour. I don't read it. If it's anything like her previous messages, it's an all-caps novel-length assault about how evil and trampy and disgusting I am. I block her number and hope that's the last I ever hear from her for the rest of my life.

The internet isn't being much nicer, to be honest. I know, I know, the last thing I should be doing right now is scrolling through Twitter and Tumblr, but I can't stop myself. Gossip blogs have already posted videos from multiple angles of our argument, along with pictures and transcripts. The top three worldwide trends on Twitter are "#EmmyLovesAlfie," "Emmy is a whore," and "Bar161." Fans keep tagging me and Alfie in their tweets and posts, congratulating us on getting together. That's awkward.

Others are sending me death threats, telling me that if I break his heart they'll hunt me down. I want to send them gifs of me rolling my eyes and tell them there's no chance of me breaking Alfie's heart. But I can't say anything. I can't explain, can't defend myself. Anything I say will just make things worse. All I can do is lurk online, and shift between laughing and crying and laughing again at some of the ridiculous things people are saying.

Trolls are on high alert. In the last five minutes, I've been called a homewrecker, a greedy bitch, a cheating whore, and so much worse. Men in my replies offer me their penises while calling me a slut.

What really hurts, though, are the comments about my sexuality. People are saying I only said I was bi so I could sleep around. More say I'm adding fuel to the garbage fire of stereotypes that bisexuals are burned with every day. Straight and gay people alike are using me as an example of why they would "never date a bisexual." I've been branded a bad bisexual. Everything I was afraid of is coming true.

And the headlines. So many headlines.

JESSIE LOVES EMMY LOVES ALFIE!

CHEATING SCANDAL! YOU'LL NEVER GUESS WHICH BRIGHTSIDER IS A HOMEWRECKER!

EMMY KING "BAD FOR THE WORLD"! STAR'S EX TELLS ALL!

IS JESSIE TELLING THE TRUTH, OR IS SHE A CRAZY EX-GIRLFRIEND?

LESBIAN DRAMA! CLICK TO SEE THE LATEST EMMY KING LOVE TRIANGLE!

But it's not even true. I didn't cheat on anyone. I'm not what they say I am. They see pictures and headlines and videos and assume they know the whole story, when those are only a few pieces of the thousand-piece puzzle that is my life.

I don't get a wink of sleep. By the time Chloe wakes up, I have a splitting headache, a heaving stomach, and a heart that hurts more than both of them combined. People keep calling, texting, and emailing me, but I ignore every ping of my phone, instead replaying last night's mistakes in my mind over and over again.

Regrets. Too many regrets for one night. I broke all my rules, my sobriety streak went from six and a half weeks back to zero, and I can't even begin to think about the damage I caused the Brightsiders. I crawl into the bathroom and throw up for the sixth time . . . only now I don't know if it's from alcohol poisoning or pure anxiety.

"Damn, Emmy," Chloe says as they rub my back. "You must've downed all the tequila in the bar last night."

My groans echo off the toilet bowl. "Feels like it."

"I'm so sorry," they say, "about everything that went down with Alfie."

Ryan walks in with an ice pack, and I sit against the tiled wall and hold it over my eyes. I don't exactly remember when he arrived this morning—somewhere between the third and fourth time I stuck my head in the toilet—but I'm glad he's here.

"I'm sorry, too," he says. "If I had known how you feel about Alfie, I would never have made you promise to stop being with him."

"No," I mumble. "I'm the one who's sorry. I'm sorry I lied, and I'm sorry I'm always getting myself into trouble. I'm the one who threw the match into the dumpster, and now I have to burn in it."

"It's not that bad, honey," Chloe says. "You can handle it."

I frown. "But I fucked up huge this time. And I don't know how to unfuck it. I feel like I'm never going to be enough."

Chlo claps their hands loudly, and I jump. "We made a promise that we'd stop trying to please everyone. So no, you're never going to be enough for some people. None of us will be."

"Pfft," Ry says. "Fuck those people."

"Exactly," Chloe adds.

They're right. People are always going to have an opinion about everything—from my queerness to my hair color. And for some, it will never be enough. I need to figure out what's enough for me.

"I know what I need to do," I say. "But first I will require a lot of ice cream."

Chloe laughs. "Maybe wait until you stop puking first. Then we can spend tonight eating Ben and Jerry's and watching cheesy rom-coms about people who soothe their heartache by eating Ben and Jerry's."

That makes me laugh. I suck in a slow, deep breath. "Thanks for being here, my loves." I rest my head on Ryan's shoulder. Knowing I have my friends to support me makes me feel like I can actually get through this. This is what true family feels like. They're here with me, caring for me, loving me, laughing with me, at my worst. They are my ride-or-dies.

Chloe's phone buzzes, and I hear them gasp.

"What?" I say, peeking out at them from under the ice pack.

"Um," they say, reading something on their phone. "Jessie got arrested this morning."

Ryan and I gasp. "WHAT?"

"The cops were called to Bar 161 after she started throwing bottles, but she fled the scene before they got there. Then at around five a.m., cops pulled her over and got her for another DUI."

Chloe hands their phone to me, and there on the screen is Jessie's mug shot. "Fuck. This is bad."

"Don't you start blaming yourself," Chloe says. "This is on her."

"Is she going to jail?"

Chloe scoffs. "No, she's white."

"Truth," Ryan says as he scans the article on Chloe's phone. "According to this, she'll probably get off with community service."

After seeing Jessie explode last night, I hope she gets some help. But as for me, I'm done with her. For real this time.

"Good riddance," Chloe says before helping me off the bathroom floor. "Come on, let's move this party somewhere more comfortable."

After giving me a long, comforting hug, Ryan leaves to check on Alfie. I tell him to tell Alfie I'm sorry, and he nods.

Chloe and I spend the afternoon in bed, watching movies and eating ice cream. Then I start getting my life together.

I can't deny it anymore: I need help and this time it needs to hold. I need to stop trying to handle everything on my own. I need to talk to someone who can help me find ways to cope with being famous, who can guide me through my struggles with my parents and relationships, who can help me heal. It makes me shake with nerves to admit it, but I can't do this on my own. It's time for me to find professional support.

I call Sal to beg for forgiveness, and then we work with PR to write a public statement taking responsibility for my behavior and committing to seeking help. Sal gives me the number of a therapist, and I promise to book an appointment for tomorrow morning.

Sal wants me to talk to Alfie. She says we need to find a way to move forward. She got an angry call from Tucker from the record company, but somehow she managed to talk him into giving me one more chance.

"I reminded him," she says through the speaker phone, "that 'ILY' is the company's biggest hit in years, and that you were the one who wrote it. That song saved you."

I promise her that I'll meet up with Alfie and Ryan tomorrow and make things right. I don't tell her that I have no idea how the hell I'm going to do it.

Once I've got plans in place to fix this mess, I run myself a hot bath and try to relax. Then I wash my hair, brush my teeth, and put fresh sheets on my bed. I fall asleep with a new sense of determination. My life isn't over. This is not the end for me.

I'm just getting started.

CHAPTER FORTY-ONE

Thunder rumbles outside my window, waking me up. I check my phone: seven a.m. My appointment with my new therapist isn't for another three hours. I roll over to get more sleep, but open my eyes when I hear something that sounds a lot like a guitar.

I sit up against my pillows and listen carefully, recognizing the tune. Am I hearing things? I start to wonder if I'm dreaming when the music grows louder, coming from outside. I wrap my covers around me and climb out of bed, wobbling sleepily into the hall.

I knock on Chloe's door, but there's no answer so I open it a crack.

"Chloe," I whisper. They push their eye mask up over one eye to see me.

"Are you playing music?" they ask me, their voice croaky from sleep.

I shake my head. "I thought it was you."

Thunder booms above us, making us both jump.

"Jesus Christ!" Chloe says. "It's the fucking apocalypse." I jump onto the bed with them, waiting for the thunder to fade. When it finally does, we hear the music again.

"I knew I heard something," I say. We follow the tune down the stairs and through the house. But when we walk into the kitchen, we don't hear it anymore.

And then a honeyed voice begins to sing, making my heart skip a beat.

This can't be real.

"Tell me you hear that, too," I say to Chloe.

A smile spreads across Chloe's face. "I hear it." They grab me by the shoulders and push me forward. "It's coming from the front porch. Go see what's up."

I run to the front door and swing it open.

There he is.

Alfie is at the door, playing his guitar and singing "And by the Way." His hair is dripping wet and hanging messily over his shoulders. A puddle forms around his boots. He reaches a high note and squeezes his eyes closed to hit it just right. When he opens them again, they pierce right through me.

I look over my shoulder at Chloe, and they're grinning. Then they blow me a kiss and start walking back up the stairs to give us some privacy.

I turn back to Alfie as the chorus rolls around. He's belting it out like the words are flowing straight from his soul.

Maybe I'm fallin' . . .

 . . . *maybe I'm stallin'* . . .

 . . . *maybe I'm fakin'* . . .

. . . maybe I'm breakin' . . .

. . . but my heart just keeps comin' back . . .

. . . to you.

Thunder shakes the house, but I stay perfectly still. There are so many questions I should be asking right now, but I'm mesmerized by the magic of this moment. From the front step of Chloe's house, with the rain plummeting down, palm trees swaying from the storm, Alfie is like that one ray of light that pushes through the dark skies. The chilled breeze licks at my skin, but hearing Alfie's voice keeps me warm.

I've got an arrow in my heart, and it's carved with your name . . .

. . . I've got an arrow in my heart, and it's carved with your name . . .

. . . I've got an arrow in my heart, and it's carved . . .

We linger for a second after the music fades into the wind. He stares at me with his big, Bambi-like eyes, as though he's waiting for me to speak first. So I do.

"Alfie?" That's all I can say. Even though I'm looking right at him, I still can't believe he's here.

"I wrote it," he says.

"Huh?"

"The song," he says. "'And by the Way.' I wrote it."

I furrow my brow. "But Ry said he—"

He shakes his head. "Because I asked him to. But Ryan didn't write it. I did."

"Why?" I ask, narrowing my eyes. "Why would you ask him to take credit?"

He groans, wipes a hand down his face. "I was scared. If people knew I wrote it, I was afraid they'd figure it out. They'd know who it was about."

My mouth goes dry. "Alfie."

"It was about you, Em," he says. He's giving me that intense stare again, but his eyes look pained. "It was always about you."

The lyrics race through my mind.

I've got an arrow in my heart, and it's carved with your name . . .

> *. . . at first I thought it was just a phase . . .*

. . . the rhythm of my heart has stayed the same . . .

> *. . . one day a switch flipped and then . . .*

. . . all I could see was you . . .

> *. . . my heart just keeps comin' back . . .*

> *. . . to you.*

It's like a veil has been lifted from my eyes. It was about me. This whole time, it was about me. I cover my mouth with my hands and feel tears on my cheeks.

"Are you okay?" he asks, his face crinkled with worry.

I'm too overwhelmed to speak, so I just nod. And then I shake my head. Because I don't know if I am okay or not.

He flips the hood of his jacket over his head and takes a step back.

"I just needed to tell you that. I couldn't stand the thought of you thinking . . ." He glances away and sighs. "I didn't want you to believe for a second that what we were doing was ever just fooling around for me. I thought I was the one with the lovesick heart. It didn't even occur to me that you might feel the same way."

He stops at the steps and looks up at the gray sky. "Anyway. I can tell by your face that you don't want me here. This was a mistake. Sorry." He steps out into the rain and walks solemnly along the path.

"Are you fucking kidding me right now?" I yell at him.

He stops, turns around, and shields his eyes from the rain, looking at me in confusion.

"What?" he asks. His voice is low, serious.

I walk to the steps and clutch the railing, screaming at him through the rain. "How can you seriously think I would let you leave after all that? You don't show up in the middle of LA's only thunderstorm, at seven a.m., tell me you wrote that song about me, and then sulk off into the rain. That is *not* happening."

A slow smile spreads across his face. He runs back to me, dropping his guitar on the porch. The second he's close enough, I crush my mouth to his. The rain drenches us to the bone, but I don't care.

He stops and leans back a little, pushing my wet hair behind my ear. He's looking at me like he's never seen me before. "Is this really happening?" he asks.

"Yes." I kiss him harder, taking the collar of his jacket in my hands and pulling him out of the rain and into the house. My fingers shakily undo the buttons on his jacket while I find the door with my foot and kick it closed. Alfie slides his arms around my waist and lifts me up, and my legs wrap around his hips. I push his jacket off and let it fall to the floor.

He presses me against the door and moves his hands to my thighs, squeezing them in a way that makes me gasp into his mouth.

"Wait," I say, trying to gather my thoughts. "Waitwaitwaitwait wait."

"What?" he whispers.

"I just—" I suck in a deep breath. "I'm still a little confused. Why did you tell Ryan it didn't mean anything? When he busted us in the James Bond room?"

He cringes. "I freaked out. Ryan scared the hell out of me with all his talk about our lives blowing up and what would happen if Sal found out. I'd been so wrapped up in finally being with you that I didn't let myself consider all that. So I panicked. If I'd thought for a second that you wanted me to fight for you, I would have. I swear."

My gaze trails down his arm and lands on that damn tattoo. I press my finger into it. "And what about this? *Only fools*? What's up with that?"

He looks down at it. "That is why you shouldn't get tattoos when you're heartbroken."

I raise an eyebrow at him, waiting for him to elaborate.

He grimaces. "Ugh. This is so embarrassing. I got it because I was feeling sorry for myself. I wanted to brand myself a fool for letting myself fall in love. It was supposed to be a warning to myself to not let it happen again."

"Well," I say, grinning cheekily. "I'm sorry to say you are most definitely failing at that."

He laughs. "So, have I redeemed myself yet? Are you satisfied?"

I pretend to think it over, just to make him sweat. "You have redeemed yourself."

I kiss him again, then pull away. "But I am not satisfied."

He pouts, and I grin.

"Upstairs," I whisper, gesturing to the stairs behind him. "Bedroom."

He glances over his shoulder, then back at me, his eyes wide. "Are you sure?"

I nod and kiss him again. "Yes," I say.

He smiles against my lips. "Yes."

I lower my legs to the floor and we race up the stairs, taking them two at a time. The second we reach my room, he throws his arms around my waist again and scoops me up. I laugh and pepper his neck with kisses while nervous butterflies swirl in my stomach. We fall onto the bed, and my temperature rises as he lowers himself on top of me. Heart racing, palms sweating, breath shallow.

He sits up on his knees to take his T-shirt off, and I climb under the blankets. I stare up at Alfie, his tattooed arms reaching out for me, and smile. I can't believe this is happening. He tugs at the hem of my tank top, and I sit up so he can lift it over my head. We're both topless, taking each other in.

I press my lips against the spot just above his collarbone, lingering there long enough to breathe in his scent. He smells like rain and Burberry. I move my mouth down and kiss the tattoos on his shoulder. He dips his head back and closes his eyes as I kiss along his collarbone. I lay down on the bed, and he reaches out to touch my skin.

"Ah!" I gasp as his fingers run down my chest. "Your hand is freezing!"

He falls onto his side next to me, laughing shyly. "Sorry." He holds his hands over his mouth and breathes into them, warming them up for me. I do the same, then tentatively touch my fingertips to his stomach.

"Too cold?" I ask.

He shakes his head. "Don't stop."

I walk my fingers up his chest, over his chin and poke his nose. "Boop."

He side-eyes me and snorts. "Such a dork."

"I know you are," I tease, tracing over his soft lips.

"Mm-hmm," he murmurs against my finger. "You're the dork." He tries to bite my hand, and I snatch it away, giggling. He shoves his arm under me and pulls me into his chest, pecking me on the forehead.

"You're *my* dork," he says, and I stifle a happy squeal. His mouth moves over mine, our lips parting so our tongues can meet. I melt into him, wanting nothing more than to be as close to him as I possibly can.

Something feels different this time. Now I know this is real. This is love.

Alfie rolls onto me, his hair falling over my face, tickling my nose. I push it behind his ears as he nibbles on my earlobe, his warm breath making me shiver. I nuzzle my face into the crook of his neck, kissing and nipping and sucking until I leave a mark.

His hand drifts down to my breast again. "Cold?" he asks.

I answer him by shaking my head and kissing him harder. He smiles against my lips. I trace my fingers over his back, following the arches of his shoulder blades, drawing hearts over his skin. He caresses my cheek as he kisses me, his tongue moving with mine.

Our symphony begins.

ONE MONTH LATER

"I'm so proud of you, Emmy," Jane, my therapist, says as she stands up from her armchair. "You've made so much progress already. I hope you see that."

"I do," I say with a smile. "I feel it, too."

She opens the door to her office, and I say good-bye.

"Have fun tonight!" she calls after me. "I'll be watching!"

I step into the elevator and let out a happy sigh. Talking to a stranger about my personal life is still taking some getting used to, but it's worth the discomfort. I've never felt more supported in my life. For the first time, I'm totally surrounded by people who believe in me. Now the only asshole I need to deal with is the one in my head, and Jane knows exactly how to help me do that.

Jane has held my hand while I waded through layers of baggage from my parents. She listened while I rehashed my relationship with Jessie. She let me scream and cry and swear about every headline and meme and Twitter troll. And every time I leave her office, it's like I've shed another layer of skin.

I drive myself back to Chloe's to meet with Zach and the rest of my glam squad.

Kass is sitting at the kitchen table when I arrive. She's flown in from Boston to be my date for tonight.

"Zach is upstairs with Chlo," she says before sipping her coffee. "He wants to do you next, then it's my turn to become a star!"

"Girl," I say, winking, "you're already a star."

Just then, Chloe glides down the stairs. My jaw drops.

"I'm a fucking queen." Chloe beams. They walk over and twirl, grinning from ear to ear.

"Yeah you are!" I say, admiring their beauty.

Their dress is a white lace off-the-shoulder number, skintight, showing off their hourglass curves. It sweeps down to the floor in a short trail that makes Chloe look taller and so elegant in a classic Hollywood way.

Zach bounds down the stairs, always a ball of energy. "Prepare to break the internet, Chlo."

Chloe struts over to the hallway mirror and strikes a pose. "Oh, I'm prepared."

Zach points to me. "Your turn, sweetie. Follow me."

I lift my hand to my temple and salute. "On my way, Major Zach."

———

After three hours of tweezing, concealing, contouring, highlighting, and styling, Zach puts the final touches on my look. Then it's time for my outfit. I've chosen a metallic rose gold skirt and matching long-sleeved crop top.

It's spandex, so it takes a few minutes to squeeze into it, and then I have to call Kass to zip up the skirt, but once it's on, it's worth it. Only an inch or two of my skin is exposed in the middle, making it subtle and edgy at the same time. It's simple, but I'm pairing it with purple lipstick and my new pale pink hair to make it pop.

"Damn," Chloe says when they see me, their eyes popping out of their head.

"Thank you!" I blush.

We stand in front of the mirror in my room, trying out different poses to find the best ones to use tonight.

"We are gonna burn up the red carpet," they say.

"The Grammys won't know what hit 'em."

We start dancing, and Chloe starts singing "Swish Swish" by Katy Perry and Nicki Minaj.

"Em?" my favorite voice calls from downstairs.

"Oooh. Your *lover* is here," Chloe teases. They take my hand, and we walk down the stairs to find Alfie and Ry waiting for us.

I didn't know it was possible, but Alfie looks both suave *and* scruffy. He's wearing tight black suit pants and a rose gold suit jacket that matches my outfit perfectly. Instead of a shirt, he's only wearing a wide cummerbund, allowing him to show off the stag Patronus tattoo on his chest—and look incredibly sexy doing so. His hair hangs over his shoulders messily, as usual, and his black-and-cream shoes shine.

He drags his gaze down my body, and I shiver. "Em. Wow. You look beautiful."

I do a weird curtsy thing for some reason. "Thanks. You look hot."

He flicks his hair back, grinning. "I try."

I turn my attention to Ry, who's wearing a classic black-and-white tuxedo. "Very James Bond."

He strikes a 007 pose, humming the theme song.

Alfie slides an arm around my waist and plants a kiss on me. Chloe swoons.

"You two are unbearably cute," they say. "You know that, right?"

We glance at each other and both say, "Yep."

"It's sickening," they say, poking their tongue out.

Ryan laughs. "Hey, you should've seen what I saw in that VIP room. If I'd opened that door a second later, I would've been scarred for life."

I cringe. "Not my finest moment."

"I'll always feel bad about that," Alfie says. "We should've told you."

"But," Ry says thoughtfully, "I wasn't exactly honest about me and Will at first, either. So, I guess I can understand why you didn't tell anyone. New relationships are weird, especially when you suddenly have feelings for someone who's always been a friend."

I laugh. "Weird is an understatement. At least you and Will could admit you had feelings for each other. Alfie and I were in total denial."

He laughs, and Alfie narrows his eyes at us.

"I wasn't in denial," he says. "I knew I loved you, babe. I just didn't know you loved me back. You were the one in denial."

I flip him the finger, and he grins. "See how she treats me?" he whines.

Chloe and Ryan roll their eyes.

"Speaking of Will," I say to Ry. "Is he coming?"

Ryan adjusts his tie. "He's meeting us there. It's our first public event as a couple. He's making this huge deal of it." He smiles. "It's actually super sweet."

I rest my head on Alfie's shoulder, careful not to get makeup on his fancy suit. "I'm happy that you're happy."

Ry winks at me. "Back at you."

———————————

The longer we sit in LA traffic, the more anxious I am. By the time we roll up to the red carpet and the door opens, I'm a nervous wreck. I haven't done any red carpets or events since that nightmare at Bar 161.

Alfie steps out first, then reaches in for my hand to help me out. We're greeted by hundreds of photographers, reporters, and fans screaming our names. Television cameras swivel to face us, people with microphones wave us over to talk to them, and fans lean over the railing to get a selfie with us.

I can't wipe the smile from my face.

Will appears by our side, and when he takes Ryan's hand it's like someone turned the volume up on the crowd. They look at each other, beaming, and I can practically see Ryan's nerves falling away. He came out to his parents as bisexual about a week ago. He told Alfie and me that it was awkward as hell, and they were surprised, but, ultimately, it went okay. Tonight, Ry's parents are having a Grammy party at their house to support him. I'm pretty sure I've never seen him happier than he is right now. It's the best.

Soon, Sal finds us and starts pushing us around from reporter to reporter to give interviews. She's warming up to me again, slowly. But rocking our performance tonight will smooth things over with her for good. And that's exactly what I intend to do.

Chloe floats down the red carpet like the star they are, talking to reporters about the new album they're working on and taking time to greet their fans.

Thankfully, no one asks me too many personal questions about my recovery. Everyone's much more excited that Alfie and I are together and Will and Ry are dating—their fave ships are finally a reality.

"Brightsiders!" a stage manager calls. "You're on after the next commercial break!"

We've been waiting anxiously in our dressing room for five minutes, but it feels like an eternity. Alfie gives the stage manager a thumbs-up as he gulps down a bottle of water. He hasn't puked once today, but I can tell he's nervous. Ry runs his fingers through his hair in the dressing room mirror, mussing it up even more than it is already. I squeeze in next to him to retouch my now-trademark purple lipstick, and he puts an arm around me.

"You ready to go out there and rock their worlds?" he asks.

"Ryan, my friend," I say, "I was born ready." I pull a tissue out of the box on the dresser and press it between my lips to get the excess lipstick off. When I remove it, there's a perfect kiss mark there, so I reach over to Alfie and tuck it in his jacket pocket.

He smiles at me and pats his pocket affectionately.

And then we're swept into the hallway and toward the stage.

I take in slow, deep breaths as I walk up the stairs behind the stage, praying to the gods of live television that I don't pull a J-Law and trip. Time seems to slow down even more as we walk onto the stage before our heroes and peers and fans.

I fumble in the darkness for the microphone stand, hearing the chatter of the audience as they wait out the commercial break. Once I'm ready, I glance over at my friends. Alfie blows me a kiss, and Ry sticks his tongue out like he's Gene Simmons. Seeing their excitement triples my own, and I straighten my shoulders, wanting to look as strong as I feel when the spotlight lands on me.

"And now," the host says from the other side of the stage, "debuting their new song, 'And by the Way,' and performing their number-one hit, 'ILY,' here are the Brightsiders!"

BOOM. I'm flooded in golden light. Ry and Alfie start slamming on their guitars. It's so surreal, hearing our music pulsing through the speakers at the goddamn Grammys. And then it's time for me to let my voice be heard.

"I've got an arrow in my heart, and it's carved with your name . . ."

I watch the faces in the front row carefully as I sing, and it's like magic. Seeing eyes lighting up, hips swiveling, people bouncing up and down from pure excitement.

Singing this song, I remember the first time I heard it. The way Ryan strummed his guitar as he sang, pretending it was his to protect Alfie. I remember how much I loved it, how the lyrics seeped into my chest and curled up in my heart.

I remember when I heard it on that thunderous morning. The smell of the rain as I opened the door and saw Alfie standing there, singing it for me. The way my heart reset itself when he said he wrote it, that it was about me all along.

> *"Maybe I'm fallin'*
> *Maybe I'm stallin'*
> *Maybe I'm fakin'*
> *Maybe I'm breakin'*
> *But my heart just keeps comin' back*
> *To you."*

And now, here I am, on stage at the Grammys. Nominated for Album of the Year. Standing center stage in front of the whole world. All eyes on me. Singing the song he wrote for me before I knew I loved him.

Then the song fades out, and I soak in the glory of the moment. What even is my life?

"I gotta say something," I blurt out, surprising even myself. "I wrote this next song during a really hard time in my life. A time that I'm still healing from. But the love and support we get from our fans, it kept me going. This next song is inspired by you and dedicated to you." The crowd starts cheering again. "Thanks for loving us so hard. You give us life. And to all those kids out there who feel alone and different and afraid, know that you are valid and worthy and welcome here. We see you, we hear you, we love you. We are you. And we're not going anywhere. This one's for you."

The lighting changes, and suddenly the stage is a neon rainbow. Alfie and Ry start playing the tune. And then I give it all I've got.

"Look at you with your hot pink hair,

Look at you with your sultry stare,

Look at you with my T-shirt on,

Look at you singing my song . . ."

I gaze over the audience as I belt out my lyrics. This time, it's not only fans I see singing along, clapping their hands, grooving to the tune we're playing, but my heroes, too. People I grew up listening to. People whose posters I had on my bedroom wall, whose albums are my insta-buys on iTunes, people I worship to this day. And they're singing along to a song I wrote.

"Cover me in love, cover me in ink

Cover me in kisses till we're so in sync,

I love who I love who I love who I love,

I am who I am who I am who I am . . ."

When I get to the line *Don't mess with the girl wearing purple lipstick,* people shout it out loud. I just about explode with happiness.

Every word flows straight from my soul and into the microphone. My voice soars, filling the whole arena. My heart beats in time with the drums.

"Oh yeah, we're here and we're queer and we won't slow down,

We're here and we're queer, white, black, and brown . . ."

We're here. A few years ago we were three closeted queer kids banging on instruments, singing to Alfie's garage door. It feels like a lifetime ago, we've come so far and changed so much.

I glance at Alfie, and he mouths "I fucking love you." Then I look over at Ry, and he winks at me. Kass, Chloe, and Will are just offstage, dancing behind the curtain. Waiting to wrap their arms around us.

"Look at you, I hope you know,

Look at you, I love you so . . ."

After everything I've been through, all the broken hearts and tear-soaked pillows. All the shattered hopes and sleepless nights. All the times I wanted to run away, and all the times I actually did.

I'm still here. I'm still standing.

Whether I go home with a golden statue tonight or not, this moment right now is what I came here for.

I'm still here. I'm still standing. And I'm not standing alone.

I've already won.

ACKNOWLEDGMENTS

So much work, love, and care has gone into this book, I don't even know where to begin. I'm just so grateful to everyone who helped turn this queer kid's story about queer kids into a real-life queer book.

Thank you to Jean Feiwel, Lauren Scobell, Holly West, and Christine Barcellona for believing in this book and for all their hard work bringing it to life. I'm so grateful to Holly for being such a rockstar editor and for being as excited about these characters as I was from the start.

Thank you to the amazing people at Swoon Reads and Macmillan who work tirelessly every day. I wish I could hug all of you and feed you chocolate.

To everyone who read *Queens of Geek*, THANK YOU. Your enthusiasm for my dorky characters continues to blow me away. One day I hope to cosplay with all of you and geek out about our fave fandoms together.

To all the early readers of *The Brightsiders*, thank you so much for sharing your invaluable insight, thoughtful feedback, and encouragement. I hope I did good.

To my parents and siblings, thank you for always being there for me, even when I throw a curveball or two your way. A lot has changed over the last year, so it means the world to me to know I can always count on your love and support.

To my chosen family, what can I say? You helped inspire this story. Thanks for choosing me, too.

FEELING BOOKISH?

Turn the page for some

Swoonworthy **EXTRAS**

A COFFEE DATE

between author Jen Wilde and her editor, Holly West

Holly West (HW): What book is on your nightstand now?

Jen Wilde (JW): *Rage Becomes Her: The Power of Women's Anger* by Soraya Chemaly. It's an eye-opening and timely look at the history of female rage and its vital role in societal and cultural change.

HW: What's your favorite word?

JW: *Debauchery.*

HW: If you could travel in time, where would you go and what would you do?

JW: The future. Something like the year 2050, just to see if we make it out of this mess all right. And to pop in on my future self and see what my golden years will be like.

HW: Do you have any strange or funny habits? Did you when you were a kid?

JW: I twirl my hair constantly. Technically, it's an autistic stim, but some people think it's a strange or funny habit. In high school, one of my teachers gave me an award at assembly for being a Champion Hair Twirler. I was sitting in the audience, twirling my hair, when she announced it, haha.

HW: What's your favorite thing about being a Swoon Reads author so far?

JW: Working with such a kind, encouraging team of women. And meeting readers! Swoon readers are the coolest.

HW: Did *Queens of Geek* being published change your life?

JW: Absolutely! It launched my writing career and introduced me to an amazing world of writers, editors, and book lovers. But the most unexpected, meaningful, life-changing thing for me was seeing how many people related to Taylor and her anxiety. Before *Queens of Geek* was published, I was worried that people wouldn't understand Taylor, because I'd always felt like people didn't understand me or my own anxiety. But so many readers have contacted me to say how much they relate to her and that her experience with anxiety made them feel seen and validated. It made me realize I'm not alone.

HW: Do you have any advice for aspiring authors?

JW: There's a ton of advice out there, but figure out what works for you and forget about the rest. Writing is different for everyone—some people are plotters, others are pantsers, some write every day, others write when they can. But if you love it, if it lights you up, keep going.

HW: Where did you get the inspiration for *The Brightsiders*?

JW: I've always been kind of fascinated by the perks and perils of fame. The way the media treats famous young women says a lot about who we are as a society. The misogyny and bigotry that runs through our cultural veins reveals itself in news headlines all the time. Only in the last few years, thanks to social media, have these biases started to be called out. More specifically, *The Brightsiders* was somewhat inspired by the media's treatment of celebrities like Britney Spears and Kristen Stewart—good girls who fall from grace or behave in ways that society deems unladylike, and so are trashed and mocked as punishment. I wanted to write a story like that, but from the celebrity's point of view, to explore the intensity and ridiculousness of it all, and I hope I achieved that.

HW: What was the hardest part about writing *The Brightsiders*?

JW: All the characters! This is the biggest cast I've written about, and it was challenging to keep track of everyone and make sure they all had dialogue and weren't showing up in scenes they weren't meant to be in—or weren't forgotten about entirely.

HW: What's your process? Are you an outliner or do you just start at the beginning and make it up as you go?

JW: I am a hardcore plotter. In fact, I probably spend more time plotting and outlining than I do actually writing. Before I start a new book, I write character bios, get an idea of what they look like, what they're afraid of, what they want, even what their favorite TV shows and foods are. I use a plotting method used to write screenplays to outline the main beats of the story, so I know what needs to happen and when. That being said, I still get new ideas or head in different directions once I start writing. The outline is just a guide, and it can always be changed if I feel like it's best for the story.

HW: What do you want readers to remember about your books?

JW: That my books made them smile. Made them feel seen, validated. That they felt safe in my stories and will always have friends in them.

DISCUSSION QUESTIONS

1. What songs would you put on a playlist for this book?

2. Which character did you relate to the most and why?

3. Who would you cast in a movie version of this book?

4. If the Brightsiders were a real band, would you listen to their music?

5. Of all the locations in this book, which one would you most like to visit?

6. What was your favorite quote or passage?

7. Did *The Brightsiders* change your perspective or opinion about something?

8. What do you think the main themes of the story were?

9. What do you think the future holds for Emmy and her friends?

THE BRIGHTSIDERS SONG LIST:

ALL FOR YOU (By Alfie)

We were just kids,
Making noise in the garage
Making movies on our phones
Then you turned us into stars

We were just freaks,
Dreaming big in the garage
Blowing off steam after school
Then you turned us into stars

Every word, every strum, every beat
  of the drum
We're the show, you're the heart
We're the end, you're the start
Together forever, no matter what comes
It's for you, every second, all for you

You're everything we need,
Everything we ever dreamed,
Everything we do, we do for you,
All of this just for you, you, you

You come to every show,
Know the words to every song,
Make sure we feel the love,
You're the reason we stay strong

You come together in times of need
When one of you falls, you lift them up
When one of you rises, you cheer them on
You're our inspiration, our family

Every word, every strum, every beat
  of the drum
We're the show, you're the heart
We're the end, you're the start
Together forever, no matter what comes
It's for you, every second, all for you

You're everything we need,
Everything we ever dreamed,
Everything we do, we do for you,
All of this just for you, you, you

We've seen strangers become friends,
Heard stories that broke us, woke us,
  spoke to us
Strong as stone, powerful as lions,
In the crowd, you shine like diamonds

You make us come alive,
Send us soaring, send us high,
Make us better, make us bolder,
Because of you, we can fly

Every word, every strum, every beat
  of the drum
We're the show, you're the heart
We're the end, you're the start
Together forever, no matter what comes
It's for you, every second, all for you

You're everything we need,
Everything we ever dreamed,
Everything we do, we do for you,
All of this just for you, you, you

You're everything we need,
Everything we ever dreamed,
Everything we do, we do for you,
All of this just for you, you, you

All of this, all for you
All of this, all for you,
All of this, all for you.

FLUID (By Alfie)

The world says we gotta follow,
All the rules we've been assigned,
But who are they to tell me who I am?
Who are they to decide?

Smile, submit, stay in line, say please,
They want us to be sweet and soft,
Seen not heard, pure and perfect,
We don't have to do what they expect

Can't you see, it's just not me,
Sometimes I look the part, but
I'm not the kind to follow the lead,
It's not who I am deep in my heart

I won't fit, won't fit your criteria,
You can't make me feel inferior

I won't follow, won't follow your reign,
Wild hair, wild heart, nothin' you can tame

I won't run, won't run from the fight,
Being me, being free is my right

We can be all, we can be none,
We can be fluid, we can be one,
We can shine bright, bright as the sun

They want us to perform,
To join the ranks of suits and ties,
Do what men do or be warned,
Do this, do that, be one of the guys

Can't you see, it's just not me,
Sometimes I look the part, but
I'm not the kind to follow the lead,
It's not who I am deep in my heart

Not trying to cause trouble,
Just trying to be true to my soul,
Not trying to find feathers to ruffle,
Just trying to make myself whole

I won't fit, won't fit your criteria,
You can't make me feel inferior

I won't follow, won't follow your reign,
Wild hair, wild heart, nothin' you can tame

I won't run, won't run from the fight,
Being me, being free is my right

We can be all, we can be none,
We can be fluid, we can be one,
We can shine bright, bright as the sun

I've only got one message to give,
Set fire to the rules of the world,
I've only got one life to live,
I won't spend it hiding my colors

No one deserves to live in a box,
When the world is one big paradox,
So, come on, leave your shame at the door,
Be out and proud, it's what living is for

I won't fit, won't fit your criteria,
You can't make me feel inferior

I won't follow, won't follow your reign,
Wild hair, wild heart, nothin' you can tame

I won't run, won't run from the fight,
Being me, being free is my right

We can be all, we can be none,
We can be fluid, we can be one,
We can shine bright, bright as the sun

AND BY THE WAY (By Alfie)

I've got an arrow in my heart and it's
    carved with your name,
I've got an arrow in my heart and it's
    carved with your name,
I've got an arrow in my heart and it's
    carved with your name,

I didn't mean to,
I didn't know I could,
Is this life's cruel joke
Or just mirrors and smoke

Someone please, reboot my heart,
Someone please, hit restart,
Because I know how this will end,
And there are 99 reasons for me
To lock up my heart and swallow the key,

Maybe I'm fallin'
Maybe I'm stallin'
Maybe I'm fakin'
Maybe I'm breakin'
But my heart just keeps comin' back
To you.

Round and round and round and
    round and round,
To you.

And by the way,
I'm a fool for you.

At first I thought it was just a phase,
A fleeting spark or a glitch in my game,
So I wait,
And I wait,
And I wait,
And I wait,
And I wait,

Nothin'.

Since then our lives have been
    nothing but change,
And yet the rhythm of my heart has
    stayed the same,
It's hard for me to remember when,
But one day a switch flipped and then,
All I could see was you,

Maybe I'm fallin'
Maybe I'm stallin'
Maybe I'm fakin'
Maybe I'm breakin'
But my heart just keeps comin' back
To you.

Round and round and round and
    round and round,
To you.

And by the way,
I'm a fool for you.

Round and round and round and
    round and round,
And by the way,

I've got an arrow in my heart and it's
    carved with your name,
I've got an arrow in my heart and it's
    carved with your name,
I've got an arrow in my heart and it's
    carved . . .

ILY (By Emmy)

Look at you with your hot pink hair,
Look at you with your sultry stare,
Look at you with my T-shirt on,
Look at you singing' my song

We wave our rainbows in the air,
We sprinkle glitter from here to there,
We fight for our rights, speak our truth,
We are the future, we are the youth

I'm going for the win, I'm going for gold,
I wear my heart on my sleeve 'cause
   I'm just that bold,
Oh yeah, I'm here and I'm queer and
   I won't slow down,
We're here and we're queer, white,
   black, and brown

We wave our rainbows in the air,
We sprinkle glitter from here to there,
We fight for our rights, speak our truth,
We are the future, we are the youth

Cover me in love, cover me in ink
Cover me in kisses till we're so in sync,
I love who I love who I love who I love,
I am who I am who I am who I am

So don't box me in, don't box me in,
I won't be boxed in
Don't mess with the girl
Wearing purple lipstick

I just wanna reach people just like me,
I just wanna show people just like me,
You don't belong in the shadows,
You weren't born on the sidelines,

You entered this world with all eyes
   on you,
And that's the way you can live it, too

We wave our rainbows in the air,
We sprinkle glitter from here to there,
We fight for our rights, speak our truth,
We are the future, we are the youth

We wave our rainbows in the air,
We sprinkle glitter from here to there,
We fight for our rights, speak our truth,
We are the future, we are the youth

Look at you making hearts with your
   hands,
Look at you rockin' with the band,
Look at you, I hope you know,
Look at you, I love you so

**Sometimes you've got to live
outside the lines.**

Keep reading for an excerpt.

CHAPTER ONE

The door of the bus hisses as it folds open, and a burst of warm air swirls around me. I heave my suitcase down the steps and squint through the glare bouncing off the sidewalk.

I'm here. I'm actually in Los Angeles. After spending years daydreaming about this moment, it's happening. And it's even better than I imagined, because this is real. The sun is burning my pale skin, the smell of freshly brewed coffee and exhaust fumes fills the air, and I'm kicking myself for thinking my fave plaid shirt was a smart outfit choice in this weather. But it's all okay, because I made it.

I open Google Maps on my phone and check the street signs. I've stared at the map of West Hollywood so many times in the last few months that I could probably find Parker's street in my sleep, but the part of me that likes to be in control needs to have the map ready, just in case.

"Okay," I say quietly to myself. "I'm on Santa Monica Boulevard. Good."

I start walking, dragging my suitcase with its one busted wheel behind me. It's Sunday afternoon, and there's a chill vibe in the air. Tattooed people in printed shirts and oversize sunglasses sip cocktails at trendy outdoor cafés. Locals stroll along the sidewalk, and I smile at their dogs. Bars are painted turquoise and lemon yellow, and there's so much stunning street art that I don't know which one to Instagram first.

I can see why Parker, my cousin, loves this neighborhood. Its Old Hollywood vintage-style neon signs and proud queer culture are a perfect fit for him. Compared to our gray hometown of Westmill, Washington, it's like being on another planet.

Just as I'm thinking of home, I get a text from my mom.

Mom: are you there yet? Let me know you're safe xo

I'll reply later. There's too much going on here that I don't want to miss, and if I'm honest, the last thing I want to do right now is think about home.

That town was suffocating me. Closing in on me like the walls of the trash compactor on the Death Star. I made it out just in time to avoid being crushed by the weight of utter normalcy and conformity. Being here feels like breathing after holding my breath my whole life. I'm free. Free to be exactly who I've always wanted to be.

While waiting at the famous rainbow crosswalk, I arch my back to stretch out muscles that are still stiff from being stuck on a bus for eighteen hours. If I were anywhere else, I'd want to find a place to shower and nap and recover from my journey, but not here. All I want to do is dump my suitcase and start exploring this town. The air is filled with limitless possibility that gives me a buzz when I breathe it in.

This is where people who love creating fictional worlds as much as I do all gather to make magic. The world's most iconic stars have been born here. My heroes have walked these streets.

Emotion swells in my chest, and I squeeze my eyes shut. I can't believe I actually made it.

Finally, I can stop dreaming and start doing. No more long, rainy nights standing behind a deep fryer, feeling a thousand miles away from where I wanted to be. No more hiding in the back of classrooms, counting down the days on the calendar until I could be free.

I'm here for an internship on my favorite TV show: *Silver Falls*—about werewolves and the people who love them. This time tomorrow, I'll be sitting in the writers' room, taking notes and listening to ideas and trying not to fangirl all over everyone. I'm about to take my first big leap toward my goal of creating my own TV show. I'll intern this summer, hopefully find a job as a personal assistant to a showrunner, then work hard and pay my dues for a while. After a few years, I'll be promoted to writer. My days will be spent crafting story lines and creating characters I've always wanted to see on my television. Then, maybe by the time I'm in my thirties, I'll have proven myself worthy of getting my own hour of airtime. I'll be Bex Phillips: showrunner.

That's my plan, anyway. Mom always says, "Every house needs a blueprint and every dream needs a plan."

I check the map on my phone again. One more block. I look up just as two pretty people with long legs and colorful hair walk by. One wears a T-shirt with HELLA BI printed on it, and the other has a denim jacket covered in buttons that proudly support trans pride. They don't notice me staring at them—they're much too infatuated with each other. They hold hands and giggle as they walk by, and I'm filled with such hope and joy that all I can do is swoon.

I'm home.

When I turn down Parker's street, I still can't wipe the smile from my face. It's lined with palm trees. The sky is a perfect blue. I feel like I've stepped into a postcard. But the closer I get to his building, the higher my nerves rise.

I made it to LA, which means there are no excuses now. Is it possible that some part of me believed I'd never actually make it this far? Did I feel safer holding on to a dream that was so huge, I never thought it would ever come true? What do I do now that it has?

I mean, it's not like I'm the first eighteen-year-old stepping off a bus in LA, carrying a suitcase full of dreams. Everyone has heard those stories of young hopefuls flocking to Hollywood, chasing fame and fortune. But this town is notoriously tough on new arrivals. I could get eaten alive. I could end up back in Westmill with my tail between my legs and my dream crushed to smithereens. God, the jerks from school would love that.

My heart starts racing. Sweat drips down my back, and I'm not sure if it's from the California heat or my sudden burst of anxiety.

Limitless possibility . . . that's a lot of pressure.

Walking the streets of my heroes . . . that's a lot to live up to.

Stop dreaming and start doing . . . that's a lot of responsibility.

Jesus. This is actually happening. I'm here. It's all on me now.

I cannot fuck this up.

Check out more books chosen for publication by readers like you.